WRECKAGE

—The—

of

EDEN

OTHER BOOKS IN THE AMERICAN NOVELS SERIES

A Fugitive in Walden Woods

The Port-Wine Stain

American Meteor

The Boy in His Winter

ALSO BY NORMAN LOCK

Love Among the Particles (stories)

—*The*—
WRECKAGE
of
EDEN

Norman Lock

Bellevue Literary Press
New York

First published in the United States in 2018 by
Bellevue Literary Press, New York

For information, contact:
Bellevue Literary Press
NYU School of Medicine
550 First Avenue
OBV A612
New York, NY 10016

Library of Congress Cataloging-in-Publication Data
Names: Lock, Norman, 1950- author.
Title: The wreckage of Eden / Norman Lock.
Description: New York : Bellevue Literary Press, [2018] | Series: The American novels ; 5
Identifiers: LCCN 2017014712 (print) | LCCN 2017020737 (ebook) |
   ISBN 9781942658399 (E-Book) | ISBN 9781942658382 (softcover)
Subjects: LCSH: Military chaplains—Fiction. | Dickinson, Emily, 1830-1886—Fiction.
   | Women poets, American—19th century—Fiction. | United States—History—19th
   century—Fiction. | GSAFD: Biographical fiction. | Historical fiction.
Classification: LCC PS3562.O218 (ebook) | LCC PS3562.O218 W74 2018 (print) |
   DDC 813/.54—dc23
LC record available at https://lccn.loc.gov/2017014712

Bellevue Literary Press would like to thank all its generous
donors—individuals and foundations—for their support.

 This publication is made possible by the New York
State Council on the Arts with the support of Governor
Andrew Cuomo and the New York State Legislature.

 This project is supported in part
by an award from the National
Endowment for the Arts.

Book design and composition by Mulberry Tree Press, Inc.

Manufactured in the United States of America
First Edition

1 3 5 7 9 8 6 4 2

paperback ISBN: 978-1-942658-38-2

ebook ISBN: 978-1-942658-39-9

For Dorothy Hub, who, in her time,
also withdrew behind the hedges,
though she left no words for posterity

She dealt her pretty words like Blades—

—Emily Dickinson

The
WRECKAGE
of
EDEN

Dear Emily,

We were together perhaps a score of times—alone, just half as many—frank, as frank as our New England reticence would allow, less often than that. Once, I had foolishly hoped for affection, even intimacy. Do you blush? It could not have escaped your notice that my interest in you was more than a passing one. I admitted as much. But you have retired from the world, even as narrow a one as Amherst, and I have resigned myself to your indifference and my own inadequacy.

Your last letter (it had the finality of a judge's gravely gaveling after sentence had been passed) seemed as absolute as the Arctic, which not even poor John Franklin could overcome, and was quite as cold. Cold may be too harsh a judgment on you. But certainly there was no warmth. It was—how do I describe the feeling that came over me after I had read it through a second time and returned it to its envelope? Austere. I would think you were a Calvinist if not for your poetry, which is sometimes irreligious. I prefer your verses on the hummingbird, the oriole, the bee, even the dank and nocturnal toad to the somber ones that can inspire me with a nameless dread, as though I were officiating at my own funeral.

Because you will admit me no farther into your house than its anteroom, where the light is dim, I am writing these pages to remind you of who we once were. I expect no answer, except as my own mind can supply, knowing you as well as any mortal can. (Or am I still guilty of the old vanity?) If this reminiscence should be read by others, who may not have heard of us, I can only hope they will judge us kindly. We are no other than we could have been.

Robert

THE MEXICAN WAR

He will refund us finally
Our confiscated gods—
                    —Emily Dickinson

–1–

AFTER CHAPULTEPEC, I SUCCUMBED to vainglorious fancies unworthy of a man of the cloth, but even an ordained minister ought to be forgiven one of the lesser transgressions to which youth is liable. Frivolousness weighs scarcely more than a feather on the scale of moral conduct. I was only twenty-four and backward in the ways of the world when I put myself at the service of God and General Winfield Scott. Before that, I had been to Boston and, once, to Concord for a meeting of the Female Anti-Slavery Society. There I'd heard Mr. Emerson and William Lloyd Garrison speak and had caught a glimpse of Henry Thoreau, who seemed a clownish fellow. When I was a small boy, I'd been taken to Philadelphia to the coal wharves on the Schuylkill River, to cheer the striking workers, by an uncle who believed in the rights of man. Much later, I attended the seminary at Gettysburg to learn the ways of God. But mostly my travels prior to the Mexican War had been confined to Hampshire County: I had been as far south of Amherst as the confluence of the Connecticut and Chicopee Rivers, notable for brown bullhead, pumpkinseed, and shad. I'd been north to Greenfield, east to Pelham, and west to Chesterfield, there to view working conditions at the tanneries—also with my egalitarian uncle, who, during his own youth, had been enflamed by Robespierre and the Jacobins. Of the great and sprawling world, only a corner was known to me; the rest was as blank and mysterious as Terra Incognita on old Ptolmey's map.

When I embarked on my Mexican adventure as an army chaplain, I half-believed that my religious zeal and character would be tested as David's had been when he went among the Philistines. I did not bear arms against Nicolás Bravo and his swarthy troops, not even so primitive an instrument of destruction as David's sling. Instead, I carried the Gospels, as the Franciscan friars had amid the Aztecs of Montezuma's empire three centuries ago.

I refused to admit to myself that the likely reason for my having enlisted in "Old Fuss and Feather's" army was conceit. The national pastime of annexation and the personal trial in which I hoped to have my faith and manhood assayed were, both of them, vanity. In truth—by now, I ought to be able to distinguish it from falsehood (except for the lies I tell myself)—I was like a boy parading before a mirror, dressed in his father's uniform. I'm afraid that even then, in 1847, I was unworthy of my calling. I've often wondered if He did, in fact, call me, or if I might have misheard Him. Did He whisper "man of God" in my ear? Perhaps

He meant me to be a farmer—a man of *sod* . . . or a school-master, bricklayer, or fisherman: a man of the *rod* . . . *hod* . . . *cod*.

I can almost hear you laugh at my simple rhymes. Yours are sometimes *odd*, Emily! Shall I send you *Walker's Rhyming Dictionary* at Christmas? In return, you can send me an ear trumpet, so that I'll never again misunderstand the Lord's wishes. If only uncertainty could be so easily removed!

In truth, I feel as hollow as a termite mound.

In truth—in truth—in truth! How I've come to loathe the phrase!

On one occasion when we spoke together frankly—frankness is nothing if not intimacy—you said, "There is neither an absolute truth nor one true faith. Or do you think that God does not love the Mussulmen or the immodest butterflies, which decline to keep the Sabbath, except as pagans do?" I became indignant in the way smug young men will who hear their ideas, acquired secondhand, flouted. I felt myself stiffen inside my seminarian's black frock coat. My throat tensed in righteous anger. I recall having simpered platitudes, and, when you took no notice, shaking a finger at you as if I were Cotton Mather admonishing a back-slider. You called me "obnoxious," which I knew I was. I could see myself strutting sanctimoniously on the bank of Mill River, as though I were watching an actor perform in a melodrama. A not very good actor who would and did "tear a passion to tatters, to very rags," as Hamlet said. Much later, I realized the correctness of your remark; moreover, it did not cheapen truth, but, rather, it exalted faith by introducing a necessary doubt. When truth is absolute, faith perishes. Religion requires a heresy to oppose if the faithful are to taste the honey of salvation.

Did I *believe* when we marched into Molino del Rey to reduce the citadel?

The question is better put "in what did I believe?" Was it God, the sacraments and articles of faith, the union, or merely in the gaze I saw each morning reflected in my shaving mirror? The meaning of that glance was too ambiguous to decipher. I know its meaning now. Nearly two decades later, I can read the lines in my once-smooth face with the canniness of a phrenologist. If you were here with me, you could read it for yourself, Emily. The secrets of a person's character, like the shining words spelled out by snails on philodendron leaves, are legible to your eyes.

On my face, you would read the weariness, cynicism, and jadedness of a man much older than my forty-two years. A legion of souls was winnowed by war; the kernels were swept into an ash pit, and dry husks are all that remain of youth and high ideals. A young seminarian, I had fancied myself a man of principles, but, like seed sown on stony ground, they did not thrive.

This recollection is fast becoming a confession. Better that you are not here to hear it; otherwise, I might not have the will or courage to make it. In fairness to you, Emily, I'll make room for your "remarks" as though I had you before me.

My belief in what have you was tested immediately

following the Battle of Chapultepec, accounted a glorious victory for the United States, when thirty San Patricios— named for the mostly Irish immigrants who had joined with the Catholic Mexicans against us—stepped off into eternity or nothingness. The thirtieth of the condemned men, having lost both legs, had to be helped on his way. The gallows was placed where the traitors could watch our marines tear down the Mexican tricolor and raise "Old Gory" in its stead. The patriotic spectacle was the last thing they saw of earth. (The sky above Mexico City is radiant in September.) The Irishmen didn't wait alone on the rough platform to hear their final departure called. German immigrants and a contingent of negroes also stood like passengers with train tickets in their pockets.

Clothed in a youthful certainty, like the freshly ironed gown of a seminarian, I was nonetheless troubled by the hanging of those deluded renegades, but there was nothing I could have done for them, except to offer up a silent petition to an equally silent God. I was an army captain under orders, as well as a chaplain. The fit belonged to the United States, the sick and wounded to the army surgeons; only the men's souls were mine. I applied the balm of salvation, or, if too late for an infusion of grace, I helped to bury the dead with prayer and tenderness. I often watched myself with satisfaction and approval.

You must be appalled, Emily, but you were always stronger than I. When the Christian revival at mid-century thrilled many a soul in Amherst, you were as unwilling to make a show of your faith as a modest woman is of her petticoats. You chose to be shunned, together with a tiny faction of "no hopers," rather than be enrolled among the "saved," who paraded their faith like a new hat.

Mount Holyoke Female Seminary

Dear Mr. Winter,

Grace refused to visit me—though my classmates swooned in droves, as if at the arrival of a handsome swain bearing Chocolates & Valentines. I would not put on Piety for fashion's sake.

Emily

While you were wrestling with God and Euclid in South Hadley, I was standing in a scorched ruin in Huamantla, a Mexican town in the state of Tlaxcala, rich in dust, heat, scabby dogs, dirty children, and idleness, which is everywhere apparent among the dusky races. You could have reasonably expected the town to pass into oblivion unnoticed even by its inhabitants, who seemed half-asleep. I would not have been surprised had they lain down for their siesta one afternoon never to awaken. Huamantla, however, was to have a tragedy, although one too sordid for an ancient Greek to have considered worthy of pen, parchment, and the Athenian stage.

On the preceding day—that would have been the ninth of October 1847—soldiers under the command of Brigadier General Lane had ransacked the cantinas and, becoming stupendously *borracho*, had parted women—señoritas and señoras both—from their clothes. A number of dark ladies had also been "outraged," a quaint expression, as though they had suffered nothing more grievous than a rude remark. Next, inflamed by liquor and lust, Lane's men set a portion of the town ablaze and murdered a number of Mexicans to avenge the death of Sam Walker, a captain in the Texas Rangers.

Huamantla would be buried under history's grim accrual, which seems to consist largely of broken pots and bones. Soon, our army would pass like a scythe along the National Highway, from Mexico City to Veracruz. In December, we would begin to reap all murdering, thieving Mexican soldiers and rancheros. With the war in its second year, the Polk administration was impatient for a final victory. The "greasers," after all, were no match for America's men at arms, the uniformed archangels of its Manifest Destiny.

But on that blue October morning, standing amid the wreckage of Huamantla's main street, I was interested to hear a lieutenant of marines belittle the previous day's massacre. You couldn't call it that, not according to him. It was nothing next to the Battle of Bad Ax in 1832 or the Cutthroat Gap Massacre in '33, when two tribes did their damnedest to slaughter each other down to the last redskin.

"Huamantla will be remembered as an incident, if it's remembered at all."

Vacantly, he stared—his name was Pearson—at the broken glass, the charred walls, the bits and bobs that had, like the clay roof tiles, fallen helter-skelter into the now-deserted street. There was a foulness in the air, such as flies love, and the stench of burning wood persisted in the scorched timbers. In my fancy, I could smell the spilled blood of Mexicans seeping into the dust. The blood was dark, like them. Suddenly, my guts knotted, my eyes stung, and my sight went momentarily black, as it will in strong sunlight.

Lieutenant Pearson was eloquent on the subject of mitigating circumstances. "What do you expect when the greasers sneak into our garrisons and knife us in our sleep?" He took off his cap and mopped his glistening skull. His bald head was unpleasantly moist, his cap rank with sweat. "Stinking Mexicans are almost as bad as the Indians, the Chinks, and the niggers."

I had joined the Anti-Slavery Society while in Amherst, and the lieutenant's bigotry, which had been given emphasis by a gob of brown tobacco spit, made me uneasy. I hadn't the courage to rebuke him or even to frown in disapproval.

Pearson was a rough sort of man, flinty, irascible, and gloomy. He had the sunburned, weather-beaten face of the rancher he'd been until he lost his wife and children to typhus. He had enlisted in time for the Second Seminole War, with every intention of making an end—brave or ignoble, it didn't matter—to a disappointing life. Instead, he killed enough Indians and fugitive slaves to earn a battlefield commission.

He put his cap back on and returned the damp bandanna to his pocket.

"Let's get out of the damned sun," he said.

The dry season had come early to the Central Mexican

Highlands, and the sun beat down unmercifully on all who dwelled below.

We left the glaring street and went inside a cantina that had survived the pillaging. It was a dirty, flyblown place, but its thick adobe walls allayed the noonday heat. We sat at a table decorated with a sugar skull from a previous Day of the Dead. In Catholic Mexico, I felt like one of the Canterbury martyrs, sent to the stake by Bloody Mary for his faith.

"Whiskey and *cerveza*!" Pearson shouted to a man dressed in the white cotton blouse and pantaloons of a Mexican peasant. Like soldiers everywhere, he knew enough words in the native tongue to ensure that his appetites could be satisfied.

The Mexican paused in his war against the flies, waged with a rolled-up newspaper. He put two glasses and a jar of *pulque* on the table beside the sugar skull. Then he returned to his makeshift bar to prepare the corn-brewed beer called "*tesgüino*" by the natives.

"*¿Y el otro hombre?*" he asked, whisking into froth an amber-colored concoction.

"*Sí, sí. Whiskey y cerveza para mi amigo también*," said the lieutenant while the *camarero* poured each of us a glass of the milky fermentation of the sap of the maguey plant, plentiful in the high country of Tlaxcala. "A whiskey will do more good for your soul than prayer, Padre."

I'd managed to keep my pledge of temperance, a difficult moral victory for a man in the army, but I didn't want to give the lieutenant cause to heckle me. A shepherd should appear to be no better than his sheep if he is to bring them to Jesus. Subtle reasoning worthy of a Jesuit! By the second glass of that most ardent of spirits, each chased by *tesgüino*, I was extolling my Christian virtues to the lieutenant, who seemed not to hear me.

"Anybody who can drink this piss isn't human!" he growled, sniffing at his cup as you would a sour dishrag and then setting it aside with an expression of disgust.

Rare among women, Emily, you aren't shocked by the vernacular, which, you once told me, is "the language Adam and Eve spoke carelessly in Eden before the world grew strict."

"Mexicans are human beings!" I shouted, loudly enough to scatter flies that had been milling about on the sticky table. The native whiskey had penetrated the rusted works of my Christian principles like a lubricating oil.

"Mexicans are no better than dogs," snarled the lieutenant.

"I like dogs," I replied stupidly.

"You're lucky, Winter, to have only the soul to worry about." He clenched his teeth, as though he feared his might escape its noxious prison.

You once said that I had a surname fit for an allegory. Remember, Emily? "Mr. Winter, his heart, a cinder." You wondered what Hawthorne could make of such a name. Since the war—I mean the latest in our sanguinary history, hardly more civilized than that of the Aztecs—I seem to have grown as cold as a snowman, and as ridiculous. But I'm afraid that my faith has never been more than lukewarm.

In a tongue thickened by *pulque* and prejudice, the lieutenant railed against martial law declared by General Scott at Tampico. Intended to safeguard Mexican property, the order was disliked by the army and by Secretary of War Marcy, who considered it a weakness.

"At Jalapa, they hanged a private in the Eighth Infantry for killing a Mex squaw," said Pearson with a scowl.

I was transfixed by a bright shimmer of oak leaves outside the cantina window and, for the moment, could not break the thread of my stare. I was unused to strong drink. I recall a fierce yearning to be once again in Amherst, where the leaves would be starting on their slow and spectacular end. I pictured you in your front yard, collecting them to press into the pages of a book.

Such a slight young woman! I had thought then.

You're said to be plain, but I saw a pleasing arrangement of features, a tidy figure, and a fair complexion. You may have possessed none of the so-called feminine graces, but I thought you agreeable, even comely, when you unconsciously struck a pose that did you justice. On that golden, luminous afternoon, your hair shone with a liveliness found, at all wakeful hours, in your amber eyes. There was *that* about you, Emily: the lambency, archness, and intelligence of your sherry-colored eyes. And when I heard you speak—well, all else was beside the point.

"With what art does nature embalm its corpses!" you said about the autumn leaves.

The point in the fall of 1847, however, was Mexico and our hatred for its swarthy inhabitants.

"We were sent here to kill Mexicans," the lieutenant said with a grimace that revealed chaw-stained teeth. "Polk wants it, Marcy wants it, the people want it, I want it, and so, Parson, do you."

He said that or something like it. I was having trouble distinguishing his words because of the flies droning in my head and the sound of your voice, Emily. You had just said something important to me back in Amherst, and I was desperately trying to make it out.

"What is it? I didn't hear you."

You flitted among the leaves, a demure little bird.

Abruptly, Lieutenant Pearson rose, staggered, and knocked over the wooden chair, which had been gaily painted blue. It was then I discovered that my head had come to rest on the table, next to the sugar skull—a memento mori, which Mexicans give their children to eat.

You see how impossible it was. A people who could make light of death and its dread mysteries. A people who believe in Extreme Unction and the sugar skull. Death is unreal there, though the corpses lying in streets and fields from Veracruz to Santa Barbara must have been real enough even for them.

Impossible to make an annual holiday of death! To give children sugar skulls and toy skeletons to celebrate their macabre festival!

The lieutenant threw his empty glass at a lithograph of the Sacred Heart hanging on the whitewashed wall. The noise of its splintering on the stone floor of the cantina rudely woke me from my reverie.

"What is it?" I cried out.

In my stupor, I'd imagined that General Rea had stepped out of the roaring sunlight and into the dusky cantina to avenge Huamantla. I wanted to protect you from the general, Emily, but my legs were not working the way they should. Besides, you were fading, and then suddenly you were gone—back to your father's house no doubt.

"See this?" said Pearson, his voice rising on the last syllable, to finish with an expression of bewildered inquiry.

I gave him what attention I was able while the somnolent Mexican ceased momentarily his campaign against the flies in order to witness the latest idiocy of the gringos. Unsteady on his feet, Pearson unbuttoned his tunic and removed it, as though by sleight of hand, so that I was left wondering how the crumpled garment had gotten from his naked torso to the sawdust-strewn and spittled floor.

"Look! *¡Míralo!*" he commanded in the languages of the conqueror and the conquered both. The Mexican leaning against the bar seemed unaware of his defeated status. Instead, he smiled at me from under his bandit's mustache, as if to say that the lieutenant was *loco*—crazy *borracho*.

Pearson's back was a parchment scribbled over by a rawhide lash for his having violated Scott's declaration of martial law. Only by the perjury of the captain under whom he served had Pearson kept his commission. He was too good an officer and too skillful with the musket and the knife to reduce to the ranks.

"I was flogged for stealing a crucifix! It was a pretty thing," he said wistfully. "Not plain like ours."

I had been inside la Catedral Metropolitana in Mexico City, which had been built on a sacred precinct of the Aztecs. It was extravagant, richly appointed and furnished; its decoration bombastic beyond reason and propriety. Standing in the nave, among the Tuscan columns, I'd felt strangely light-headed; I was uneasy in the presence of such pomp. I admit also to having been envious and ashamed. I would have gone to the altar and asked for forgiveness had it been in a decent Protestant church. I was confused, as if I had been standing in a brothel, although I'd had no experience of low haunts of any sort. I'd been tempted to trespass like other men, so that I might better understand them. Besides, a virtuous character is strengthened by temptation, and in a world where all is good, there can be no good men. (I was beginning to excel in specious reasoning.) If I had not spent my days among rough soldiers, I might be a different kind of minister and a different sort of man. I'm unused to nice manners, elegant suppers, banter over port and cigars, and the sweetness and tempering influence of ladies in parlors and ballrooms. Grace, for me, is theological.

Later, on the afternoon of the Día de los Muertos, I watched a priest kneeling before a gaudy crucifix. Dressed in lace and finery, he looked more like a court dandy than a divine, and I despised him. I was more impressed by the *ofrenda* in an arcade across the street. On that makeshift altar were *flores para los muertos,* flowers for the dead, tall white candles, childlike paintings, rough-hewn crosses, rosaries, a Blessed Virgin, and an *el Señor* pointing to His red valentine of a heart. Miniature skeletons grinned beneath tiny sombreros. Pineapples, tortillas, gourds, apples, tamales, strings of red and green peppers, jars of *atole,* and clay bowls brimming with *mescal* or *pulque* had been set out for the refreshment of the ghostly visitors.

I watched young women, faces painted in imitation of *calaveras,* skulls, perform the dance of death. Each became la Calavera Catrina for the day, the Lady of the Dead, descended from Mictecacihuatl, custodian of bones. The bread, *pan de los muertos,* was decorated with bones made of frosting. Everywhere on the hot white streets fell the lengthy, almost palpable shadow of the underworld.

In the cantina in Huamantla, the lieutenant had gone red in the face. He took a step toward me, as though to issue a challenge or an invitation—to dance, perhaps, the Mexican waltz. Then he fell across the table, upsetting the empty *pulque* jar and the sugar skull, which rolled across the floor toward the door like a living thing wanting to get out.

I was stricken with what might have been the sickness unto death. It comes to each of us from time to time in advance of the harvester of souls—a grim reminder of our common end.

Although its jaws were clenched, the sugar skull spoke in a language I understood. "I was killed by an American soldier. I was only a boy. Maybe he got tired of shooting dogs."

I could think of nothing to say to the dead boy.

Then a voice like Lieutenant Pearson's began a recitation of Mexican atrocities against Americans, "the Dawson Massacre, Goliad Massacre, Crabb Massacre . . ."

The sugar skull answered in kind. ". . . the bombardment

of Veracruz, the martyrs of Chapultepec, the slaughter at
the rancho of Guadalupe by Los Diablos . . ."

For a time that could have existed only in my febrile
imagination, the two voices wove a gristly counterpoint,
whose themes were murder and revenge.

"What do you expect from people whose ancestors wor-
shipped Mictlantecuhtli?" asked the lieutenant, although
he was lying unconscious on the dirty floor.

The Mexican barkeep spoke from under his sombrero,
"Mictlantecuhtli is a blood-soaked skeleton; his bony
jaws and bared teeth are ready to rip the dead to pieces
or to swallow stars as they vanish from the night sky. His
tongue is lewd, shameless, and expectant—an organ for
the satisfaction of base appetites. The god adorns himself
with a necklace of human eyes; his ear spools are fashioned of human bones; his skull is dressed with owl feathers. I do not see his heart."

The man had spoken in English, or else my scant Spanish
had improved while I'd been inside the cantina. Strange,
I thought, that he seemed to be taking a siesta, lying on
top of the crudely built bar painted blue like the chairs and
decorated with golden moons and stars. He spoke again,
in a faraway voice—unless the voice was mine. I was fascinated by the lurid mythology of the country and had
come to know it by my readings in *The True History of the
Conquest of Mexico,* a sobering account of Christ Militant's
"terrible swift sword."

"The god's earthly priests send him souls to judge and
govern," said the Mexican from within a profound inertia,

which could easily have been mistaken for a trance. "There are five priests in all—four to lay hold of the sacrifice, the fifth to open the abdomen and extract the heart. All six bear the death sentence on their clothes, written by a scarlet jet of blood."

He'd spoken as if he had been witnessing the brutal spectacle with his own eyes, which remained hidden beneath the straw disk of his sweat-stained sombrero.

I wonder what thoughts passed through the minds of thousands of ecstatic worshippers, some of whom had shed blood of their own in a delirious imitation of the ritual by amputating their limbs and sexual organs, in order that the land would be nourished and Divinity appeased. When eviscerated corpses were flung down the temple stairs to the *apetlatl,* a terrace at the foot of the Pyramid of the Moon, constructed to receive them, when the severed heads had been placed on the rack of skulls, when the viscera had been fed to zoo animals—did the spectators shiver in delicious terror of what might one day befall them, high above the plaza, when the fifth priest offered up their savories to their sanguinary god?

I pictured myself as a sixth priest, my gory hands around the sacred heart of Jesus. Do you wonder at such blasphemies? The river of blood has many tributaries.

By the end of my service in Mexico, my imagination had grown extravagant, even ghoulish. I've always suspected that the *pulque* was at fault, or else the *mescal* I drank for the pain after receiving my wound at Galaxara Pass. That was in November 1847. Our wagons had been traveling through the ravine under General Lane's command when two hundred of Rea's lancers swept down on us. I remember a red rag tied to each sharpened point. A lance caught me in the thigh; I tumbled from the wagon and managed to scrabble into a ditch partly hidden by sagebrush. By God's mercy or a momentary oversight on His part, a Louisiana dragoon leaned from his saddle and swung me up behind him, like a hawk forking up a rabbit in its talons. If the dragoon had stopped to ask which of the two I would rather he saved—my skin or my soul— I would have chosen the former with little hesitation. I had looked death more or less in the face and found that, where courage was concerned, I was a rabbit.

Awake, the Mexican had taken up his newspaper and was once more swatting at flies. For no good reason, I hated him.

I rushed from the cantina into the blinding street and was sick. Lying in the dust, I wished that la Calavera Catrina would take me in a bony embrace or that a Mexican bandit would come and beat me without mercy, so that my hatred could find justification in a brutal nature too great for an ordinary man to forgive—even one pledged to turn the other cheek. I felt unequal to both my commission and my ordination and wished for a life free of the obligations they imposed.

At the foot of the Malinche volcano, Mexico had become unbearable.

–2–

ON THE BOAT FROM VERACRUZ, I could not help imagining our reunion. I had been given a hickory stick at the field hospital to use while my wound healed. In Boston, before boarding the coach to Amherst, I stopped at George Simmons's haberdashery and purchased a fancy gold-topped stick to lean on manfully. It was a showy thing, and I wielded it with panache. I hoped that my picturesque invalidism would excite a tender solicitude. I wanted to impress you and could not have known how much even then you despised flummery.

Do you remember what you said after you'd floated into the parlor and settled your skirts in the visitor's chair, as if to insist, however quietly, on your own transience?

"You've arrived in time for skating; the boys have swept the ice clean of snow."

I could feel my face flush, as if with windburn on a raw winter's afternoon. Like a child who is ignored, I kicked over the tapestried footstool.

"Your leg, Robert?" you said in the interrogative tone you frequently assumed.

"Graced by a Mexican bullet," I replied, hoping a clever pun would please you.

You compressed your thin lips into the barest of smiles.

I had lied, of course; it seemed heroic to have suffered a wound from a musket ball rather than one such as a pig might receive from a boy with a pointed stick.

"Does it pain you?"

I took heart in your voice and face, which now seemed satisfactorily pitying.

"Not at all," I replied with a cavalier gesture.

"Good," you said, and I grew annoyed that you seemed inclined to let the matter rest.

You were aware of the wars being waged in the forest. You heard the alarms raised by red squirrels ambushed in their leafy coverts by the neighbor's cat. You thrilled to a flicker's enfilade against a dead elm trunk, to the attack of the broad ax wielded by a lumberman, and, in early spring, to the boom of thawing ice splintering in zigzags across the pond. As our conversation wended, however, I became convinced that the Mexican War could be of little import to one of Miss Lyon's young ladies. You lived far away from smoke and casualties, except for what a mouse trap or a drafty flue could produce.

"We put up so many jars of piccalilli relish, Robert! The cauliflower were plentiful. I'll give you a jar to take home with you for your aunt. How is Miss Winter? I have not seen her in an age. I hope her lumbago does not overly trouble her. Does she still enjoy piccalilli as much as she used to?"

I played with my stick. I remember how the ferrule gleamed in the light from the parlor window. It made a dazzle amid the heavy furnishings. I was transfixed, and, for a moment, forgot my grievance.

"What a handsome stick, Robert!"

"Thank you. It is because of my *wound*." I imparted to the word a dying fall in the hope of turning the conversation from cauliflower to Galaxara Pass.

"I'm sure you were well looked after."

"As well as one can be under the most appalling conditions," I replied peevishly.

"No doubt you gave a good account of yourself."

Wishing to steer the conversation into a flattering light, I'd begun to relate my encounter with Rea's horsemen, when I veered, according to the mind's waywardness, toward the subject of Huamantla. I relived the "incident" vividly, as if the town had materialized in the Dickinsons' parlor. The words that came to me—accompanied by a vile smell, which overwhelmed the pleasant odors of baking bread and pine sap—seemed to belong to Lieutenant Pearson.

"The Mexicans got what they deserved," he snarled, or I did. "They're no better than the mangy dogs they eat." Looking into your eyes, I realized, gratefully, that the voice, whoever had uttered it, had been heard only in my mind.

I was not myself, Emily. I'd lost my way while we were bringing fire and the sword to the Mexicans. The sketch that, moment by moment, we make of ourselves had smudged. The coarse language I had used *was* Lieutenant Pearson's, although he'd fallen two months earlier in the Atlixco Valley. I gave him water to drink from my canteen as he lay gasping on the parched earth, and, at his end—an agonizing one—I held him in my arms and whispered words of spiritual comfort, in which I did not wholeheartedly believe.

After Huamantla, I'd broken with the lieutenant, and, at that electric moment when he was about to cut all ties with the living, I did not truly wish him well. I was obliged, however, by considerations beyond personal likes and dislikes. I tried to summon, for the occasion, an image of the glory that awaited him. Instead, I pictured the pathos of the scene rendered in oils, in the heroic style of Watteau's *The Death of Montcalm*, transported from the Plains of Abraham to the Mexican Highlands, in the shadow of Popocatepetl. God, what hopeless, hapless creatures we are, whom a housefly can distract from the contemplation of eternity!

"Robert, would you like some tea?" you asked, ensconced in Amherst.

I was offended by your cheerfulness; it jarred with my somber fantasy.

You went into the kitchen and returned with tea and scones, which were, in your case, nibbled at and, in mine, gnawed on—not in hunger, but because of an obscure fury. You went on to give me news of your family, of friends left behind at the academy, and of friendships newly made at Mount Holyoke Female Seminary.

"I am mostly shy of people, preferring to bind some few kindred souls to mine than to spread a jam of universal sweetness," you said, picking a crumb from your plain dress. "A sorority of young ladies can be tedious. I dislike gossip unless it trills."

Your voice came from far away, reaching me at the Chapultepec Castle walls, where I'd drifted on the boat of reverie. I tasted black powder; the smoke from musketry and cannon were everywhere thick and noxious as incense. I was kneeling over a dead marine; his chest had been blown open a moment before by a Mexican large-caliber musket ball. My bloody hands had been rooting helplessly inside him. What had I hoped to find? He wore a stunned look on his face. I had thought to see the hope of heaven in his still-opened eyes, but they were blank and staring. Hurriedly, I said the words of my office over him, afraid that he had gone on unprepared for the obligations of immortality.

I knelt over the lieutenant, the marine, and many others during my nine months at war. They departed this world for some other, as well as lodged deeply in my mind. They had power over me, could disconcert and disturb my self-regard. By my disquiet, I know that I was not entirely the frivolous man that I supposed. I pray that I was not.

Your voice drew me back to Amherst and the wintry parlor. I arrived with a stinging in my eyes, which had been overwhelmed by the memory of the Mexican sun, which is to New England's like a gold doubloon to a dull one-cent piece. You had been prattling about your brother, Austin, and your "dear friend" Abiah Root.

I expect you bristle to read the word *prattling*. Well, you were not always a sibyl, for whom every word is serious.

You soon left Miss Root and an encomium on her qualities for Silliman's chemistry.

"To think that the world is made of potions, such as a magus or a charlatan would have concocted! I do believe God created the world in Mr. Hooke's laboratory and, according to Dr. Lyell, spent a dreadfully long time in doing it."

You seemed a capricious schoolgirl, yet there was sense in your whimsicalities.

"For geology, we have Mr. Hitchcock, who discerns 'the divine character' in rocks, which were once thought to exist solely to break plowshares and to bruise our heels when, on picnics, we walk barefoot through the grass."

"I doubt God would have had the vanity to autograph His handiwork," I said with the self-importance of a youthful scholar.

"He must be at least a little vain—his flora is so showy."

You begged my pardon and rustled from the room and returned with a notebook filled with volcanoes and antediluvian creatures sketched in your peculiar hand.

"Dr. Lyell has given Bishop Ussher and his chronology a terrible knock. Abiah will not forgive him for meddling in God's business, not after having needlepointed, on the finest linen—oh, with such industry!—a motto concerning the seventh day, called 'rest.'"

I was too distracted to pretend to be dismayed by your casual blasphemies. I was much like a chess player who, in thinking over his next move, does not realize that the game has been lost.

"Mexico is blessed with volcanoes!" you exclaimed, as if in praise of fertile plains and navigable rivers. "Amherst, alas, has none, and Father won't allow an eruption in the house. I must keep myself stoppered and let the lava flow within, or else I will inflame the town."

I remembered the serape I had brought home for you. I'd left it in the vestibule, after I had taken off my winter things. I hurried to get it, forgetting to limp.

"I bought you this in Veracruz," I said, feeling suddenly foolish.

You untied the brown-paper parcel and beheld an emphatically red native shawl.

"Robert, I am a plain New England wren, not a parrot of the Yucatán."

You smiled, and I wondered if I ought to feel insulted. You stood and swung the gaudy thing around your shoulders, loosening, while you were at it, a clutch of coppery hair.

"Shall I walk abroad and shock the town?" you asked, striking a saucy pose. "Happily, the time of feeding witches to the fire is past." You took off the serape and tossed it on a chair. "I will wave it at Father and, when he charges me, dispatch him with a sword. My words have no effect on him."

I must have appeared downcast, because you said with charming self-effacement, "I'm impossibly provincial, except in my imagination, where I will wear your colorful gift as the robin does its red breast and the cardinal his cassock. And when I'm cantering on my night mare down the streets of dear dreary Amherst, I'll answer the curious with a stately nod of my head like so—a gesture quite in keeping with birds and ecclesiastics."

Pleased to see you merry, I laughed at your pantomime of bird and churchman.

"Shall we walk to the brook?" you asked.

I inclined my head in what I thought was a fair approximation of a gallant. My manners were not rustic like

Thoreau's, but I suffered from a shyness made worse by a very young man's infatuation with a girl standing before him with the assurance of a sovereign. You must've sensed my discomfiture, for, having started for the entrance hall, you stopped and came back to the parlor again. Do you remember? You favored me by putting on the serape, despite your misgivings.

"Pray there is no Papageno in the woods," you said with a smile.

We took the least trafficked way to Mill River, outside of town.

"If we *are* seen, we'll say we are two strolling players preparing our roles for an amateur theatrical; I am the mad Ophelia, and you, sir, are the brooding Prince of Denmark."

I felt buoyed up, Emily! I would have thrown away my dandy's stick, if not for the lie—no, not a lie, not truly, but an exaggeration. Who among us is not liable to hyperbole at one time or another? Why, isn't it the very soul of your poetry?

We entered a thickset woods without a trace of Mozart's bird catcher in it. Dead leaves, downed in November, crackled beneath our boots. The afternoon was cold, and you wrapped yourself in the serape, draped over a prosaic and far more suitable "Yankee" coat. How exotic you looked in your "plumage"!

"I'm glad of it, though it alarms the birds and would, were she skulking amid the maples, offend Miss Lyon. But it is warming, and I thank you for the gift."

You stooped to pick a milkweed, the sharp edges of its

dried pod opened, revealing tufts of cotton teased by winter's winds.

"Do you remember when we were here last?" I asked, wanting to move the conversation, which had been brittle as the icy leaves underfoot, toward an emotion—one we two had shared.

"It was in late autumn; the leaves still clung to the maple trees, though they had turned scarlet and gold."

They had reminded you of your mother's ruby ring, which, unlike the leaves, could not tarnish, although, in time, it would fall from her shriveled finger. What a morbid fancy you have! I'd thought then. I felt a tenderness for you I could not explain otherwise than love.

"You were entreating me to settle, once and for all, the matter of your vocation," you said with a hint of sternness, even disapproval in your voice.

"I was in doubt." And I remain so, though I've learned to live with it as Lord Byron did a clubfoot. By the way, your father did right to forbid his poems in the house. They're much too sensational for a former student of Miss Lyon's seminary for young ladies, or so I've been told.

"I feared for your soul and for your poor aunt's purse, which had shrunk to keep you at school."

"Emily, I wanted your opinion!"

"I was sixteen and not sufficiently grown up to have an opinion."

"You are one of the most opinionated young women I have ever met."

"And as changeable as a weathercock."

"I admired you, Emily." It was admiration I had professed, but my voice had been sullen.

"Whatever for?"

I hesitated, unwilling to admit the source of my regard, which did not lie entirely in an appreciation of your character. "You seemed a sensible, sober girl."

"Feathers! You mistook my qualities, which are dominated by a flightiness much less useful to me than to the bird. You wanted me to nudge you into your cassock, Robert, when I scarcely knew the cloth and fashion of my own approaching adult life. You wanted to discuss belief. Why, I was more interested in the heresy of the dragonfly and the beatitude of the moth, which, in trying to put on a halo, scorches its wings in a candle flame. Have you considered the dragonfly, Robert?"

"No, I can't say that I have," I replied in annoyance.

"It is astonishing to me how it hovers at the border of entomology and mythology. If I could only make myself small, I would saddle one with a hyssop leaf and ride into a dell peopled with satyrs and nymphs. Does one say *peopled* in the case of chimeras? Or should I have said—to be respectable and Christian, as I was brought up to be—that I would *flutter* into Eden as it was before the first couple. I sometimes think that if the Garden were ever to be found again, as ancient kingdoms sometimes are by travelers, only ruin and death would remain—except for the birds, which keep canonical hours."

I leaned against a maple tree and picked at bark.

"Their notes never sour, not even those twittered by jays,

the most unmusical of the tribe. I should love to visit Brazil and hear the toucans! I would go to Mexico if it were not so perilous. Tell me about the birds of Mexico, Robert— or, if you prefer, the tigers. Are they truly fierce? I know them only from Blake." And then you recited his poem in a strangely yearning voice.

"Leopards, tigers, play
Round her as she lay;
While the lion old
Bowed his mane of gold,

And her bosom lick,
And upon her neck,
From his eyes of flame,
Ruby tears there came;

While the lioness
Loosed her slender dress,
And naked they conveyed
To caves the sleeping maid.

"Wouldn't it be fine to keep a tiger in Amherst and take it walking on the Sabbath while the congregations are preening in their pews? It saddens me to have been born a Calvinist, although the fault's not mine, but my paternity's. I would like to have sat on Sunday mornings in the dust-moted gloom and read the stories told in leaded glass. I'd have listened attentively to the lowing of sheep and the stiff wings of archangels beating the crystal air sky blue. I'd

have turned a deaf ear to the minister, whose mouth was
certain to taste of the coddled egg he'd eaten that morning and whose ears sprouted tuffets in their 'porches,' as
Shakespeare would have put it. Calvinism is too plain for
those who room in a nutshell—the walnut's, in particular,
whose gnarled tenant is said to resemble the human brain.
In mine, the Lord's star is still hanging above the barn,
although partially eclipsed by time. How awful to have
been born a Hittite and obliged to worship the hippogriff!"

Your flight of fancy, delivered without pause, left me
reeling. I made no answer, because none was possible in
that seeming rout of sense. You had managed to drive me
off as effectively as if each word had been a stone. I sat
on a stump, my stick between my knees, and brooded "in
character."

You made some noises to a sparrow, and I made a face.

"What *is* the matter, Robert?"

"I didn't know you spoke Sparrow."

You glared at me, and I almost repented of my sarcasm.

"It is a language more ancient that Egyptian, and the
sparrow understood me perfectly. And I won't thank you
for your sarcasm, Mr. Winter, nor for that sour face you've
put on. There's enough vinegar in it to pickle a cucumber."

"You confound me utterly!" I scolded. "Speculators taking stock of you would soon be bankrupted."

I sat on my stump and stewed. I wanted to apologize, but
you had driven me nearly mad with your chatter, which, I
now suspected, was a fire screen to keep my ardor at a safe
distance. You dropped a dead leaf, which winter had reduced

to a skeleton, bowed your impish head, and approached me cautiously, like a reluctant penitent.

"I am sorry, Robert, if I have said anything to annoy you. At times, I can be an irritating creature—everyone says so. More than once Miss Lyon threatened to wash my mouth with brown soap. I told her I wouldn't at all care for the taste and, as to hygiene, I preferred my brush and powder."

I couldn't help but smile: You were so impertinent. What changed you into the Belle of Amherst, wearing a ghostly white dress, in a house you keep to like an anchorite? Where did all the fire and foolery go?

"For once, Emily, I wish we could talk seriously."

"If we must, let's do so by the water. Rivers are oceans for those who live inland, and nothing sobers like an impression of infinity."

We passed in silence until we came to the river, then watched ice floes slip toward their polar destination. Most of the river had frozen; up the next reach, I saw a lone skater tracing figure eights like a schoolboy learning his numbers. But here where it raced and tumbled down a weir in a "mournful solfeggio," the white-capped water was free of ice. You stood mutely for the longest time, until I began to fret.

"What are you thinking now?" I asked.

"American rivers naturally speak English, Mexican rivers Spanish. Did your brain translate them when you were in the 'infernal zone'?"

"They . . ." I paused in order to contrive an effect that might endear me to you.

"And what might they have said?" you asked before I could finish my thought.

You were looking at me curiously, your head turned to one side like a wren's, the bird you always claimed to be.

I meant to tell you that the rivers had talked to me of you. But I did not say it. I said nothing, and you turned away before I could catch the look on your face.

"Imagine the Rhine speaking in Low German!"

I sighed, got to my feet, and, taking your arm, began walking toward town.

You were cheerful, and to act the man I did not feel myself to be, I donned a genial mask. My heart, however, was caked with river ice, or so it felt while the maple trees closed ranks and the creeping vines untied my bootlaces. The hike out of the woods seemed arduous, as if I were carrying a haversack on my shoulders, but it was melancholy and disappointment that oppressed me. In Mexico, I had thought of you often, Emily. But on that winter afternoon, in those woods I had recalled vividly and tenderly, I could think of nothing to say.

"What is it you wished to tell me?" you asked, coming to a standstill. A waif of a girl, you held me fast, like an anchor, nonetheless.

I could not have moved to save myself from a leaping catamount, so gravely did your hazel gaze transfix me. In such a moment did a still-reticent Vesuvius contemplate Pompeii.

"It has been on your mind all afternoon while I've been fidgeting."

I suppose you'd read my mind. You had the keen perceptions of a mentalist even if you did not always choose to exercise the faculty, which is only an unnatural degree of sympathy. To be too much in other people's minds can turn a person's wits.

I shook my head and said, "Nothing."

"I have been selfish and beg your pardon. I ought to have asked about your many months away and the awful war. But it makes me nervous, Robert, to imagine men as beasts, no matter how noble the cause for which they flay and slay one another. Was the cause a glorious one for you?"

You looked into my eyes, and I into yours. The ice that had packed the chambers of my heart thawed, so that I had to turn my gaze away, or else you might have seen my tears. And then you astonished me by taking my hand and holding it in yours, while silence dropped its gentle rain over us like mercy.

"I don't know," I replied, peering through the trees toward Mill River, which I heard but could not see. It was uttering syllables with the gravity of Daniel Webster. It was a New England river, after all, and could be depended on to speak solemnly.

"You are a good man."

"No——"

"Yes, you are, for I think it is only good men who cannot make up their minds. Bad men have only one thought: the evil that they do. A good one revolves around an issue like a top."

"And if he should come, at last, to rest in error?"

"We are all errant."

"A clergyman ought not to be." It was a vainglorious thing to say.

Something Lieutenant Pearson had said about the Seminole War rose from the obscurity in which my mind was mired: how the marines had fought the Indians and their black allies from boats as they made their way slowly through Florida's mangrove swamps. "It was not the enemy that scared us, but the tangled immensity."

"To be human, he must be lost," you concluded. "Otherwise, he is a wooden Jesus on a varnished cross."

With the strain of emotion, my breath had been making ghosts in the cold air. In spite of your art of persuasion, which I considered often specious, I was not convinced. I tried to recall what I had believed on leaving the seminary and what I'd thought on the journey to Mexico with the expeditionary force. In my memory, I saw only a callow young man, who imagined himself a Joshua, victorious before the walls of Chapultepec Castle, in Mexico City. ". . . and it came to pass, when the people heard the sound of the trumpet, and the people shouted with a great shout, that the wall fell down flat, so that the people went up into the city, every man straight before him, and they took the city."

"Won't you tell me about the war?" you asked with a sympathy I accepted as if it were love, for I guessed that you could bear me no stronger kind of affection. At least it was not idle curiosity on your part.

"No," I said sadly. "Thank you, no," I added wearily.

I had itched all day to tell you of the stirring events I had lived through since we'd last been together and how—in the presence of mortal danger—I had neither shirked nor cowered. But I no longer had a taste for it—no longer saw the danger as a gold watch with which to dazzle you into a mesmeric trance.

"If you should need an ear, you'll find mine not made of flannel," you said, with an easy cleverness you could not help.

I smiled, in turn, picturing a moppet's cloth ears. Seizing the moment—most men in love are opportunists, despite the bridle of affection, which partly reins in their egotism— I asked if you ever thought of marrying. Do you remember?

"Oh, I don't think I shall marry on this side of heaven. Once there, I'll have my pick of suitors, who will not mind a plain face. In fact, I will have no face at all, nor will they, if we are to believe the stories we are fed like porridge. We will wear shining raiment and new shoes, and I'll think back on what a strange thing a serape was, unless, to put me at my ease, the Almighty dons one to dim the painful radiance of His glory."

"There are many who would marry you now," I said both doggedly and sheepishly.

"My dowry is worthless in men's eyes."

We left the woods and walked into town. You had given me the serape to carry, "so as not to excite gossip among the bonnets." On Main Street, you remembered an errand with which your father had charged you that morning: to buy a tin of Cavendish. We went inside the spiced and fragrant gloom of the tobacconist's. I yielded my bruised sensations to its balm and briefly felt at peace. You gave me a tin of perique "in gratitude for friendship's gift," which I accepted as I would have your love.

"You forgot the relish for your aunt," you said when we were once again outside in the cold, which had increased with the lengthening shadows.

"I'll get it another time."

"Please come tomorrow, Robert!" you said in a frightened voice that surprised me. "Say that you will come to me tomorrow."

–3–

JORGE LUIS MANZANERO HAD SKIN THE COLOR OF ADOBE and hair as black and lustrous as wet slate. He belonged to General Scott's Spy Company, recruited by Lieutenant Colonel Hitchcock to gather intelligence behind enemy lines and, when possible, assassinate its leaders. Manzanero had once been a highwayman on the road between Mexico City and Veracruz. To my surprise, I found him genuinely remorseful when I was sent to give him the spiritual comfort of my office.

Mexico is a Catholic country, but Manzanero was raised in the Protestant faith by a German couple who had emigrated from Pennsylvania in 1825, after the overthrow of Iturbide's empire and the founding of the Mexican Republic. He spoke German and English as well as he did his native tongue. After Santa Anna abolished the

Constitution in 1834, Manzanero's meager holding, which he'd farmed with the help of a cousin and a mule, was expropriated by one of the dictator's minions. Homeless and destitute, Manzanero had briefly been a thief and twice cut a rich man's throat before joining the insurgency in the Yucatán.

I met him in Perote—that would have been in June 1847. He was waiting for me at a table in the back room of a ramshackle bodega. I remember the dust in the air. The table was covered by a thin layer of it, in which he had been idly tracing the outline of a horse. When I stepped into the room—it was all one shadow and smelled musty like a cave—my mouth was dry, and I spat a brown jet of spittle into a dented spittoon with the carelessness of a desperado.

"*¡Hola,* Padre!" he said, knowing me by my buttons and hat.

He wiped the dust from the table with his sleeve and nodded for me to take the chair opposite. I sat, and for a long moment we regarded each other. I felt uncomfortable, knowing something of his history. Doubtless he had misgivings of his own. I did not cut an impressive figure, nor did my face, which was boyish and open, inspire confidence in a man who had lived meanly and violently. My eyes did not look as though they could search his soul without coming away trembling and appalled. I knew this at once and felt the sweat start on my forehead, as it had often done when, a seminarian at Gettysburg, I would sit for examinations. (There, in 1863, 8,000 men would fail the challenge to their longevity.) What was I doing in a bodega smelling of sour wine, stale tobacco, and sweat? I might have made a nice living in New England. I'd been offered a pulpit in Granby and also in a small Ohio town, but I had chosen to go south with an army of hardened hearts and intemperate souls.

"What is wrong, Padre?" asked Manzanero. "You look as though you might cry."

I grew furious and spoke rudely to prove that I was a man. "I have gotten dust in my eyes, coming to this miserable hole. What is it you want? I've better things to do with my time than sit here picking fleas from my beard!"

"But you have no beard!" replied Manzanero, roaring with laughter and smiting the table with the flat of a rough brown hand. It was thickly matted with black hair, and I felt disgust rise in my gorge.

I must have looked as the steer does the moment the sledgehammer is brought down on its head.

"That was some joke, friend!" he said, wiping his mouth on his sleeve. "More wine!" he shouted to the barkeep. "No, we'll drink tequila—me and the padre. We will drink to our acquaintance and then to our friendship, and by the third drink, we'll have forgotten who we are."

If I were to save his soul, I knew I must drink with him, even at the risk of my own. He was important to the prosecution of the war. After Manuel Dominguez, the first Mexican to be recruited into the Spy Company, Manzanero was the most daring. They would ride into Mexico City on burros, like any other peasants from the countryside hoping to sell apples and onions in the marketplace.

While there, they would purchase intelligence concerning the garrison from their informants. Captain Walker, whose inglorious death lay four months in the future, had sent me to dissuade Manzanero from leaving the company. He had expressed "doubts concerning his soul." He was ill—perhaps mortally—but he could still be useful, the captain had said. Walker had ordered me to "offer him the hope of heaven if he'll continue to work for the Americans, who are doing God's work in Mexico." I was dubious, but I did as I was ordered.

The barkeep brought our drinks, and I prepared to immolate myself with the juice of the blue agave plant.

"We should talk first," I said, setting my glass aside. "I've been sent to advise you——" I almost said "my son," but I knew how fatuous the phrase would have sounded in the presence of a man who had had no real father and who, if he wished, could stretch out his hand and crush my windpipe as easily as a ripe pear. I coughed, as though his fingers were already around my neck.

"Drink up," said Manzanero, who then followed his own advice. "It's hot out. Where is the rain? There should be rain this time of year."

I swallowed the harsh liquor and put my glass down on the table in a manner that signified resoluteness.

"No more. I've come to comfort you."

"Go ahead." I couldn't decide whether he had meant to encourage or to challenge me. He leaned back in his chair and waited for me to speak.

"I will not talk of sacred matters in a barroom." The rebuff had sounded grand, and I was pleased with myself.

"Hombre, you are right! We must go to church."

He threw a handful of coins onto the sticky table, shouted a few words to the barkeep, and led me outside into the intense sunlight, which not even the dust in the air could lessen.

His manner changed as we walked along the street, empty of people at the siesta hour. He'd become thoughtful, and the swagger was gone from his walk. In the bodega, I had thought him to be a man in his early middle age, but now, in the unmerciful light, I saw that he was older. Without the bravado, he seemed tired and melancholy. He led me to the porch of a small church built of adobe bricks and terra-cotta roof tiles.

"This is a *Catholic* church," I said.

"*¡Sí, sí!* I know what it is, Padre, and for sins such as mine, I need the help of the saints and the forgiveness of the Immaculate Heart of Mary."

"I understood that you were a Protestant."

"I am, señor. But when I was a very small child, my mother—the one who brought me into this miserable world—would take me to a church much like this one, where I would pray to the statues, beg for forgiveness, and weep with her at the Stations of the Cross."

"I am a Lutheran minister, not a priest. I have no authority here, no . . . power to absolve sins, except in a general way. It would be a blasphemy for me to attempt it."

I was angry for reasons more complicated than my lack of suitability.

"You are one of God's ministers," said Manzanero reasonably.

"One of His *Lutheran* ministers."

"In Mexico, there were many gods. Now there is only one."

"I don't know what words to say."

"Come, Padre, and God will whisper them in your ear."

I followed him into the church. What else could I have done? We walked across the nave, which was cool and cast in a twilight comforting to the senses. He stopped at the altar rail, genuflected, crossed himself devoutly, and got to his feet again, as if he were once more a boy standing beside his mother. He looked at me expectantly, and, embarrassed, I did as he had done. The gesture was not without reverence—because I was afraid. The God of the papists was, for me, a stern, unloving father. I trembled in His presence.

Manzanero led me to the confessional booths at the back of the church and nodded for me to take my place in the priest's cabinet, and then he entered the penitent's compartment and shut himself in behind a tarnished velvet drape. I found it pleasant, sitting in the dusk. I closed my eyes and wished that I might fall asleep and wake to find myself somewhere else. My masquerade made me uncomfortable, as did the nearby presence of a murderer. A pastor is rarely presented with a sin blacker than adultery or covetousness. The idea of the Spy Company also disconcerted me. Espionage seemed unworthy of a democracy and a country of frank, fair-dealing men and women. It seemed medieval—a heinous practice of the Inquisition. Worse, I felt like a spy in the house of God, desecrating it by my unlawful usurpation of the priest's role, no matter how much I detested it.

Through a wire grille between us came a polite cough, which lengthened into a catarrhal hacking. I opened my eyes and applied my ear to the lattice.

"What do you want to tell me?" I asked, not knowing what else to say.

"I want to make my confession, Padre," replied Manzanero, who appeared to be willing to overlook my ignorance of Catholic ritual.

"Do you do so freely?"

"*Sí.*"

"Continue." I gestured imperiously, as I had often seen the bishop do, though I had no audience in the cramped cabinet with its sour odor of mildew.

Manzanero began a lengthy recitation of offenses and villainies. His breath, so close to my ear, moistened it and produced in me a feeling of revulsion, which shamed me. Now and again, his breathing grew rapid while he told of some transgression that especially troubled him. The close air of the cabinet, the smell of spiced meat on his breath and of stale tobacco in his heavy mustache, the enormity of his actions and of my own—all combined to bring me near to fainting.

Suddenly, I pictured myself as an Aztec priest scooping out Manzanero's heart with my hands and tossing it rudely on the altar, the way a butcher does a handful of

tripe. I had defiled God's house, and so I began to pray—
not for the miserable sinner on the other side of the wall,
but for myself.

Can you forgive my terror, my weakness, my self-pity? If
anyone can, it is you, Emily.

"I forgive you, Robert." There, I've said it for you. I think
I need your blessing more than God's.

Drone, drone, drone—Manzanero's penitential voice filled
the confessional with waspish syllables. The booth was furnished with a prie-dieu; I knelt on its small bench and supported my head with my hand, the elbow on its little desk.

Do you know what the "Little Ease" was, Emily?

It was—and may still be—a prison cell in which one can
neither lie down nor stand. It must be an exquisite torture.
It was much in use by the priest hunters during Queen Elizabeth's reign. I would be frivolous to compare my quarter
of an hour in the confessional to the hours and days spent
inside the Little Ease by the recusants. Yet I am often guilty
of frivolity, and I tell you, Emily, I felt a fearful cramp while
I sat inside my compartment—a cramp in the soul, whose
cause I knew to be that divine faculty's weakness in me.

While I did not follow much of what Manzanero said,
I attended to a crime that, to him, was more flagrant than
the rest. I'll write it as I remember it, and you can peruse
it if you wish. I'm aware of your curiosity concerning "the
careless sleeve of Death," in the words you once intoned
over a fox, its leg half gnawed, dead in an iron trap. I stood
unmanned while you looked with ferocity at "another trespass of the accursed race of Adam."

From the other side of the wall, Manzanero said, "Captain Walker ordered me to break into the home of one of Santa Anna's puppets—a grandee who gave *el presidente* gold in return for the protection of his house and person. There are many such men in my country, if you can call them 'men.' Maybe also in yours."

I made no reply.

"The house—a fine hacienda—was at Santa Rita, near Veracruz. I broke into it through a patio window, after giving the dog chained up outside some poisoned meat. The family was asleep upstairs. It was very dark—there was no moon that night, and a heavy mist from the Gulf covered everything, so that my boots were wet from the grass. I lit a candle and was startled to see myself in a mirror hanging above a fancy carved chair that looked like a throne. Maybe Santa Anna sits in it when he comes to Santa Rita to receive his tribute of gold pesos, I thought before I spat on it.

"I went up the staircase with *cuidado*—with great care, you understand—testing each footfall on the carpeted treads before putting my weight on them. In other words, Padre, I went like a thief, only I had not come to ransack *el señor*'s valuables, but to take his life."

He paused to collect himself, and I heard how labored his breathing had become while he relived his dark passage through the sleeping house, which was also one through a soul with its chancel light put out.

"Continue," I said and hoped that he would not. The poisoning of the dog had shaken me, and I hated Manzanero for that unspeakable cruelty.

"I crept into the bedchamber and saw the man I was to kill asleep next to his wife in a big carved bed. In their nightclothes, they looked like two ghosts, if ghosts sleep. I drew my knife—a knife such as butchers use to flay a carcass—and drove it into the man's heart. The blood came . . . a great deal of blood that quickly soaked the sheet and the nightdress of the woman next to him. She woke and, seeing my face above hers, screamed. She screamed once, for I had already cut her throat before she could think of screaming a second time. I hurried out of the room and, at the top of the stairs, I encountered a young man, also wearing a nightshirt. The scream had awakened him. He stood there with sleep in his eyes—I saw them clearly by the light of my candle. He looked surprised—no more than that—to see me coming from his parents' chamber. Without thinking, I drove the knife, soaked with their blood, into his gut, and he fell backward down the stairs."

Manzanero had reached the end of his inventory of horrors. The ensuing silence rang in my ears like the sound that follows the ringing of a bell after the last peal has died away and the listener strains in vain to hear its echo. He was waiting for me to say something.

"God be with you," I said, unable to find any other words in me or in the missal on the shelf of the prie-dieu. My rudimentary Spanish could not unlock its secrets concerning papist sacraments.

My benediction had not satisfied Manzanero.

"Am I forgiven?" he asked sharply.

How in His name could I know? I had no business in a

Roman Catholic confessional, no dispensation to intercede on a sinner's behalf, and no insight—of earthly or divine grant—to see into a mercenary's heart.

"Yes, you are forgiven," I said, though I considered him unredeemable. "Go with God."

And still he was not satisfied!

"What is my penance?" he asked gruffly.

"You will say the Lord's Prayer twenty times before you sleep tonight."

"Is that all?"

He seemed offended, as though the penance I had meted out to him was too slight for the enormity of his crimes. I wished I might tell him to hang himself as Judas had done. I wished I might, at the very least, tell him to go to blazes.

"You will not drink tequila for a week—no, for a month. For one month, you will abstain from drinking spirits—and also from women." What was a month of abstinence to a dozen years of drunkenness and fornication? To murder? "Two months! For two months, you will practice virtue."

And still he wanted more punishment!

Do you know how Giles Corey, of Salem, answered his judges when they punished his silence by *peine forte et dure*? They had placed him naked on the ground, covered with boards, and, one by one, they piled rocks on top of him. "More weight," he said, refusing to plead his guilt or innocence to witchery. Thus did Manzanero that afternoon in la Iglesia de la Nuestra Señora, and I did not know whether to admire or condemn him.

"You will do as Lieutenant Colonel Hitchcock and

Captain Walker order," I said, recalling my purpose in coming to meet Manzanero: to put his conscience at ease, so that he could continue his infamous work for the army, for the rest of his natural—or unnatural—life.

"*Sí*, I will do as the officers wish."

"As *God* wishes," I said sternly, feeling a surge of authority.

"His will be done," the penitent replied, crossing himself. "Pray for me."

I searched my mind for something to say, and could think of nothing more apt than the fifteenth verse of the fifth chapter of the Book of James. It had been intended as a prayer for the sick, not, as in the case of Manzanero, a bad conscience. I said the words anyway.

"'And the prayer of faith shall save the sick'"—I added the words "*at heart*"—"'and the Lord shall raise him up; and if he have committed sins, they shall be forgiven him.'"

"Thank you, Padre."

"Thank you, Señor Manzanero," I said, without knowing why.

Content at last, he yanked the curtain aside and stepped out of his compartment.

We left the church together and walked toward the garrison. I felt a distinct lack of grace on the dusty street. Some men dressed in the ubiquitous sombrero, white cotton pantaloons, and peasant's blouse were squatting in a ring while two cocks bloodied themselves to the death with metal spurs tied to their twiggy legs. I hurried into an alley and was sick. Vomit streamed from me like dirty water. I brought up an ancient bile, a nameless hatred, and a grudge against God—God forgive me. I emptied myself until I felt as though I had pulled up a rancid, vile thing as one might a toadfish from the mud with a rusty hook on a string.

Manzanero had followed me into the alley. He gave me a handkerchief with which to wipe my mouth. I was grateful. There was sincerity in the offer and genuine solicitude in the act. Had I misjudged him after all?

He took me to a food stall and bought me a glass of lime juice to refresh my mouth. He offered to buy me a *taquito*, a native food that I had come to relish, but I could not forget the poisoned meat he'd fed to the dog. He ate a chorizo, like someone who has made a good confession and swallows the body of Christ with gusto.

−4−

THAT NIGHT, I WENT UP ON THE BATTLEMENTS of the Fortress of San Carlos, where we were garrisoned, in order to be alone with my thoughts. To say that I went there to forget them is nearer the truth. One can stand only so much perplexity. Even Christ wept in frustration and—I say the word, though I be damned for it—*resentment* in Gethsemane. The night was cool, as it invariably is in the Mexican Highlands. I looked out from a coign of vantage onto fields of maize and, closer to hand, at a dry stream-bed meandering among apple and pear trees. The corn was sere because of the drought, the fruit withered. Providence or a sated Mictlantecuhtli would shortly send rain to the parched fields and orchards and flood the stream. Even now, it was filling the pockets of the clouds on the lee side of the Sierra Madre Oriental.

A pretty figure of speech, don't you think? Perhaps I should have been a poet, too. We could have riddled each other with guilt and imagined we were happy.

As the shadows merged into darkness, I paced the battlements, stopping to watch the sun bleed molten gold onto the shoulders of the Cofre de Perote, an extinct volcano stark on the horizon. With good reason, the Aztecs had exalted Huitzilopochtli, a warrior who each night fought against the darkness until the sun could once again claim its precedence. Men and women had been sacrificed to him as our own Lord had been done away with on a hill of skulls, to become a symbol, which is both less and more than a man.

In a letter written sometime after Lincoln's death, you said, "All can seem lacunae when the mind's a blank." You might have been talking about that June night in Perote. I was empty, and the world also seemed empty. Perote was not a town in the hill country of Judah, nor did the Star of Bethlehem shine. The light had wavered on the dead volcano until, like an altar candle, it was quenched, signaling the day's recessional. I was cast adrift in a lightless firmament. Little by little, my eyes grew used to the darkness, which was not absolute as I'd first imagined, but studded with a myriad of stars. The coming of that light had taken an age, and my loneliness was almost past enduring. Leaning over the parapet into the engulfing night, I saw Manzanero's face like a projection of memory's magic lantern—a ghostly souvenir of an afternoon in which the profession of faith and the solemn vows of ordination had weakened and the sickness of the world had touched me like blackwater fever.

Manzanero died a month after I'd heard his confession. Whether by a royalist's bullet or rope or by mortal illness, I never heard. At the time, I wondered if a premonition of his impending death had caused him to seek forgiveness. He only half-finished his penance. I don't know in which of hell's denominations his soul is lodged, unless my fumbling intercession saved it from eternal pain. Otherwise, it was, as the Mexicans say, "*De nada*. For nothing."

I no longer fear hell as once I did, but atop the walls of San Carlos, I trembled.

"The night is filled with daggers," you said on the eve before I left for the Mexican War. You'd given me an Indian pipe picked from the woods behind your house, "like a lady sending a fellow to the lists with a chaste kiss and a wish that he returns with his armor like new." You withheld the kiss, however chaste, and the wildflower I would lose before I had crossed the Río Grande.

I'd have been happy to remain in Amherst, but you did not care to have me near. My infrequent visits and our letters, carried by strangers like writs or notices of overdue accounts, would be sufficient for you. Emily, if you had only *asked*, together we might have increased the circumference of Amherst or traveled on a lengthening radius to the western territories. We needn't have stopped until our backs were to the continent. You could have gone even further, on "the frigate that sails the mind's unfathomable ocean." Such fancies *your* mind has spun out of nothing more substantial than sea foam! I'd have been content to be a master's mate, mopping the spilled ink from your desk. I tell you I'd have been happy to watch you hammer words into sense, according to your mind's peculiar inclination.

The stars above the Mexican hills seemed to have dulled to paste—a crust on the black bowl of space, like dottle in a pipe. The day's allotment of radiance had been spent, and I wished for nothing more than sleep and its effacement until reveille should wake me to myself again. I was about to leave the battlement, when Captain Walker appeared. He did so with the abruptness of a ghost, which he would become in October, during the Battle of Huamantla. By the light of the greasy torch he carried, I saw the fatal wound. Aghast, I crossed myself; I must have worn a remnant of the afternoon's mummery on my soul. I can't explain my apostasy in any other way except that the night had become suddenly uncanny.

"Good evening, Padre," he said mildly.

The look I gave him was one of both terror and pity.

"What is it?" he said. "You don't look well."

I could not take my eyes from the ghastly hole in his chest!

"Chaplain Winter, what is the matter?" he demanded, irritated by my bewilderment.

"I'm sorry, sir, I—— I do not feel myself tonight."

"I hope to Christ you didn't eat any greaser grub!"

"No, sir."

"The meat is dog, you know, and God knows what shit they use for fertilizer."

He leaned his elbows on the crenelated wall and gazed through a thick embrasure at the black sky and still blacker fields unrolling from the fortress toward Paisaje del Cofre de Perote. The summit gleamed eerily for reasons best known to natural scientists or necromancers. I could not rid my mind of the unholy thought that I was talking to a dead man. I wanted to retire to my quarters and ponder—no, *forget* the day's events. I was overwhelmed and needed the blankness of a dreamless sleep.

"You did a splendid job of persuading Manzanero of the rightness of our cause."

I was no longer convinced of its rightness. Not entirely.

Walker turned to me. "You do believe in what we are doing here?"

"I don't know."

"Good God, man, we're doing His bidding! You, more than anyone, should know that. Or do you think He wants his chosen people to occupy only a portion of the Americas? He did not make us rabbits content to scrabble in some meager warren. He bestowed on us breadth of mind and largeness of ambition. He knows that we can make Mexico glorious, the jewel of our empire. Mexico is wasted on the Mexicans. You surprise me, Padre."

Vexed, he drew me roughly to the embrasure. I shivered at his touch. Was he an honest ghost ignorant of his end, or a diabolical one seeking to enlist me in his racial dream of Manifest Destiny just as I had sought earlier that day to bind Manzanero to it?

I smelled the coming rain in the air. It was an intimation of the unrevealed future that waited expectantly, like the captain's phantom wound, which would, four months hence, bleed beyond the skill of any man to staunch.

"Look at that enormous plain. When rain comes, it will burgeon with maize and apples, pears and plums; fish will run again in the streams. It is a paradise, the lost Eden, from which our race was cast out and to which we are fated by blood and nationhood to return."

> Down white graveled paths
> Walked the bright connubial pair—
> Embowered in a fecund Paradise,
> Pruned & weeded by Negro gardeners.

His face was close to mine; I smelled the dried sweat in his clothes and the stew he'd eaten for dinner on his breath. Once again, I felt like vomiting.

Walker hissed like the serpent itself, "Jesus would have been seduced by Mexico and California! He'd have eagerly let the devil make Him emperor over them."

How should I answer such blasphemy? I wondered.

"Well, Winter? What do you have to say?"

Walker demanded an answer, and I was no martyr willing to give him an honest one. I have often thought of Martin Luther, who refused to recant despite the threat of torture.

I know myself too well; I'd have renounced faith and God Himself to escape the pain of the Vatican's inquisitors.

"They are a great prize for our people and a glorious offering to Him, who has given us this rich land to conquer."

My zealous rhetoric appeared to satisfy the captain. He turned around, and, in his ashen face, I saw the death of many. The words he uttered next could only have come from a dead man who had been made privy to the future. God knows why I had been chosen to hear them.

"America will become fabulously rich, while Mexico will grow ever poorer. There will come a time when, to escape poverty and the violence and corruption born of it, the Mexicans will, by stealth and at great risk, return to their lost territories and, from there, infiltrate into the far corners of America. They will be despised and persecuted and, in their turn, they will hate us. A day will come when we will build a wall to keep them out, one as formidable as the walls of the Fortress of San Carlos. Like dogs digging beneath the rusty gate of Paradise, they'll try to slip inside. Mark my words, Winter, much blood will be spilled to keep them out."

I nodded, feeling weak and unwell, as if *my* blood had been drained.

Walker held the lantern to my face.

"You look like hell, Padre. You should go to bed."

I said good night and hurried to my quarters, where I quickly undressed, prayed, and snuffed out the candle. I shut my eyes, hoping to quell the riot in my brain, but the oblivion I had wished for eluded me. I wanted to pray again, but failed, although I chastened myself by kneeling on the stone floor and once—desperate for peace—lashed myself with a leather belt. Years later, by the Mississippi River, I would see a negro slave's flayed back and recall the night of my mortification and feel ashamed.

Whenever I was in earshot, Lieutenant Colonel Hitchcock liked to say, "There's nothing more useless to an army than a chaplain."

He was right. In the end, I could do little else but pray over a corpse.

The Mexican War is said to have been a magnificent victory for the republic. By the Treaty of Guadalupe Hidalgo and the Gadsden Purchase five years later, we came to possess Texas north of the Río Grande, the territories of Arizona and New Mexico, and Alta California, an area larger than Europe. We acquired a western border on the Pacific and had only to await the fullness of time and aggression to fill in the blank spaces between two great oceans in order to own a continent. Nothing stood in the way except hostile Indians and an immense geography. I know, without benefit of Captain Walker's prophecies, that the Indian problem will be finally solved and geography subdued by ax, plow, black powder, Hood's theodolite, iron rails, and war—always more and more war.

When I returned to Amherst in February, Austin showed me a letter you'd written him. It betrayed that impudent way you had—so charming to me—before you became "peculiar."

Mount Holyoke Female Seminary
Thursday Noon

My Dear Brother Austin,

News of the War has been slow to arrive in South
Hadley. I wonder if we have won, or lost. Miss
Lyon refuses to confide the crumbs of intelligence
shared at High Table to the infants in the Nurs-
ery. Several of the Seminary's Young Ladies have
purloined tableware to defend their honor—though
I do not think spoons & butter knives will be of
much use against the Aztec horde.

Your Affectionate Sister,
Emily

You were not yet eighteen and can be forgiven your frivolity. No doubt you've sobered after what the recent war has
cost us in men of a generation lost; in the corruption of
our national virtue, assuming virtue and nationhood are
not incompatible ideas; and in the blighting of the human
spirit. The vast annexation of Mexican territory made us
worthy of fraternal slaughter.

On the boat trip north to Boston, I engaged in little
self-reflection except for the kind that happens in a mirror,
into which we gaze in admiration (if we are handsome or
comely) or to assure ourselves of our existence (if we are of
a metaphysical bent). I was boastful and boorish like the
rest. I know that I gave no thought to the spectral night on

the battlements, with the ghost of Captain Walker, and I tried with some success to forget Manzanero and my folly. Mostly, I dwelled on you, in anticipation of our meeting at the house on North Pleasant Street, which, as I said, turned out to be a disappointment.

–5–

"You've come for your piccalilli," you said in answer to my knock at the door. "I expected you first thing! Your delay speaks ill of your character, sir. Next time, I shall blow my bugle at dawn, so that you will think yourself whisked back to some dreary garrison or that Saint John's Horsemen are on their way to prize up the dead like so many mealy potatoes."

When in a galvanic mood, you would often jolt me senseless, until I could but stammer a reply, usually insufficient or beside the point. Worse were your impertinences, which might have made a lady blush and a gentleman squirm.

"I'm afraid you've shown yourself unworthy of my piccalilli, Robert. We'll see if you can redeem yourself in my eyes, which, according to Austin, would have been uncommonly pretty if only they'd been more pleasingly arranged. My features do seem a trifle skewed, as if they'd begun to migrate and, having grown weary of the effort, came to rest in transit. There is no help for it. I am as God made me. Isn't it wonderful that He makes so few mistakes when He is about His creation? I'm the exception that proves the rule. Does that make me living proof of God's existence? You must save your answer till we're alone, so as not to shock the grown-ups. Father is waiting in the parlor, where the rack and thumbscrews have been prepared."

You led me into the parlor, where a handsome man of middle age, with a patrician nose and air, was waiting to receive me. The room was bright, as was your father's hair, shining like copper in the light of the fireplace. The floor was varnished to a sheen and islanded with a rug of deep blue sown with pinks, the furniture sufficient and sturdy, as became a New England house, and the limestone fireplace proportioned for a man to stand beside without seeming to be engulfed. It was too pleasant a room for an inquisition.

"Father, I believe you are acquainted with the Reverend Winter, lately of the war with Mexico. Mr. Winter, you know my father, Mr. Edward Dickinson."

Nervous, I gave him an exaggerated bow, which might have been mistaken for ridicule. He remained seated.

"It is good to see you again, Mr. Dickinson. I hope you are in good health. And Mrs. Dickinson?"

"Tolerably," he said as his eyes bore into mine.

He seemed to be enjoying my uneasiness and to be intent on prolonging it, until you said, after a discreet glance at my walking stick, "Won't you ask Mr. Winter to sit down?"

"Please do," he said, gesturing toward the sofa, on which the dog, Carlo, lay asleep.

I complied, while you perched birdlike on the ottoman in front of your father's chair.

"Shall we have tea?" you asked brightly.

"If Mr. Winter wishes," he said—reluctantly, I thought.

You sprang up from the ottoman.

"Emily!" he admonished. "Where are your manners?"

"I beg your pardon, Father, but you know how fuddled I become when company calls."

You curtsied to us both and flew into the kitchen with a rustle of skirts. We were left with the feeling that we had been mocked.

"You must forgive my daughter, Mr.—or do you prefer Reverend, or Captain, perhaps?" He regarded me coldly.

"Please call me Robert."

He looked askance at me, as if I had been a rat catcher inviting him to look inside his grubby sack.

"I shall call you Mr. Winter, if you have no objection."

He seemed determined to deny me even the smallest authority to which I might reasonably lay claim.

"None at all, sir." Not in this world or—I expect—in the next would I address him as Edward.

I crossed one leg over the other and saw that I had brought snow inside on my boots and that it had melted in a puddle on the floor. I was mortified and wished that I were somewhere else—even the Fortress of San Carlos, where a ghost walked the battlements, croaking about the American future and the Mexicans' revenge.

"You have been to Mexico," said your father. I could not decide if his words had been intended as a question or a declaration.

"I have."

I nearly began a recitation of the past year's events but decided I might appear prideful in his eyes. What's more,

I knew that your father was a Whig and had been opposed to the war. "He'll disapprove of you, you know," you'd said. "You had better hide behind your cloth." I had taken your advice and come dressed as a minister of God and not a chaplain representing a militant Christ bearing "His terrible swift sword" against the enemies of the chosen people in the New World. I was beginning to understand that I had been in Mexico not for the reasons I had supposed, but to consecrate President Polk's territorial ambition, and that of slavery's apostles.

"Doubtless, you witnessed many gory scenes," said your father in a tone of voice suitable to the denunciation of unspeakable crimes.

"I regret to say that I arrived home with a poorer opinion of men."

He nodded in what I took to be agreement. By his humorless face, however, I knew that a low sort of person like me could expect no pardon from the "Squire of Amherst."

"At such times as these, misanthropy comes out in us like a rash. May I inquire as to your politics?"

I had none, nor had I rehearsed an answer that could have satisfied him. You chose to arrive at that moment with gilt-edged cups and saucers and a pot of India tea. I have always suspected that your intervention was not by chance, Emily. In any case, I was saved from the pillory and allowed to speak thereafter of less weighty matters.

You laid out the tea things on a table whose pedestal had been carved into a pineapple—an American symbol of hospitality, betrayed by your father's peevishness, which you managed to ignore.

"What do you think of our new looking glass, Robert?"

Disapproving of such intimacy of address, Edward hemmed into his china cup.

You rose and went to stand before the mirror.

"Each time I look at it, I am reminded of a monkey." You spun around to face me and said, "Oh, Robert, when I was at school last fall, a menagerie stopped in front of my window! How strange to see bears and monkeys on the lawn of Miss Lyon's school! You would have thought she would be furious, but I suppose she is inured to the antics of little monkeys." You turned again to the mirror and pulled a simian face. "Well, I oughtn't to mind the resemblance—they are so very clever."

"Emily, must you chatter so?" scolded Edward.

"Pray, Father, what else should a monkey do?" you replied with a mock seriousness that dissembled your insolence.

In his annoyance, the teacup rattled on its saucer. The clock thudded out the seconds one by one.

You looked at me with mischief in your pretty eyes and asked, "Did you happen to see monkeys when you were in Mexico?"

You had come away from the mirror, and, shooing Carlo from the sofa, you sat down beside me. If your father had had a glass eye, his ire would have shot it across the room.

"You are indecent, girl!" he barked.

"Nonsense! There is no more decent girl in the entire Amherst sorority of female fools and busybodies!"

"Emily!"

"Well, Robert?"

So unnerved had I become that I stared at you without comprehension.

"Did you see monkeys in Mexico?"

I put down my cup and, distracted, did not pick it up again. "I saw spider monkeys in the lower elevations."

"How fortunate for you! I am sure their antics made you laugh. I must tell Austin—he has never seen a monkey except in Mr. Elliot's stereoscope. Would you care to see London? Mr. Elliot would be delighted were you to take an interest in his views, although his London is not so interesting as Mr. Thackeray's or Mr. Dickens's. Have you read *Nicholas Nickleby*? I think it very fine indeed, but what cruelties there are in the world! I can scarcely credit them!"

I began to fume. What do you know of cruelty? You are a brash young student at the South Hadley seminary, of gentle background and more than modest means. You may have suffered a toothache or a hangnail, but I've seen men's arms and legs blown off. I've prayed over departed souls gone to whatever comes next. I was preening myself in self-righteousness—you know how I was in those days. A prig. I bore a sense of injury as pleasant as hunger about to be appeased by Sunday dinner.

"Emily, why don't you play something for Mr. Winter?" said your father hotly, his face the color of a turkey wattle.

"I shall be happy to, my dear."

You flounced to the piano bench, sat, and settled your skirts. Vexed, your father leaned back in the easy chair.

"She's a most irksome young woman!" he complained, while you began to play "The Juniata Quick Step."

"Something less jarring to the nerves!"

"He means a plain tune for a plain New England girl."

The tune modulated into a dirge.

"Father would prefer to hear one of Isaac Watts's dour hymns." Your fingers paused on the keys, before walking soberly onward into one:

"Time, like an ever-rolling stream,
  Bears all its sons away;
  They fly, forgotten, as a dream
  Dies at the opening day."

You sang badly, I thought.

The hymn came to an abrupt halt. If fingers can be said to pout, yours did. "In heaven, our ears will have their fill of common measure," you carped, turning the pages once more to Mr. Burditt's quickstep. "While here on earth, I prefer something lively."

Your fingers pounced. The parlor jangled. Carlo, the dog, whined. Your father breathed heavily, and, given his beet red complexion, I feared for his heart. And then you stopped again and closed the piano lid with a bang, which made the dog jump and your father grumble like a grampus in its sleep.

We fell silent, Edward, no doubt, to repair his frayed nerves.

"Yes, a most irksome young woman. I fear for the peace

of my house when she is in one of her moods. Pity Miss Lyon! Her patience almost certainly reached its limit with Emily to try it. She has refused salvation, you know, to her family's shame."

I would not let him draw me to his side. I wanted to be your champion, your cavalier. Had I had a sword instead of a walking stick, I'd have flourished it in your father's face.

"What do you think of her, Reverend Winter? Is she very wicked?" Having been asked for an ecclesiastical opinion, I couldn't very well admit my fondness for you, which he would have scouted.

"No, Mr. Dickinson," I replied with the dawning of a smile, which I suppressed. "She is high-spirited. She will quiet in time, when she comes to marry."

"She will never marry."

"But surely when she is older———"

"She will never leave this house," he said like a judge pronouncing sentence.

I persisted. "Someday she will want her own life."

"It is quite impossible."

"What if a man were to ask for her hand?"

"No man would dare!"

I nearly asked him why he could not picture me as an eligible suitor, but the sternness of his countenance forestalled questions. I never did discover the reason for his dislike. Of course, I know now that no man would have pleased him as a son-in-law.

"It would be cruel to keep her here . . . a spinster."

"She is unfit for anything else, and she must help her

mother, who suffers from sick headaches. No, Emily's place is here."

"What of Miss Lyon's and Emily's poetry?"

"The seminary is not congenial for anyone whose nerves are tightly strung."

I was about to raise an objection, but he cut me off.

"I know her better than she knows herself. I am her father, after all. As for her poetry, she can scribble here to her heart's content. The world comes in at her window; it is enough."

Have you really been content to be as you are, Emily, or was it Edward's doing? If that is the case, I curse him and consign him to the tyrants' hell.

Carlo began to bark. Your father took a wooden darning egg from your sewing basket and shied it at him. He yelped and ran to his wicker bed and lay down on the serape I had given you the day before. Did you put it there, or did Edward to spite me—to spite us both? I didn't understand any of it. The dog licked its paw. I thought your father a brute and wished circumstances allowed me to rebuke him. "I have cried to see him beat the poor horse," you told me later. "Father has a fearful temper. I know how to handle him—*just*—but you must take care, Robert, not to provoke him." It was a ghastly afternoon.

Your mother entered the parlor, wan and haggard. She held a handkerchief dampened with spirits of ammonia. I could see she was unwell. I stood to greet her. She nodded and sat on the rattan rocking chair.

"It is Mr. Winter, Mother," you twittered, taking the

handkerchief from her hand and dabbing her forehead with it. "He has just returned from the Mexican War. He's come to pay his respects." You had spoken as though she were deaf or in her dotage.

"I am pleased to see you again, young man," she replied with difficulty, one side of her face stiffened by neuralgia. "I hope you did not suffer much."

"Hardly at all," I said, ashamed of the walking stick in my hand. "It is nothing, ma'am."

Your father grunted from his chair. I'd have liked to break my stick over his head or shy the darning egg at *him*.

"Has Emily looked after you?" She glanced at the walnut table, where the tea things sat. "I see that she has. My daughter is a capable young woman."

"I've committed to memory Mother's copy of *Letters to a Young Lady*, by the Reverend John Bennett, gone to heaven, who, when he was among us, had much to impart concerning the proprieties."

"I was telling our guest what an excellent homemaker and companion Emily will make when she has sufficiently matured," said Edward with a fulsome smile.

"Father rules me like a *patron*!" you jeered, with a glance at the neglected serape.

"Emily has all the graces," replied your mother. "You are a good girl, Emily dear."

"I'm a good girl," you parroted. "Robert has been telling us all about the monkeys."

"Monkeys, you say!" Your brother, Austin, had arrived, his boots sopping. "Hello, Robert! I'm glad to see you."

We shook hands amiably. He sat on the ottoman, you on a cushion on the floor next to Carlo, whose tawny curls you stroked absently. "You must tell me about them, Robert."

"We have heard enough about monkeys!" growled Edward. "Such talk will distress Mother."

"Will it upset you, Mother, to hear about the monkeys?" Your innocent tone concealed a barb intended to wound Edward. Even in my nervous state, I could feel it.

"Oh, I——"

Before she could reply, Edward had turned to rebuke his son. "Good heavens, Austin, look at the mess you've made on the carpet! How many times must I tell you to use the front-door scraper on your dirty boot soles?"

I glanced at the floor, where my own boots rested guiltily.

"Odd, is it not, that boots should have soles when so many who stand in them do not?"

Edward glared. I withered, but you would not be cowed. In fact, you almost smiled.

"I'll clean Brother's mess. Austin, talk to our guest awhile. I fear we have bored him."

You went into the kitchen and returned with a brush and bucket. My nose was stung by a caustic smell. While I answered the first of Austin's questions concerning the war, you scrubbed the carpet.

"Mr. Winter, I'll thank you to speak no more of unpleasant matters!" ordered the mogul of North Pleasant Street. "Mrs. Dickinson is delicate."

"Yes, sir," I replied with ill-concealed anger, while my mind recoiled from the genteel madness of the Dickinsons' parlor to grim memories of the madness I'd witnessed in Mexico.

I was again at Chapultepec Castle, where thirty soldiers of the Saint Patrick's Battalion twisted on the gibbet like apples on a tree—soon to fall and rot. I saw a Mexican woman lying in the street like a broken doll—black eyes fixed on eternity or vacancy. I recalled the peculiar odor of scorched wood and roasted flesh and how fat flies settled on the dead. "Our Words are too nice to render stench & gore. They decorate Corpses as prettily as flies do, armored like a Shogun's warriors in bottle green & bronze." You wrote those lines to me during the late war. I seem to have been always at war, even in peacetime, which is nothing but a prelude to the next conflict—an interlude between brutal acts, when actors and spectators stand about and drink tea.

"Unpleasantness does not belong in a well-regulated home," said Edward as a gentleman might talk of a maggot he has just discovered on his dinner plate.

"You must be careful of what you say, Robert, or Father will force his castor oil on you."

I feared for the teacup in his hand, but he turned his anger abruptly to solicitude aimed at your mother.

"Emily, my dear, you should be in bed. Daughter, put the bucket away and take Mother upstairs."

You got off your knees—a most unladylike attitude, more becoming to a servant girl—and set the bucket in a corner of the room with an unnecessarily loud clatter.

"I should be going," I said, rising from the sofa. I couldn't leave fast enough.

"Will you be staying long in Amherst?" asked Edward.

His eyes burned beneath his beetling brow. I could have lit a lucifer with them. How have you stood him all these years? I would have lost my wits and been manhandled into an asylum, or lost my temper, murdered him, and been hanged.

"I must be in Springfield, Illinois, in five days' time. I am to be the chaplain at the fort there."

"I will say good-bye, then," he said. "You must visit us when you are next in Amherst."

He opened a newspaper, and I understood that I had been dismissed.

Austin rose and warmly clasped my hand. I saw my humiliation reflected in the young man's eyes.

"Good-bye, Mr. Winter," your mother said as you led her from the parlor. "Please give my regards to your aunt."

I thanked her and, with a glance at you, left that most unwelcoming of houses. The urge to smash the jar of relish in my hand was almost irresistible.

−6−

I LAY ABED IN MY AUNT'S HOUSE and watched a spider write its morose tales in cursive filaments. Your penmanship, Emily, is hardly more legible than its. I've had to strain after sense over a letter or poem. But I'm grateful for the expense of time and ink and thought—though they do seem "dashed off"—and hope to receive others. I'll need them now that you are no longer "at home" to guests.

Austin writes that you seldom leave the Homestead. Except to take the air or tend the garden, you are secreted in your opalescent shell. But I see through you, Emily. It's all a ruse, because your poems are as angry at God as ever, although the anger lies too deep for common intelligence. You aren't the dotty Belle of Amherst you would have us believe. Rather, you are the Tigress of Amherst, and I've discerned your fugitive tracks on paper as an Indian does his prey's imprinted on the ground. I sometimes think I ought to set off and rescue you. I'd storm the house as once—in a kind of dream—we rushed the walls of Chapultepec and took Mexico City for the United States.

The afternoon following my hasty withdrawal from your family parlor, Austin visited me at Tess's house, where I stay whenever I'm in Amherst. (I write what is common knowledge with us, in case other eyes should happen on these pages.) If you can find the energy, I'd like it if you could visit her. Do you recall the house? The white clapboard one next to the grange. She is getting on in years. Who knows when she will be called to the Land of Canaan? I *must* believe in the hereafter; the damp earth is unhealthful to lie in for any length of time. Tess always liked you, although she thought you were too skittish.

She let your brother inside—despite her reservations concerning "clodhopping young men"—and we sat in her cheerful kitchen, enjoying the smell and warmth of a currant cake baking in the oven. It had snowed overnight, and the window ledges, fence posts, and garden wall were iced with white frosting—please pardon an obvious metaphor.

We should not scorn the obvious thought simply because it occurs to ordinary people not endowed with uncommon faculties.

"Emily asked me to come," said Austin, as snow melted from his overcoat and trouser legs.

"You've been wallowing again," I said, pointing to a puddle on the floor. He replied with a grin so delightful, I had to laugh. "You're a walking snowman who should on no account be allowed indoors."

He handed me an envelope addressed to me in your spidery hand.

"Emily hasn't been herself. Last week, I brought her home from Mount Holyoke. She was unwell."

"I hadn't realized," I said contritely, "or I wouldn't have walked with her all the way to Mill River in the cold. You must tell her how sorry I am."

"She wants to see you before you go. We've hatched a plot between us. It's all in the letter."

"I'll read it now, shall I?"

"Yes, she's expecting an answer by special courier . . . me." He beamed again—he used to be a jolly fellow, like many of the ginger-haired tribe, whom the advancing years will grizzle.

I gave him hot coffee to drink while I teased the meaning out of your letter. I've saved it—well, I have everything you wrote to me, except a bundle of poems lost at Charles Town in '59.

North Pleasant St.
Tuesday Morning

Dear Reverend Winter,

I write *in haste*—like any Gothic heroine whose
Ogreish father is waiting in ambush for her to
commit further Missteps & Misdeeds. I am—as
doubtless dear Austin has told you—"under the
weather"—a curious phrase, because I cannot
imagine being "Over it," unless I were a Condor
or—to be baldly patriotic—the bird stamped on
our specie, disliked by Dr. Franklin for a rapacity
alien to the Virtues of a Republic.

I will meet you here in two days hence—at the
stroke of one, in the afternoon. Be sure to wipe
your boots! Father, whose feathers you ruffled, will
be in Boston on legal business, & Mother in her
room, entertaining her complaints.

In case you have forgotten me, my hair is red, &
my feet will be shod in dainty slippers suitable for a
Caliph's daughter. Poor Carlo continues to sulk and
has sworn to me in DOG that he will have nothing to do with his assailant, who fancies himself
Edward Dickinson, *Esquire*.

Hush! I hear his footsteps and so must dash——

Your ACOLYTE

I read the letter again to assure myself that I'd deciphered it correctly. Your handwriting is a mare's tail one needs to curry. Your odd twists and turns of speech and your maddening dashes can confound me; you're too clever by half for a man like me of no special wit or intelligence.

"Tell her I will come," I said to Austin, who got into his overcoat, pulled his hat down over his ears, and left with a slam of the door.

The noise brought my aunt into the kitchen, alarmed her cake would fall. "Your friend is a galoot," she said, having once heard the word used to describe a New Bedford man.

"He's young," I said, believing that in youth lay the absolution of youth's errors. At two months shy of twenty-five years old, I pictured myself as a man already treading the foothills of middle age. The sensation was agreeable.

Aunt Tess took the cake from the oven to cool, bustled militantly as maiden aunts do—kitchen rituals are mysterious to those of us who are served their suppers on a plate—and left with a parting adjuration: "Don't you dare touch that cake, young man!"

I had more on my mind than cake, however much I loved currants.

I put on my coat and wool hat and left the kitchen, whose inside windowpanes were wet with condensation. I stomped about the snowy yard, too old to make snowmen, not old enough to curse the cold. Young men like to feel themselves on the brink of tragic outcomes. When I was a boy of ten or twelve, I'd stalk a nonexistent bear through a nearby New England wood, pretending it was Lapland or the Schwarzwald. How grand to imagine myself mauled! With my last ounce of strength, I would slay the beast with a sharpened stick and then—succumbing to the elements— expire picturesquely on ground hallowed by my blood, after which I'd hurry home to hot milk and scones.

I walked around town, wishing I had on my uniform instead of civilian clothes, which I wore without distinction. I waved through the window of the barber's, where the old man who used to cut my hair was stropping a razor. I waved to Mrs. Oliver, who was leaning over the counter inside the millinery shop, where she was buying a bolt of dimity to make summer dresses for her daughters. I knocked on the window of Garrett's hardware store. Sam stepped outside onto the pavement, wearing his denim apron, as he did at every hour of the day and, for all I knew, wore over his nightshirt, to sell iron hinges and fishing hooks in his sleep. Upon seeing my fancy stick, he asked about my wound. I kept silent, as I knew brave men must, until they get their snouts in a glass of whiskey. He soon grew bored by my reticence and, after nodding farewell, went back inside to his kegs of nails.

No one else bothered to acknowledge my presence. I might've been in a sleepy Mexican town while the inhabitants were diligently taking their naps.

I walked down High Street toward the river with no other end in view than to rid myself of nervous energy. In my strange, impatient mood, I felt as tightly drawn as a bowstring or a trebuchet, ready to hurl myself into some vague action. I was angry with your father, but my anger was likely the result of the buffeting my faith and intellect had received while I was in Mexico—assaults, I was sure, that I would not have experienced in a Connecticut or an Ohio pastorate. I remember raging with my stick against the Christmas ferns, green above the snow.

"Mr. Winter, you are an ass!" I said aloud.

I chastised myself for inaction and indecisiveness. It has always been thus: I go forward because it is the only way open to me. Who knows, perhaps my progress—fitful and unplanned—is a delusion. Although I have traveled much and far, in actuality I may have been as bound to one place as you, Emily, are now to your Homestead. I imagine you make a formidable ghost.

What is the place from which I have not strayed?

I do know that it lies inside my mind—or soul, if you prefer the word. What "it" is, however, I've yet to discover.

I stood by the weir where you and I had paused two days before. Broken ice swept down the river, sped up as it neared the falls, and then, with a rush, fell down like a boat smashing on the rocks below. Though the drop was no Niagara, the noise of water cascading with its freight of ice was loud enough to drown out any other. A Red Indian could have crept up behind me and taken my scalp or a thief my wallet, which had been fattened by my army pay. I'd meant to buy you something else, after having seen the serape appropriated by Carlo for his bed. I had intended to look for a gift while walking, more or less aimlessly, through the streets of Amherst, but my mind had been distracted. I promised myself that I would get you something before I left for Springfield. But what? The usual presents a young man might give a young woman whom he admired, but to whom he was not engaged, would have probably ended in your sister Vinnie's dresser, or as a plaything for the dog. You never cared for tawdry stuff that finds its way into bottom drawers—"cramped hostel for spiders." Like Thoreau, you would have been happy with an acorn or a pebble.

Hearing a noise, I spun around, almost wishing to see an Indian or a bandit standing in front of me. But I'd heard only a bashful squirrel, whose twitching gray tail I managed to catch out of the corner of my eye before it disappeared into the underbrush.

I thought of you in your room, sitting at a desk no bigger than a child's and writing, as other women knit, row after row of words—enough by now to fill a steamer trunk, which will never cross the sea, except as may be sent by mesmeric currents to kindred souls. I am not one of them. It pains me to admit it, but I'm not like Sam Bowles or your Mr. Higginson, of Cambridge; I have no appreciation for your crabbed verses, even if I honor them for having come from you—through what storms and upheavals only God knows.

"And what if God is no poet?" I hear you ask. "What if He is a strict grammarian who condemns verses that are not always grammatical, whose rhymes are improper, and whose meaning—like His—is not always clear? At His vast age, I think it likely He prefers Alfred Tennyson to Mr. Whitman, who is too newfangled, and to me, who is too nervous."

"What do you know of God, Emily? For nearly twenty years, I have been His minister."

An acorn dropped from on high, making the tiniest of thunderclaps among dead leaves veined with ice.

"You are the vainest man I know, Robert Winter!" you scold me from afar.

Impulsively, I hurled my walking stick into the river. Its gold ferrule gleamed briefly in the winter light before it disappeared. The gesture held a certain glamour that pleased me. Immediately, I was sorry for my intolerable conceit. I got down on my knees and began a prayer that went nowhere, like a letter mailed without a stamp. I stood and dusted the snow from my trousers.

How many times have we beseeched God to make Himself known to us, even if He chose a cat—or Carlo the dog—as His vessel, ignited the smallest shrub, or dropped a shining angel's feather on the lawn? It does not seem too much to ask of a father—the Father of us all, as is said.

Once, when I voiced that puerile complaint, you replied with vehemence enough to shake your slender frame, "I would sooner expect Father to speak kindly to me or stroke my hair or ask to read my poems."

Mine? I didn't really know him; he died of diphtheria when I was two. I recall a big man, his arms matted with dark hair, a cigar whose end was always wet clamped between his teeth. I remember the feeling of his cheek against mine and the chafing bristles of his beard. Little else.

"It's enough to reconstruct a man," you said grimly. "Or a beast that smokes cigars."

Mother died when I was fourteen of cholera. I went to live with her sister-in-law, Tess. So much for the family tree. It has been well pruned by a variety of deaths. At least none of us has been hanged or drowned, shot through the guts or eaten by cannibals. Not yet. There's time enough for fate, accident, or cosmic drollery to devise an ingenious and uncommon end.

I walked back to town and found that I did not miss my stick at all.

–7–

ON THURSDAY, I WENT TO YOUR HOUSE. When you opened the door, you blushed as if I were a lover instead of a friend. I'd have renounced my ministry to have been the former. You were shy, but bold enough to let me in "without a fig leaf for what the neighbors say."

"Your mother is asleep?" I asked while I stood in the hall and unwound the scarf from around my neck.

"She's gone out with Tim, the stableman, to visit Miss Hub, who is sick. When Mother is not overcome by melancholy or illness, she does much good abroad. She is often 'away' even when she is at home: Her thoughts will sometimes wander! She is lonely and must find society however phantom."

"What time will she return?" I asked apprehensively. I did not care to be found alone with you. My heart was in turmoil, and I felt guilty for my thoughts.

"She'll be at least an hour yet. She's gone halfway to

South Hadley, where dear Miss Lyon reigns over her charges—I nearly said 'hostages,' but that would've been unkind, which I hope never to be."

I hung my hat and coat on the coat tree in the vestibule and followed you into the parlor. You sat in Edward's easy chair "to spite him" and gestured toward the sofa for me to sit.

"Your leg is healed?" you asked politely, glancing down at it.

"Pardon?"

"Your walking stick . . ."

"I threw it in the river."

"Pity, it was a handsome addition," you said without a hint of irony or a smile. "You and your stick looked well together."

I could think of nothing else to say but "Thank you."

"I'm glad you made a speedy recovery; a wound to the body takes the mind away."

"What is that you're reading?"

You were holding a book bound in morocco.

"Oh, it is one of those books you cannot put down for fear the story will go on without you."

I made a sour face—a plain man can sometimes tire of riddles, Emily!

"*Emma,*" you said. The name meant nothing to me.

There followed an expectant pause such as an angler senses between the nibble at his hook and the tug at his line.

"Jane Austen's novel. Oh, if Father were only like dear kindly Mr. Woodhouse! What a heaven home would be!

The fire's nearly famished. Would you be so kind as to feed it? It will take coal, but it prefers wood—its nose is uncommonly discriminating. It is especially fond of apple wood."

I put wood on the grate and, stooping on the hearth rug, applied the bellows vigorously.

"The fire thanks you and wishes you to know that it will raise no objections if you care to smoke. You may purloin a pinch or two of Father's Cavendish from the jar. He owes you that much! Was he very rude? Did he hurt your feelings? Do I talk too much? I do, you know, although only when my interlocutor is congenial. You *are* congenial, Robert, if overly earnest. You must go into the kitchen and pinch some of Mother's leavening. I do talk too much once the cork is pulled. It is a fault for which Miss Lyon has more than once reproved me."

I fiddled nervously with my pipe, like an actor with a prop who hopes to hide his feelings for the heroine behind a distraction. You watched my hands curiously while they spilled tobacco onto my lap. I felt myself to be on the wrong side of a row of glowering footlights.

"What would you say to me and have me say to you?" you asked, as if you, too, were an actor preparing for a play—a farce or some nonsense by Goldoni.

I took advantage of your sincerity. "Do you want me to stay, Emily?"

"Yes, but you must slink away like a poor blind possum before Mother arrives home. I would not know how to explain your presence without blushing bright as a cockscomb."

I was annoyed and said with more acid that I'd intended, "Would you like me to stay *in Amherst*? I'd give up my commission if you asked me to."

"I shouldn't if I were you, Robert. Commissions are not for the asking. Besides, there is nothing here in Amherst to keep you close."

"I have feelings for you, Emily. Tender ones." *There!* The truth was out.

"They say even an earthworm has feelings—they are that common."

"Wouldn't you like to leave *this*?" The sweep of my hand took in the house, Amherst, your father's oppression, your mother's travail, and your gradually diminishing circumference.

"My thoughts go with you, and that is sufficient, for they are the better part of me; the rest is naught and fit only to molder here with Father. He is the rasp that sharpens my nails and tongue and the flint that sparks my anger. What would I be without my anger? It is not small, but large, like that of Moses when he broke the sacred Decalogue against a rock. I'll stay and goad Father and my muse. They seem somehow related."

"There is nothing I can say to convince you, then?" I asked despondently.

"Keep me in your thoughts, and I shall get about as well as Mungo Park in Timbuktu."

The wood on the grate crackled like a volley of musket shot. I felt like a man whose turn had come to stand before a firing squad, which would put an end to the quandary of his life.

"Robert, you are to be spared!" you said brightly. "Be glad I care enough to send you on your way. I can be electric, like the eel that stings."

I sighed and said no more.

"Shall we view the house, as Father says to lesser folk, like an emperor eager to show off his domain?"

Moping, I followed you into the kitchen.

"Here is a room over which he does not preside, where Mother is at large amid the pots and knives. She is free to admire her preserves sealed in wax, shrouded in dust, and guarded by a spider, which is what became of the dragon and its golden hoard in our modern age. See how richly the peaches glow, and this jar of honey—gold assayed by honest bees!"

You handed me a dusty jar, which I churlishly refused.

"The bees will be disappointed to have their labor spurned. But I'm not the least put out. We are friends and must be tolerant of each other's moods, which are sometimes dark. Besides, you accepted my gift of piccalilli, which made the cauliflower glad."

You returned the jar to its shelf, the dragon's lair, and led me upstairs to your room.

"Here is where I receive nocturnal callers. They bring me poesies while Carlo brings me bones, fleas, and doggerel. One must take care to weigh the souls of those who stand at the door to her sepulcher, as the Egyptian Ma'at did the souls of the dead. I'm sure mine must weigh no more than a feather—I am so unfledged."

Your room was austere; nevertheless, the cherry desk and chest in which you kept your poems in the dark "like potatoes growing eyes," the sleigh bed "for visiting polar regions," and the painted walls that shone with afternoon light like the honey in the jar created a pleasant refuge. But still your demons—"Compulsion & Ambition"— would harry you after the candles had given up their ghost in rising threads of sooty smoke. I doubt you realized then the true nature of your calling, except, perhaps, as a voice insisting—more imperatively as time passed—on the destruction of Father, form, and the wretched play in which you had been cast as ingenue.

"My father's mansion has many rooms—mine is both a sanctuary and a scarlet prison."

Increasingly, you would shut yourself away while I yielded to coercions that had nothing to do with art or revenge, if that is not too strong a word for the passion that inflamed you like a carbuncle needing to be lanced. Increasingly, Edward and Calvinism would lie athwart desire like an oak tree fallen across a stream.

"Have you read it?" I asked, having noticed a copy of *Jane Eyre* on your desk.

"Not yet. Abiah says it is very exciting. I wonder if I shall find it so and if my poor heart can stand it."

You nibbled on Chocolat Menier embezzled from the kitchen.

"Father gives me books, then begs me not to read them,

all except *Letters on Practical Subjects, to a Daughter,* which I pretend to read as once the fair Ophelia did to gull Prince Hamlet. She also had a father, poor child."

"It's all a charade!"

Your eyes widened. "What is, Robert?"

"Your fluster, your *fluttering*! You're not the naïf you would like us to believe."

"You look as if you've eaten sour cherries." You joined me at the window, which faced the cemetery across the street. "I'm growing root-bound like those poor clods."

"I wish for once you would really talk to me!" I cried, at my wit's end.

"What would you have me say? Public figures are not allowed to prattle. The private Emily is a tender animal inside a pretty shell."

I ought to have left you then and there.

God only knows what vagary prompted your next remark. "What will Amherst say when the Mexicans come to town, dressed in sombreros and serapes, and set up flower stalls on the town common? We have our own 'donkeys' hereabouts, who bray together on Sunday morning. A fiesta may be gay for some, but I fear that most of the town's good Christian folk will be intoning anathemas."

"Why would they come?" I asked in anger and astonishment, recalling Captain Walker's ghostly prophecy.

"To take back what we've stolen from them."

"Don't be silly!"

"I hope to be here when they do and welcome them to Amherst. I'll wear my serape and give them bread and piccalilli. How furiously Father will glare at me!" You laughed strangely. "Now you must go, Robert; Mother will be here soon. Hold out your hand."

I did as you asked.

"Imagine that I have given you a small parting gift."

I played my part in the pantomime, letting my fingers briefly touch your palm. Did you even notice that I trembled?

"What is it?" I asked stupidly, looking at my empty hand.

"Anything you like, though some would call it 'possibility.'"

You smiled; I shook my head. I did not know what to make of you. I never have.

"The secret is not to choose," you replied to my unspoken question.

I went into the hall and put on my winter things.

"I'll walk you to the gate," you said, getting into your coat.

"Are you well enough to go outside?" You had a cough, which worried me.

"Well enough."

We paused at the gate. Suddenly, I glimpsed the world beyond it, as if through your eyes. I saw the factories of Amherst and their billowing stacks, the sad dray horses, the drivers in their leather aprons, unshaved and uncouth. I heard the factory whistles calling men to account and the rattle of iron wheels over dirty streets. The earth was spoiled, and the people had lost their places in it. They ate bitter herbs and pricked themselves on thorns. They hated one another in their shame, which they did not understand, and they made war on one another for reasons they also did not understand.

"Will men make war in heaven?" you would ask in a letter written during the Utah War, called the "Mormon Rebellion" by some. By then, you'd become an Amazon pretending to be a pygmy. "They seem to enjoy it so."

I forget how I answered, if I did answer. Unlike you, I saw only as far as my eyesight allowed; I did not have second sight and my faith was never strong enough to pierce the night and obscurity.

"Good-bye, Robert. Please write to me with your address in Springfield."

The gate opened and then closed behind me. I almost leaned over its ornamental iron spears to kiss your cheek.

"Leave him," I said, attempting once again to incite you to revolt.

You knew whom I meant without having to be told. "Father does me less harm than a husband would."

"Even Mr. Newton?" I asked slyly. I knew of your admiration for the young lawyer in Edward's office.

"I put him on like spectacles. My sight is sometimes poor."

I walked into the world, which had changed in a harrowing instant. Turning to wave one last good-bye, I thought I saw the flaming sword and the fiery cherubim standing on either side of you. The gate had closed, and I had been shut out, while, by His magnanimity, you had been allowed to remain in His garden to prune the fruit trees, make Indian

bread, collect honey, and put up peaches and pickled asparagus in jars.

I hurried down North Pleasant Street as though chased
by lightning bolts and an infernal spawn. I had received
a grim revelation and wished that it could be erased from
my memory. Even then, I knew that time did not belong
to God, but was the Devil's realm, in which I would—in
time—forget. Your mother passed me in the wagon. Her
pinched face was lost in the shadows of her coal-scuttle
bonnet. Tim, the stableman, sat next to her like a grizzled
Charon.

Having reached the edge of town, I gazed at the snow
and wooded steeps of distant Mount Holyoke. I considered making a pilgrimage there, but I was no holy man
with a craving for mortification. I was tired, fretful, and
nettled by uneasiness.

Your voice wound through my thoughts like an adder—
something you'd said earlier, a reproach. "You don't see us
clearly, Robert." Whom had you meant by "us"? You and
Edward. The Dickinson tribe. You and me. Your heart is a
locked room as mysterious to me as the one in which you
receive your nocturnal visitors.

I walked home to Aunt Tess's and, like a child, lay down
with the blanket pulled over my head, afraid and sick at
heart. I knew that my eviction had been final. Perhaps in
Springfield, I thought, I will find a bone of faith to gnaw on
. . . a rag of belief to rest my head upon.

I was not long in Springfield when a letter—your blood-
less surrogate—arrived, to unsettle me again.

North Pleasant Street
Amherst

Dear Robert,

My Fate is imperial—my realm the polar page—
my subjects are Words. I would be more comfort-
able addressing them, wearing one of Austin's frock
coats & a pair of striped trousers, but the town
would sneer.

The Weather here—so you know—is impend-
ing: One feels it everywhere, but I can no more tell
its future than I can my own—except that it will
be bleak.

Love—like water—is liable to pour, slow, drip,
& finally sink into the ground, where Generation is
hit or miss. I *almost* miss you, Robert, well enough
to enclose a kiss or, since I am chaste, a lock of hair.
But I don't endorse Idolatry.

I remain your FRIEND—
Emily

P.S. According to the *Springfield Republican*—
which is Gospel—there is rioting in Paris, Berlin,
& even in London, where John Milton sleeps in
stately company. Thus, do men with bloodshed
affirm universal brotherhood.

THE MORMON REBELLION

Narcotics cannot still the Tooth
That nibbles at the soul—
—Emily Dickinson

–1–

I DID NOT SEE YOU AGAIN until I brought the child home to live with Tess. That would have been in the fall of 1855. I stayed in Amherst long enough to see her settled. When I visited the house on North Pleasant Street to pay my respects, you were shy. I was embarrassed, your mother distant, your father furious. I recall little else of that afternoon except your smile, which seemed frozen, as if you, too, had suffered an attack of neuralgia—or a toothache. My visit concluded, you walked me to the gate, just as you had done seven years before.

"Your face looks as though it pains you, Emily."

You gave no reply.

"I think my visit has distressed you."

"Some days the rafters splinter and suns are let inside, which sting sight black."

Your eyes slid from mine.

"Your father could not wait for me to go."

"Emperors have cares lesser mortals cannot comprehend," you uttered as if by rote. You seemed uncommonly listless that afternoon.

"I hope you'll visit Charlotte sometimes. I fear she will be a lonely little girl."

"Then we shall be great friends."

Your eyes had returned to mine. They held them not with brazenness, but with kindness.

"It will be a comfort for me to think so," I replied gratefully.

We stood in the yard, minding the rattle of dry leaves and the chafing wind, which caused your eyes to weep. You daubed at them with your handkerchief. In the house opposite, a woman peered through a curtained upstairs window, as though we were there solely to gratify her curiosity.

"Vulgar minds will think you've made me cry." You glanced sharply at the woman at the window, who did not bother to flinch.

"Do you miss poor Ruth very much? Of course, you do! Please forgive a spinster her insensitivity."

"You're not yet twenty-five!"

"A widow apprentice, then."

Why must you always demean yourself? I wondered. I think now that you were bent on becoming invisible. By a cruel instinct, you favored obscurity, like the mole. I could've throttled you and given the harpy pressing her baleful face against the window a choice morsel to carry to her sorority of gossips. They could have worried it to their evil hearts' content until, like dogs, they tore it to shreds.

"We named our daughter after Charlotte Brontë," I said to change the subject. (I lied: Charlotte was Ruth's mother's name.)

"I adore her novels, especially *Jane Eyre*!" you exclaimed with a smile, which undid the knot of anger in my throat.

"So you wrote me."

"I often think of Bertha Mason locked in her attic room—her wits turned and her nature changed from human to animal. And then the fortunate fire! Fortunate for Rochester and Jane. I keep a box of lucifers close in case I should be shut away. My ardent verses would make excellent tinder. I wouldn't care if all Amherst were consumed in a holocaust beginning with my officious neighbor's house." You sighed. "But Father would only put it out; he used to lead the fire brigade and knows how to douse a flame."

This time, you stared defiantly at the busybody across the street, and this time, she did flinch and slink away into the depths of her room.

"My bobbin will never be emptied of its thread!"

"You are half-mad already," I said, watching your face flush triumphantly.

"I will *never* be that woman!" you declared with ferocity. I didn't know whether you meant your nib-nosed neighbor or Rochester's captive wife, Bertha Mason.

Composing ourselves, we were quiet a moment.

"Your letters were troublesome," I said when the silence had grown too loud to bear.

"Did my epistolary presence in the house annoy Mrs. Winter very much?" you asked without the least expression on your face or in your voice. Your thumb, I noticed, was stained with ink—you called it your "birthmark."

"She knew of our friendship."

"It was never otherwise."

"I see that clearly now," I said, reflecting on your parting words to me before I left for Springfield.

"You don't mind?"

You had suddenly turned kittenish, and again my anger rose against you.

"Not anymore," I replied, lying once again.

"The soul keeps exclusive company. Mine is, perhaps, overly nice in its judgments."

Were you trying to hurt me?

"I should go," I said, my hand on the gate. "I leave for Springfield in the morning."

"And I have supper to make, which must be on the table at six. Father won't abide exceptions to his rule. To think that now *you* are a father!"

"Not a very good one, I'm afraid," I replied with more honesty than I could have wished.

"Charlotte will be happier fatherless."

"Why don't you leave Edward?" I blurted.

"I fear my muse would balk. She is bashful in unfamiliar company."

You turned and disappeared into the deeply shadowed porch.

I closed the gate and walked down the street. This time, there were no fiery cherubim to send me rushing home to hide my head beneath the blanket.

–2–

I WANT TO TELL YOU ABOUT RUTH.

She gave me a child and, less than four years later, died of Bright's disease. I knew no one in Springfield to whom I could entrust Charlotte, although Mary Lincoln offered to take her in. She and Abe lived nearby at a house on Eighth and Jackson streets. But Mary had the care of three young sons at home and, like your mother, was visited by headaches. Charlotte would be better off in Amherst with Tess. As an army chaplain, my life was liable to change in an instant. I could not devote myself to both God and a daughter. Yet the feeling nagged me that I did not love her enough and could not love Him at all.

I've been too brief. You want to hear how it was for me when I arrived in Springfield and how it was for Ruth and me when we courted, married, lived together, and parted at the "great divide," which all must cross in time.

At first, I lived at the army post and applied myself industriously to my trade, which was to proclaim the Gospels in the wilderness, though it was hardly that in Illinois in 1848. Except for the Mormons and Hebrew peddlers, the land was Christian. The Treaty of Fort Adams had expelled the Choctaw. The southern tribes had been exiled to the Oklahoma Territory by the Indian Removal Act. The Cherokees had toiled over the Trail of Tears, which, like death, permitted of no return. Hostiles remained to harry white settlers, but the cavalry could be relied on to deliver the renegades into bondage or to a heathen afterlife. People

in Illinois still talked of the "Long Winter" of 1832 and
the famine that followed it and how northern Illinois men
were forced to go south to "Little Egypt" for corn—which,
unlike the Word of God, was a staff of life they could not
do without. "We're going to Egypt," they'd say, like Jacob's
ten sons before them, who had gone down the Nile to buy
pharaoh's corn.

I met Ruth at a church sociable on Shrove Tuesday, the
day before the start of Lent. We ate fried doughnuts, called
"*fasnachts*," as was the custom among the Amish and the
Lutherans. I had been invited by the church's pastor to
deliver the invocation and had been struck by Ruth's calm
and candor. She was not bright or clever, nervous or ironic.
She was not, by turns, mournful or sprightly, nor was she
vexing, red-haired, birdlike, spinsterish, or eccentric. She
was a big-boned, large-hearted girl whose parents had emigrated from western Pennsylvania when she was a child.
She could milk a cow, deliver a foal, cook, sew, and put a
sick dog out of its misery. I liked her because she was unlike
you, Emily. I believed that she could make me forget you. I
almost did, but your letters seemed to insist on my recollection. They were your envoy, perhaps the better part of you.
You did not care a "fig" that I was married. Marriage was
not what you wanted. Love was not what you wanted. If you
could have passed, unmarried, into widowhood, you would
have done so gladly. You were never far from "the quiet
nonchalance of death." I think now that what you wanted
was my submission.

Ruth and I married on the first Sunday after Easter at the

Lutheran church in Springfield. Her father gave the bride away with only a sentimental reluctance. Yours would have run off the groom with his fireman's ax. The wedding was small; none had money or inclination to spare on extravagance. We were an ordinary bride and groom—partly serious, partly giddy, and partly anxious about what lay ahead. We never wasted words on the subject of faith or doubt, the covenant of marriage or its obligations. We got on with each other and got on with our life together. In time, where all things—blessed and depraved—occur, we had a child. I knew by then that naught can happen in eternity—an impious notion for a minister of God. If, as I have promised many others in their bereavement, Ruth and I meet again when time has come to an end, it will be a meeting empty of all human joy, without which life and afterlife are savorless.

I expect that my despair is felt in the marrow of us all—an "awful nullity," as you call it.

In his bones, Abe Lincoln knew the meaning of naught. We met for the first time at the law office he shared with William Herndon in the Tinsley Building on the square. After the wedding, I went there to have my will drawn. Ruth and I seldom gave thought to posterity—having trusted, if not in God and Providence, in a principle of just compensation that would transcendently balance accounts. But a child can make parents less trusting in the goodwill of others and more reliant on themselves. Ruth was determined to have children.

I liked Abe immediately; one did or did not according to his prejudices. He looked more like the militia captain he'd been in the Black Hawk War than a lawyer. He was tall, rawboned, and as awkwardly articulated as a country rube. He had a habit of leaning far back in his swivel chair, as if to ascertain the limit of gravity. I never did see him fall. He spoke in a tenor voice, which would sometimes climb into a higher register, though it was never shrill or uncontrollable. He spoke plainly in a cadence recalling Shakespeare's plays or the Bible.

After the will had been executed, he suggested that we have lunch together. I agreed, thinking we would be going to a Springfield eating house, but he opened the bottom drawer of his desk and took out apples, cheese, and peanuts, wrapped in a piece of linen that served as a tablecloth.

"I'll play Judge Solomon," he said wryly while justly dividing that simple fare.

Afterward, he went into a back room and brought out two glasses and a jar of cider.

"A man needs little else for good digestion and the well-being of his bowels."

He poured us each a glass. We drank to each other's health.

"You are a New England man," he said, quartering his apple with a pocketknife.

"That's right," I replied. "Born and raised in Massachusetts. I came out in '48."

"What did you think of the Mexican adventure?" he asked, his dark eyes piercing mine.

"I am glad it's over," I said evasively.

I'd heard that, when he had been in Congress, Abe

denounced Polk and his ambition. Before I went to Mexico, I had believed in Manifest Destiny and thought our country and the Mexicans would be well served by annexation. I didn't care to argue the point now. I knew of Abe's reputation as a debater and didn't relish being whittled like the apple whose slices he was masticating while he continued to take my measure.

I filled my mouth with peanuts, rendering speech, for the moment, impossible.

"America is not yet fully grown," he said. "God help the world when she bestrides the continent."

Choking on the damned peanuts, I fumbled for the glass of cider.

He leaned back in his chair and regarded me mischievously as I hemmed and hawed.

"You hold your opinions better than you do your peanuts."

"You must come to dinner at my house and meet Ruth," I said, attempting to change the subject.

"I will, and I'll bring Mary along. I believe our two ladies are already acquainted."

"They have a grocer and a draper in common," I said, much relieved.

Abe smiled tolerantly, while I ran a finger round the rim of my glass.

"What is life like for an army chaplain?" he asked, sweeping the broken peanut shells into his hand's rough palm—a hand that had plowed and split logs, as well as turned the pages of Blackstone's *Commentaries* by the light of a greasy candle.

"It is a great thing for a man of little faith," I replied. "He has less of it to lose."

I studied the man's shrewd yet kindly face for a sign of disapproval. I saw there what unnerved his adversaries in courtrooms and Congress. I also saw sadness, which would have endeared him to you, who, I think, judge us by the sorrows we cannot bear.

"You sound like a man trying too hard to be clever," he said, smiling.

In my confusion, I felt obliged to talk about God and His grace, His divine nature and eternal bliss. Abe rebutted my arguments, adducing man's fall from grace, his greed, and earthly misery. I lauded the just; he lamented injustice. I reminded him that the Savior promised the meek that they shall inherit the earth; he thought that, by now, they would be getting impatient for their inheritance. The antiphon went nowhere. If he'd wanted, he could have destroyed me with a word or a look. Apparently, I wasn't worth the effort. Realizing my inconsequence, I became annoyed, like a flea that, having hopped onto a stone, discovers that there's no blood to be drawn.

We were often together until Ruth died and I moved back onto the post. I enjoyed his company, and we didn't spar much over serious matters. Maybe he doubted my sincerity. Maybe he foresaw the controversies and crises awaiting him. I do recall his having grown heated one evening, concerning the Mormon doctrine of plural marriage and the institution of slavery, both of which he detested.

"Polygamy and slavery are two sides of the same coin,"

he said, brushing a fly from his cheek. "God may have given men dominion over their wives, but the law shouldn't be obliged to recognize it any more than it should the 'God-given right' to own slaves. One wife is one too many for a man to subjugate; one slave is one human being too many for any man to own."

"The issues of slavery and polygamy ought to be left to each sovereign state to decide," I replied, my hands plucking my lapels, as I had seen Daniel Webster do to great effect. "I don't approve of the latter any more than I do the former, but neither do I believe in meddling in matters of conscience."

"Robert, it seems to me that such meddling is your purpose in life: It is what preachers are meant to do."

Good lawyer that he was, Abe had cornered me, but I was too obstinate to recant. I was like a wagon master who, having realized he'd taken the wrong trail, was too proud to admit his mistake and ended, along with his party of emigrants, a pile of sun-scalded bones.

"Seems to me, Abe, that you put a preacher in the same basket as a gossip."

He smiled archly, and I felt myself sink in his estimation a little lower than the insects.

"I look after the *spiritual* well-being of my flock!" I insisted.

"I see," he said, swatting at the fly again. "You make an interesting distinction."

"Seems as if that fly has got it in for you, Abe."

"When you've got hold of a grizzly bear, you don't bother much about a pest."

I wondered whether I was the bear, the pest, or something hardly worth swatting.

–3–

I recall a summer afternoon when Abe and I took our cane poles to the river to fish for perch. Fishing always put him in a reflective mood.

"A worm doesn't have much of a life," he said, threading one from the can onto his hook. "When it's not on its belly like the serpent in the Garden, it's dangling at the end of some fool's line."

We heard a rustle in the undergrowth, which turned out to be that of a skunk.

"I know a parcel of frock-coated so-and-sos in Washington, passing themselves off as statesmen, with less character and conviction than that critter waddling through the creepers. If ever a man deserved to be called a skunk, it's a Democrat."

He spat his contempt into the water and then launched into a story.

"I once heard of a skunk that went to church on a Sunday morning and, offended by the preacher's remarks concerning its tribe, raised its tail, a rude gesture that sent the congregation running for the creek as if they'd scorched their backsides on hell's grate. When the skunk's ire had cooled, it regretted its rashness and decided to make itself agreeable to humans, who could, if they had a mind to, exterminate its entire race. So it went to a veterinary and had itself *de*skunked. The following Sunday morning, it headed for church to proclaim itself a reformed and peaceable member of the community. Well, sir, it got about as far as the churchyard before old man Hardesty's coonhound tore it to pieces."

"Meaning what?" I asked wearily, having acquired a profound distaste for riddles in your company, Emily.

"Meaning that we should not be too quick to appease our adversaries."

We watched his cork bobber trace a frantic scrawl across the water.

"Animals are the best characters for a tale," he said. "They go down like a spoonful of treacle. Jesus knew it when He spoke about the providential sparrow, the birds and the mustard seed, and the lost sheep."

He pulled in the line, unhooked the fish, and returned it to the river.

Ruth liked Abe's easy way with words but lacked his subtlety, which she did not care for. She never spoke in riddles or parables, never embellished a story, and never strayed from facts. Her life's story was a common yarn stretching from one moment to the next, with nary a tangle in between. She had no time for fancy, fragility, or talk of "infinitudes." Unlike you, she knew what life was and how to live it without fuss. My life was peaceful in those days.

Emily, what will you do if the Mexicans descend on Amherst, or the Indians, the slaves, the poor and meek, who will have yet to inherit the earth? And when they set fire to your house, will your emperor, caesar, tsar, father and his fire brigade storm the flaming walls with pikes and buckets? Will he repel the alien invaders with a stern look and the whip with which he beats his horse, while you read them poems?

That wasn't fair. You've got more pluck than I ever had. I never raised an unholy stink, never stood up to wicked men, except once outside Salt Lake City. Mostly, I've been afraid.

"The warrant of a good man's character is that he does not shirk when there's necessary work to be done," Abe once said, reproving me for a lack of conviction.

We were sitting in a pair of rocking chairs by the window overlooking Jackson Street. He'd been poking fun at passersby. The maxim had been prompted by the appearance, in the street below, of the sheriff.

"Harley is an admirable fellow. His hand might shake, but he'll shoot a bad man dead if there's no other way to keep the peace. He drinks, you know."

Abe contemplated his fingernails, which he had just pared. I clicked mine on the arms of the chair. By nature, he was a quiet man, but he would, on occasion, indulge in silences pregnant with disapproval. I would hum, clear my throat of phlegm, or make some other ordinary sound to goad him into speech.

"I won't advise you in matters of belief, Robert, nor will I presume to tell you your duty. We are friends, and I mean to remain so." He took my wrist and squeezed it harder than was necessary. "You're the body politic in miniature, and your pulse is worth taking." He let go of my wrist and returned to his rocking.

I never understood his affection for me. His heart was far greater than mine; and his uncertainty was, unlike mine, the result of a willingness to confront the worst of men and the unluckiest of destinies. He didn't hide behind a lack of finishing, a backwoods upbringing, or a haphazard education, while I hid behind doctrines that, like a headland battered by the sea, had already begun their slow erosion.

We were, all of us, wounded: Abe, in a brooding conscience no compromise could salve; you, in a heart broken by a catastrophe not even you can understand; and I, in a faith impossible for a weak man to uphold. Only Ruth seemed whole and entire until Death unraveled the plain cloth of her life.

Did I love her? Does it matter? Most conjugal pairs are guilty of halfhearted gestures, half-understood emotions, half-glimpsed truths, and a reckoning always in arrears.

The first thing Ruth bought when we set up house on Eighth Street, two blocks from the Lincolns, was a corn broom. She swept from top to bottom, washed the windows, burnished the panes with newspaper, beat the rag rugs, and, in your words,

> Spooned out Winter's dead
> From the sill inside the window—
> Each shriveled corpse,
> A tiny mummified Pharaoh.

That night, she dragged a galvanized tub into the kitchen, boiled water, and bid me wash. She looked on as though I were a boy dirty after playing in the fields. Then she put up a muslin screen and took her turn in the tub. I saw her strong young body in silhouette, defined by the light of an oil lamp. I felt the serpent uncoil in my loins, and their troublesome heat. I was uneasy but felt compelled to look at her. She appeared from behind the screen, wearing a plain nightdress. Her long, damp hair seemed indecent. She smiled gently, and I realized with a start that I, not she, was ashamed. Ridiculous man, I preened in my virtuousness while she led me upstairs, turned the covers down, and—always the practical partner in our marriage—lifted up her nightdress. She gave up her chastity as matter-of-factly as she'd given up her father's name. I felt like a sacrifice made on an altar where, in nine months' time, a child would be given to its mother's breast. The encounter had been practical and yet not without love. Afterward, we discussed neither our feelings nor the intricacies of the body's response to an experience that, I confess, was pleasurable. What she might have felt during our silent coupling, I couldn't guess, because she'd put out the light in the room, as one of us would always do.

I did love her. I know I mourned her with genuine feeling; I know my grief and tears were real. I know that I was, for a time, inconsolable. I know that I missed her keenly and, if not so keenly now, I miss her still. But it is easier to miss someone dear than to rejoice in her presence. My love, if love it was, never did flame up into ecstasy.

I should have kept the child with me even if I'd had to resign my commission and live in Amherst. Ambition did not prevent it, nor my unresolved feelings for Ruth, nor did the disconcerting thought that I would see you again. My feelings for you had flowed into the quiet backwater where we keep our memories and regrets. (I wish they had remained there.) I may have stayed in the army for no other reason than the dogged refusal to leave a path once taken— for the sake of habitude, which, little by little, replaces the soul without our realizing it.

−4−

RUTH THOUGHT MARY LINCOLN FIDGETY and considered hysteria and insanity self-indulgent. If Ruth had lived longer than her allotted span of twenty-six years, life might have rattled her, but she was pragmatic and capable to the end. She left instructions for the child's care and the house's upkeep on the back of the calendar page of the month in which she would die. The ledger where she faithfully noted every household transaction included the cost of her coffin, interment, and, afterward, a simple meal for friends. More than anything else having to do with that painful time, the discovery of that gray bound book overwhelmed me. She had written in it, in her no-nonsense way, the biography of our married life, as significant a discovery for me as any trove of love letters, of which, for Ruth and me, there was none.

I remember vividly Ruth's and my first supper at the

Lincoln place on Seventh Street, a large clapboard house, birch-colored, with green shutters, a side-gabled roof, plain corbels and cornice, two brick chimneys, a porch at the back, and a veranda on the second story. We ate celery soup and fish. I recall a pile of small bones on Abe's plate.

"Americans are fond of piles of bones," said Abe. "They are monuments to progress as it is measured by annexation and slaughter."

I knew his views on the Mexican War, the extermination of the buffalo, and the Indian Removal Act, which "Andrew Jackson and his cronies did not even bother to prettify by calling it the 'Indian Resettlement Act' or some other less autocratic and baldly extortive phrase."

"You must keep gloomy thoughts for your port and cigars, Mr. Lincoln," twittered Mary, as though she were hosting a Louisville soiree. She turned to Ruth and asked, "Mrs. Winter, is your husband dreadfully serious? I suppose he must be, having to justify the ways of men to God. Or is it the other way around? I can never remember things in their proper order. Mr. Lincoln is forever correcting me. I declare I am a flibbertigibbet!"

Amused, Abe cracked his knuckles.

Ruth stared at Mary, as she would have at one of Barnum's oddities.

"Have you heard the one about the donkey?" asked Abe.

"Mr. Lincoln, neither I nor our guests have the slightest interest in donkeys or in your foolery!"

"I'd like to hear it, Mr. Lincoln," said Ruth, not to gratify Abe, but to spite Mary, who was now glaring at her.

"Seems a might stuffy in here," said Abe. "Open the window, will you, Robert?"

"Mr. Lincoln!" Mary spoke sharply to her husband, who was picking his teeth with a fish bone.

Abe returned it to his plate and stretched his long legs under the table in prelude to his tale while I did as I was bidden. Catching a glimpse of a catalpa tree in bloom, I imagined myself outside in the summer evening air. I'd have had a volume of Shelley's or Keats's to while away the time. "Heaven smiles, and faiths and empires gleam, / Like wrecks of a dissolving dream."

Abe launched into his fable as I sat down again, and Mary fiddled with a spoon.

"There was a donkey so cussed and stubborn, it stopped one day in a farmer's field and refused to budge. Fortunately for the donkey, the farmer was a kindly soul who'd rather have taken the whip to his darkies than to his livestock. When he realized that the donkey had no intention of returning to the barn, the good man built a shed for it and each morning gave it hay and water. And so the donkey lived out its days without ambition or discomfort."

I glanced at Ruth, whose gaze was fixed on Abe, and at Mary, who, with her spoon, was pressing a crease into the tablecloth with a curious intensity.

"When the donkey finally died and was standing at heaven's gate, Saint Francis put a single question to it. 'Why do you deserve eternal bliss?'

"Without hesitation, the donkey replied, 'Because, in life, I harmed no one.'

"'Whom did you help?' asked the saint.

"'No one.'

"Saint Francis pulled an iron lever, and, before the donkey knew what had happened, it was falling through space. It didn't stop until it landed in Washington, in the House chamber, on the Democratic side of the aisle, where it was greeted by Andy Jackson and a pack of braying jackasses."

Ruth laughed, although I was not sure she saw the joke, having taken little interest in the politics of either the proslavery Democrats of the time or the liberal Whigs. Mary scowled at her husband, who looked at us with a poker face.

"Your stories are childish!" she scolded. "They might be all well and good around the stove in Merkel's hardware, to amuse the shiftless idlers who chaw and play the Jew's harp, but they are not genteel, Mr. Lincoln! You are not a gentleman, howsoever much I have tried to rid you of your backwoods ways! And will you please not crack your knuckles!"

"I beg your pardon," said Abe, his long fingers tracing a courtly gesture in the air. "I am a fool, and one day all the world shall know it." (In years to come, he would say, "I am Fool made to play the part of Lear.")

Mary replied with a sound whose spelling defies transcription: a *humph* of regret for her Kentucky home, of impatience with her husband's rustic manners, and of anger for the three of us who sat around her table like skeptics at a séance.

Supper at an end, Abe and I went into his study, while Mary praised her dining room's dark red wallpaper, embellished with a William Morris design, "purchased from Galloway and Fitch."

"I call it my 'study' to impress visitors, but mostly I take my after-dinner naps here," Abe told me.

We sat and charged our pipes with tobacco.

"How about a little glass?" he asked, a lighted pipe clamped between his teeth.

"Fine," I said, since I was safe from Ruth's reproachful eye. She was a teetotaler to spite her father, who was a sot. Contrariety can rule our lives as often as does destiny.

"And none of Mary's port, either! Damn her highfalutin ways!"

He poured us each a glass of liquor, whose burnished light entranced me.

"No better drink was ever concocted by the sons of Adam than rye whiskey." Raising his glass, he said, "To your good health, Robert."

"Long life," I replied. What irony there was in that wish, poor devil!

"Your wife seems a good sort," he said, the picture of a man at ease. He would not always be so.

"She is, but I'm afraid she might have offended Mary."

"Pay no attention to Mary! She is never so happy as when she has something to carp about. We get along well together, because I promised myself to keep her happy at all costs."

I gazed through the amber in my glass at the poplar trees, the lawn, and at Abe himself, who pulled a long face, as though he were sitting for a daguerreotypist, whose subjects always seem to frown.

"The world is better viewed through rye-colored glasses," said Abe.

You have a homely face, I thought. Like Thoreau's. Both of you, however, have virtues more important than a prepossessing countenance.

We sipped awhile in that silence known to men for whom tobacco and strong drink are enough.

"Are you looking forward to fatherhood?" he asked. His expression had become serious.

Was he thinking of his son Edward, whose death must still have been an unsalved wound in his mind—so large a mind that it needed his lofty brow to contain it? I knew that Abe's grief was immense; all his passions were. His reluctance to speak of them kept them raw.

Am I looking forward to fatherhood? I asked myself.

"Yes," I replied, after a hesitation, which he caught in the fine web of his perceptiveness.

"You're not the first man to worry over newfound responsibilities."

He pulled off one of his Congress Gaiters and scratched a toe through a sock fretted with a strand of darning wool, which took me back to Amherst and the wooden egg.

"I'm not worried."

Abe talked about his law practice and his political aspirations. He wanted to return to Washington, where he had served a term in the House until, losing his seat in 1849, he returned home to Springfield. He drawled on, pausing to tamp down his tobacco and sip his whiskey. He appeared to be speaking into his lap—he wasn't looking at me—and I was free to drift through a haze of smoke back to Amherst and my youth.

Emily, do you recall the summer day we met? I haven't thought of it in years.

−5−

I HAD WALKED TO AMHERST ACADEMY to borrow a book from Mr. Fiske, who was acquainted with my aunt. His library of works on American history was said to be comprehensive, and I hoped to find de Tocqueville's *Democracy in America* and to read it before returning to the seminary in the fall. He had volume one, which he gladly lent me, and, after a pleasant chat regarding my studies, I left him to resume his writing of an essay on "Mad Anthony" Wayne at the Battle of Fallen Timbers.

You were sitting on a bench outside North College, with a book opened on your lap. You had just taken off your bonnet to pin up a loose strand of hair, and I was struck by its coppery fineness, which seemed to catch fire in the sun. Before you could put your bonnet on again, I had seen your face clearly. At first, I thought it odd, even droll, but as my gaze lingered on it—stayed by curiosity—I saw that I'd been mistaken. Freckled and fair, your face was enlivened by hazel eyes, which, if too widely spaced for the classical ideal, enchanted me. I watched them go into eclipse beneath your bonnet's brim.

I approached you with diffidence and an overweening brashness—an uneasy combination frequently encountered in shy young men.

"What is that book you're reading?" I asked, doffing my hat like a gentleman.

Instantly, I regretted my forwardness, and I was prepared to put my hat back on my head, nod pleasantly, and walk away as fast as I could.

"Almira Hart Lincoln's *Familiar Lectures on Botany*," you said, unconcerned by my presumptuousness or the flush that I felt spreading warmly across my face. "She teaches at the seminary for young ladies in Troy, New York. She is very keen on plants."

"And do you like them very much?"

"Why, yes, I do," you replied seriously, "especially those that could not possibly take root in New England soil."

Neither of us could have known it then, but you were describing the misbegotten woman you would prove, in time, to be.

"What flower is this?" I asked, pointing to an engraving in the book resting on your lap.

"That is the *Alpinia*—kingdom, Plantae; division, Magnoliophyta; class, Liliopsida; order, Zingiberales. 'A showy and fragrant inflorescence ranging from light pinks to deep reds. *Alpinia* is indigenous to Malaya,' which, I have on good authority, is as far away from Amherst as heaven is."

You waved a gloved hand over the illustration and its gloss and said whimsically, "Of course, this is not *the Alpinia*, but only words and pictures. Miss Lincoln's book is gospel, but one must search elsewhere for the living truth."

You sat there musing and sucking your bottom lip. "Shall I tell you a secret?"

"What is it?" I asked, preparing to be perplexed.

"I am coming to prefer words to things. What book is that you have under *your* arm?"

"De Tocqueville's *Democracy in America*, volume one. May I sit down a moment? I'm feeling faint. I went out this morning without having eaten my breakfast."

You knew I was shamming; nevertheless, you made room for me on the bench—an audacity that would have shocked Miss Almira Hart Lincoln, shy, in Troy, amid her African violets.

"Thank you, Miss——"

"Miss Dickinson, resident of this town and a scholar, if an indifferent one, of this school, which, I wish you to know, sir, was founded by my grandfather, along with old Noah Webster."

My countenance expressed an appropriate veneration for your ancestor, but my interest was all in that strange face of yours. None would have called it "beautiful," but I was beguiled.

"I am Robert Winter, a student at the Lutheran Theological Seminary at Gettysburg and also a resident of this town."

"I am very happy to make your acquaintance, Mr. Winter," you replied, smoothing out the rumples in your skirt.

"Do you like history, Miss Dickinson?"

"I would like it more if it had not already come to pass," you replied wryly.

"History is time's fallen petals pressed between the pages of a book." The witticism rightfully belonged to Josiah Quincy, uttered in an uncharacteristically fanciful mood.

"I dare say you are right, but I'm of the opinion that time, being no less fleeting than impatiens or snapdragons, is unreliable and unsatisfactory. I prefer the amaranth, which is said to be immortal."

I must have appeared bewildered, because you went on to explain in that quaint way of yours, "Poetry is always fresh, except for verses penned by certain lady poets, whose sweetness turns cloudy, like honey exposed to fresh air. And languages, even dead ones, live on—in Ovid's *Metamorphoses* or Horace's *Odes*, for instance. There is also music, whose charms never fade, and pictures to look at painted ages ago that one can enjoy as if the paint had not yet dried. Even arithmetic, which I believe to be the most tyrannical subject in the curriculum, is useful when one is saving to buy a hat. But history, Mr. Winter? Fie on it! It's dry as dust, and those who teach it are old sticks!"

I felt overwhelmed, like a dory at sea, knocked about by waves.

"Do you believe in democracy?" I asked, tapping on the cover of de Tocqueville's book.

"In that I am an American, I do believe in it. But I will tell you frankly, Mr. Winter—if you can stand so much candor in one day—my house is a petty monarchy where

Father holds sway. When I left the house this morning, he was polishing his orb."

You were peculiar but, at the same time, sensible. I knew I could be no match for you in a battle of wits, never mind that I'd immersed myself in Boyd's *Elements of Rhetoric and Literary Composition*. But I could not get over my first impression: You were enchanting in your own mercurial way—an elfin being (you called yourself a "gnome")—frank, endearing, and lacking in conceit. You were a young woman worthy of my pursuit and conquest.

Forgive the words—they hardly proved apposite, but desire is as unavoidable in a young man as whiskers.

You looked at me as though your eyes were plumb bobs sounding to my very depths. I may have shivered to find myself suddenly exposed.

"You needn't fear, Mr. Winter. I shan't bite you. I am too like the tender and toothless animal that lives inside a nautilus shell."

You smiled, and I grew even fonder of your countenance. It would not have launched a thousand ships. I doubted it would have launched a waterman's skiff, but it had the power to draw me to you and to hold me in tow. Then a strange thing happened: I became persuaded that I had every right to possess you because I alone could appreciate the comeliness of your features. And by one of infatuation's paradoxes, the more I was convinced that no other young man would waste a second glance at you, the more desirable you became in my eyes.

"Will you permit me to show you the town?" I asked fatuously.

Who knew then that you would be anchored all your days to that provincial town? You are thirty-four years old, Emily, and, excepting visits to Boston for your eyes, you've stayed put, like the porcupine that turned into a cactus. I suspect Carlo was more widely traveled than you.

"I have seen it," you replied archly. "You are very bold, Mr. Winter!"

"I beg your pardon."

You were enjoying my discomfiture.

"If you would like us to be further acquainted, you must visit me at home in the usual way of a courtship. Do you mean to court me, Mr. Winter? I fear I am terribly young. But if you feel that you must, our house is the grandest one on North Pleasant Street. Father would have it no other way, even if we *are* straitened. We must, you know, maintain our 'prestige,' which I'm sure I do not care a Christmas cracker about."

I offered you my hand, which you took—albeit reluctantly—and I helped you to your feet with what I judged to be a grown-up chivalry. With the sun suddenly in your eyes, you frowned, and your freckles faded in a blush of color on your cheeks.

"I will visit you tomorrow."

"Not tomorrow," you said. "Come on Thursday, when my father will be in Boston. He is not fond of novelties."

"Will your mother be at home?"

"Certainly!" you snapped, as though I'd insinuated an impropriety.

"And is she fond of novelties?" I asked as innocently as I could.

"Not overly so, but she is not readily put out of countenance, either. Father could have glowered Oliver Cromwell into bashfulness. Yes, Mr. Winter, you must come and visit me on Thursday, when I shan't have to whisper."

−6−

Sssssnuff!

In another moment, I had been whisked from Amherst back to Springfield by a snort and snuffle that had originated in Abe Lincoln's nose. It was enough to awaken him from his after-dinner nap.

"Did that rude noise belong to me?" he asked, shrugging back into consciousness.

"It did," I replied with a laugh.

"It sounded like a train. I must've been dreaming of the Celestial Railroad and its glib conductor Mr. Smooth-It-Away. I know a good many of his sort. They would compromise their own mothers to appease the slavers."

He stretched and yawned, scratched his ear, and swept tobacco shreds from his lap.

"Mary will have much to carp about tonight. It should make her very happy."

"We should be going," I said, rising from my chair.

Abe drew a gold watch from his pocket.

"Gone on nine o'clock. The ladies will be getting agitated."

He snapped the lid shut and, with a weary sigh, heaved himself upright.

We went into the parlor, where Mary was regaling Ruth with stories of her "finishing" at Madame Mantelle's school and her erstwhile position in the Lexington, Kentucky, aristocracy. She was nattering cheerfully, but she seemed to me like a barefoot dancer mincing over broken glass or a fakir smiling on a bed of nails. Her effusions sounded hollow at the core.

Later that night, I asked Ruth, "Did Mary talk about little Edward?"

"No, but in her mind, I'm sure he was with us. She would sometimes stare into a corner of the room and groan."

In *my* mind, I repeated the words of Saint Matthew, concerning Herod's murder of the infants, ". . . Rachel weeping for her children, and would not be comforted, because they are not." Then I said aloud, "Abe worries that she will not give up her grieving for the boy."

"It's been a year and more," replied Ruth, a stolid German girl, whose philosophy was not to dwell on things that can't be changed.

"What do you think of Abe?"

"He seems harmless. Mind you, Robert, I've had enough of his fables and tall tales to see me into the next life!"

She quenched the candle flame between her fingers and went to bed without another word. The next life would come too soon for both of them, alas.

"Time consumes like a fire as it passes, and history is its ashes." Was it you who said that? I know of no one else who talks in rhymes.

When Ruth's time came, she gave birth almost effortlessly, as though the baby could not wait to begin her life. We laughed, relieved that the labor had been easy. Her mother had toiled a full day, followed by a lengthy lying-in.

"It was no harder than scrubbing a floor," said Ruth as the midwife cleaned the baby.

Charlotte was to be our only child. She brought the house alive, as children will, and kindled an affection between Ruth and me, which had grown tepid. If it was not love I felt, it was as near to love as I will likely get.

I ministered to the soldiers at the fort and preached at the Lutheran church in town. Often, we had guests for Sunday dinner; the Lincolns came on several occasions. Mary wore black, her moods were variable, and her voice would sometimes slide up and down the scale of grief like a Swanee whistle. Ruth was kind now that she, too, was a mother and could imagine a mother's bereavement. She'd listen to Mary's reminiscences and fancies, nod encouragingly, and, if they happened to be sitting on the sofa, pat the back of her hand consolingly. I do think Mary's wits were turned, although Abe spoke more kindly of them as merely being "addled."

Abe and I would trade stories and our hopes for the future. I knew that his optimism was a pretense, largely for Mary's benefit. Privately, he brooded. I recall sitting at the window of his office when, looking at the street, he said gloomily and—as it turned out—prophetically, "The Potawatomie followed their Trail of Tears through Springfield. I fear much blood will be shed and our tears will be ample."

When, at the end of June, Henry Clay, of Kentucky, died, Abe delivered the eulogy. He maintained that destiny had always put forward men that "the age has demanded." He spoke with prescience about the dangerous times ahead, admonishing the mourners, "Let us strive to deserve, as far as mortals may, the continued care of Divine Providence, trusting that, in future national emergencies, He will not fail to provide us the instruments of safety and security."

Increasingly, Abe's melancholy would overwhelm a genial nature, eclipsing it for days on end, when he seemed a man in deepest shadow. His tales became cautionary, his anecdotes somber, his fables dark; his silences grew lengthier. I would resort to his study and rest in them awhile, pleading the necessity of quiet in order to compose my sermons. Ruth had the patience of a mother and of a person whose nerves are not spun overly fine.

"Suffer little children, and forbid them not, to come unto me," she would scold with the authority of the King James Bible. There were times—God forgive me—when I resented my own child.

You must think me monstrous, Emily, but I have sworn to be honest. Self-revelation is more painful than Saint John's Apocalypse, which will not come to pass until the end of days.

That reminds me of another of Abe's fables. He had been reading aloud an account in the newspaper of the execution of Narciso López, who had led an expeditionary force of American, German, and Hungarian mercenaries to liberate Cuba from Spain. Having paused in his reading, Abe pulled at an earlobe.

"Has something put a flea in your ear?" I asked.

He laughed and proceeded to spin a yarn he called "God and the Flea."

"And when the last human being was finally dead," Abe concluded, "the flea he'd carried to the end of time hopped off his corpse and straight into God Almighty's beard."

Your recent letter, Emily, also concerned itself with the resilient pest.

The Homestead
Amherst
June 4, 1865

Dear Friend,

Lately, I have wondered if the Flea, such as tortured poor Carlo, or Lice, to be more emphatically objectionable, once inhabited Paradise. I mean the Earthly one called Eden, which was let an age ago to negligent Tenants—who allowed the Garden to grow wild. I did not think before that our Parents could possibly have *itched*—in their unabashed nakedness—from bites received from any outlaw species of Creation. Perhaps there was a Golden Age of Fleas & Men—before the Serpent had its fateful palaver with Eve—when all was peaceable & coexistent. (Lice I cannot abide & trust He would not have put them into circulation, at least before Sodom & Gomorrah.)

In church & Sunday school, vermin were not much discussed, unless it was the Mouse that had moved in behind the vestry wainscoting. Cheese & traps were set out after the Elders refused to give it sanctuary. I considered it against Christian tenets to withhold mercy even to rodents & complained so meekly, I expected to inherit the Earth before the week was out.

I like to think the Flea was once as bléssed as a dew drop or as harmless as the Commas that appear to hop about the page, excited—according to Dr. Williams—by the hysteria of my retinas. Lately, they have been washed immoderately by tears—what with Mr. Lincoln gone, & then Carlo.

What will the Nation do now that HE is a perpetual resident in Springfield, amid the marbles? What will I do now that Carlo has lain down beneath the Pear tree in the garden's southeastern corner, never to get up? Because Eternity is cold, I wrapped him in a quilt. I would spend all the words left in my Purse to bring him back again.

Write to me in care of Woe,

Emily

P.S. Carlo has sent me word from his loftier vantage that the Future is catastrophic.

P.S.S. I lied just now when I wrote that Carlo sleeps through the ages beneath a quilt. It is the red serape rather, which he always loved.

Your letters would arrive at the fort, where I'd read and keep them. There was nothing to compromise either of us, but I didn't want to give Ruth cause for suspicion. She was not jealous of me or envious of you as two beings subject to desire. What she might have feared was the intercourse of two minds exchanging thoughts whose import she could not have grasped. She might have insisted that I put an end to our correspondence, a renunciation impossible for me to contemplate. Your letters were a gift of sight to a man who had always seen things from the common point of view.

And so I cannot accept the harsh sentence you pronounced on the marvelous utterance you shape with your mouth and with your pen: "Words leave no trace and are cold besides."

You spoke from the center point of a narrowing circumference where one turns to speak to another, only to find that he is talking to himself. Why, words are your blood, bones, and very atoms! Your hammer and forge. They are all we have at the end of our allotted span and all we leave behind us. They are our posterity—yours and also mine, though mine are likely to be few and carved on a marble slab.

I know what you're thinking, holed up in your room like a female Hephaestus, smithying words into shapes at the forge of your tiny desk—your slender fingers sooty with ink.

Charlotte. Always, my daughter's name is on my mind like a cold on the stomach.

At the time, I believed that I was acting in her best interest. Her mother was dead, and I could not have cared for her properly. Aunt Tess was lonely. You would be her teacher and friend. Austin would be like a brother to her. Carlo would romp with her. Your mother would delight in her. Your father's heart would soften. Amherst is more civilized than Springfield. Illinois is nearer "Bleeding Kansas" than Massachusetts. The Indians of the western plains are more dangerous than those of the northeastern Woodland tribes. In that I could rationalize my having put a thousand miles between us is sufficient reason why I was and am unfit to be her father.

And yet I do miss her and miss—oftentimes yearn—for poor vanished Ruth. If I had been devoutly Christian and God-fearing, I would have raged against Him who took her. I'd have wept like Job. It was only the lack of an authentic vocation that kept me placid.

You once asked me why I had become a man of God.

To discover if, after having studied His way and Word, I would have cause to love or to hate Him. If I hadn't lost my father, perhaps I would not have had to wrestle with Him until, His patience grown thin, He turned His back on me. I couldn't have known myself well enough then to articulate our curious relationship. I believe now, however, that to have wrestled with divinity until "my thigh was put out of joint" may have been my true vocation. As you once said to me, "Wrestling with an angel is good exercise."

Unless I really did mishear my calling.

–7–

ONE SUMMER, RUTH AND I BOARDED a Pacific Railroad train bound for Hannibal, Missouri, to see the river the Indians rightly called the "Father of Waters." The scenery was grand, the weather fine, the other passengers untalkative, and the rapidity of our westward progress an exciting novelty for Ruth, who had never ridden by rail.

Did you go by train to Boston when you consulted Dr. Williams about your eyes? If so, you don't require my effusions in praise of travel by steam locomotive. I'll describe Hannibal, which you haven't seen and never will now that you are walled up inside the Homestead, like Fortunato in the catacombs, in Edgar Poe's oppressive tale.

The town had sprawled at the expense of the trees, with which it had been aboriginally and abundantly supplied. With its mudflats, stubble, dusty streets, and peeling warehouses, you'd have called it a "blister on creation." But the river, sown with gaily painted boats, compensated for what the town lacked in charm. Side- and paddle wheelers threshed the broad brown river, their decks teeming with fancy-dressed passengers, livestock, and slaves. The Mississippi was an extraordinary sight even for a New Englander who once had stood on the Atlantic's rocky coast and howled, for want of a destiny, into the north wind.

Ruth and I rested in a garish belvedere built on a bluff overlooking the river, enjoying the freely circulating air. We held hands like a couple just embarked on their courtship before time—that bitter solvent—could dissolve their bond of affection and marriage—that mangle—iron out their endearing differences. Being neither poets nor politicians, the talk was small.

A boy sat on the bench next to ours. He must have been sixteen or seventeen years old, a prepossessing youth whose slouch and lankiness reminded me of Abe Lincoln. The young man worked as a typesetter for a Hannibal newspaper. He was contemplating a sandwich and a slice of pie that had been wrapped in the morning's front page. I took note, among the crumbs, of the "workmanlike manner" of W. M. Smith, M.D., dental surgeon, an advertisement set in type worthy of an invitation to Christ's Second Coming.

"Most rags aren't fit to eat off," he said. "But the *Western Union* is printed with a love for cleanliness, if not always the truth."

With a glance at the headlines lying open on his lap, he commenced to eat in a curious fashion, taking a bite of sandwich and then one of pie until both had been consumed.

"To eat the sandwich first and then the pie stinks of patronage," he said in answer to our mute inquiry. "It goes against the grain of a boy raised up in Missouri to believe in democracy and the equality of all white men. Now if I were a duke, say, or a postmaster or customhouse spoilsman, I'd eat the pie and throw away the sandwich. Mine used to be the tongue of a cow who liked to chew its cud."

He ate awhile and then asked, "You folks got a name?"

"We are Mr. and Mrs. Winter, of Springfield, Illinois," I replied. "And what might you be called?"

"A number of things—most of them unflattering or downright defaming. But when she's sober, my mother calls me Sam."

"It is a pleasure to meet you, Sam."

"Likewise."

"I suppose you mean one day to become a correspondent or an editor?"

"Well, the newspaper business is steady work as long as men beat their wives or kill Injuns. And if you'll pardon me, ma'am"—he touched his hat brim courteously with an ink-stained finger—"the papers are always in demand by those who do their reading by the light of the moon cut into an outhouse door. I once saw the *San Jose Visitor* torn to flinders and nailed to the wall of a necessary house. Seems a disgraceful end for journalism. (I nicknamed the rag *The Privy Counsellor*.) No, the newspaper business will never go flat. But what I want to be is a Mississippi steam boatman."

A shrill whistle was just then announcing the arrival of the *General Putnam*.

"Do you have any experience on a steamboat?" asked Ruth, pretending to a curiosity that her eyes belied. She'd grown tired of the young man's flippancy.

"I saw a minstrel show on the *Cotton Blossom* last year and some pretty fair circuses out on the river; and, in my capacity as apprentice reporter, I go aboard steamboats to count barrels, bales, and slaves for the shipping news."

Ruth had walked to the lookout's railing to view a passing side-wheeler through a brass telescope we had brought with us from Springfield.

"There's two thousand miles of river, and a pilot needs to know every snag and shoal, bar and stump of it," said Sam as proudly as if he had already committed the dangers to navigation to memory.

"There're slaves on that boat!" cried Ruth, turning toward us, the telescope forgotten in her hand.

"The lucky ones are roustabouts," said Sam, biting off a chaw of tobacco. "They get to tote four-hundred-pound bales of hemp, sugar, tobacco, and cotton up and down gangways from here to New Orleans. Contrary to what you might think, ma'am, a four-hundred-pound bale of cotton weighs the same as a four-hundred-pound crate of cast-iron stove lids. The unlucky ones get lynched."

"It's a hateful thing to see!" said Ruth with a bitterness that surprised me.

"True," said Sam. "It would be a whole lot less hateful if you hadn't seen them up close through your glass. I always say that darkies are best seen at night, when the sight of them can't offend the finicky or gnaw the consciences of good Christians."

"My husband is a minister of God!" said Ruth angrily.

"And I'm positive that he prays for the souls of all poor

niggers," said Sam, undismayed. "'course in Missouri, we're used to seeing black people suffer at close range. The abolitionists had hoped the territory would come into the union a Free State, but the Missouri Compromise compromised the negroes here into everlasting chains. Maine got in as a Free State, only there weren't any colored people living there to speak of. Be wary of appeasement, sir," he said to me, "for on such is built the kingdom of the damned."

Abe had said much the same thing.

Sam spat tobacco juice toward the railing, but a wind sprang up and blew the brown spittle back again. The wind had also brought the stink of the tannery and of the wide mudflats where a flat boat sat piled high with grain.

"Damn!" he said, mopping his coat with a handkerchief.

So rigid was Ruth's back, which she had turned to us, I could see her corset stays pressing through the fabric of her dress.

"Mrs. Winter, I apologize if my remarks offended you. I'm a river rat and haven't had much use for manners or practice in making polite conversation, especially with ladies. Fact is, ma'am, I'm just a rambunctious no-account marking time until I get my bearings."

Sam stood and coughed like any gentleman wishing to attract the attention of a lady.

Having decided to forgive him his "enthusiasm," Ruth sat once again beside me. Sam sat, leaned back on the bench, and contemplated the river, whose boats no longer seemed gay.

A tiny silvery sound came from inside the boy's pocket.

He took out his watch and, after having told us the time, showed us the inscription on the inside of the lid: *To Tom, from Becky.*

"I won it in a poker game off a miner whose claim went bust. Every time I hear it chime the hour, I remind myself never to draw to an inside straight. You have a pleasant trip home."

Sam went on his way, presumably to set columns of type that would wrap his next day's lunch.

"What shall we do until the Springfield train arrives?" I asked.

"Let's find a present for Charlotte and a little gift for Mary Lincoln."

We strolled along the sidewalks of Hannibal, peering in at store windows. Outside the *Western Union* office, we watched Sam pick lead from a case. We sauntered past the cooperage, the rope makers, and Tilden Selmes's Emporium, where Ruth bought a christening spoon and a cloth doll for Charlotte and a tortoiseshell comb for Mary Lincoln. I bought Abe a watch fob. At the Petersen House, after his death, they emptied his pockets and found the fob, along with a pocketknife, some newspaper clippings, two pairs of spectacles (one mended with string), and a Confederate five-dollar bill. It was the string that caused me to shed tears a second time for him, after I'd read the inventory taken of his pockets in the *Boston Evening Traveller.*

Ruth and I had supper at the station saloon and dawdled afterward over a glass of ginger beer.

"I'm glad I got to see the Mississippi River, but I wish

we'd stayed in Springfield," she said pensively. I guessed that she was thinking of the black men chained up on the steamboat.

I said nothing, and my inability to offer words of comfort, consolation, compensation, or explanation (of man's behavior or God's in allowing such infamy) distressed me. I waited for her rebuke. Wasn't I a minister? Wasn't it my duty to summon words from the great store of them laid down at Gettysburg and by experience? The latter, however, had only contradicted the books that I had read, lectures I had attended, and homilies I had heard. I'd been to school in Mexico, where my Christian faith began to crumble as even rock will when water freezes in its crannies. What was the seminary next to Chapultepec, Huamantla, or Veracruz?

Emily, do you recall your odd descant on the "stone-breaker" plant?

I let Saxifrage into the little Eden behind the house & fed it stones—in recognition of its Latin meaning, "rock breaker." Dr. Harbison, who comes to take Mother's pulse, said that I had been misinformed—the plant possesses a medicinal property that can rid the sufferer of *Kidney* stones. Indeed, it has not touched a single one of Earth's that I set out for it—not even a fine yellow gravel from Puffer's Pond—which I'd have thought a delicacy. It does have the prettiest red flowers & rosettes of succulent leaves.

I've consulted Miss Lincoln's *Botany*, which

parses it thus: kingdom, Plantae; order, Saxifrag-
ales; family, Saxifragaceae; genus, Saxifraga. I
intend to cultivate my Saxifrage against the time
when I may have kidney stones or—more likely—
when my mind shall have petrified. My heart, I
fear, has already done so.

At a table inside McFadden's Station Saloon, Ruth was
agitated. I watched her finger sketch nervously in the salt
that had collected around her plate. She always did take too
much of it with her meals.

"Are you all right, dear?" I asked, without taking her hand.
I was fascinated by what she was doing with the salt, you see.

"I never thought much about their suffering." At that
moment, she was deserving of her Christian name. "I've
only ever known house slaves and those that work in the
garden. But those enormous bales they must carry! And
their backs, Robert, I saw the most awful scars on one!"

She must have known that she could expect nothing
from me.

Ruth, I wish you could have seen me at Andersonville!
If, during our brief marriage, you were disappointed in me
as a man of God, Andersonville redeemed me, though I'm
not sure God was there, either, to take note of it.

We sat while the silence lengthened into uneasiness,
and then Ruth, capable and resigned, took her napkin and
wiped the table clean of salt, as though she were at home.

Just then, a bell clanged, and the Springfield train pulled

into the station. We watched coal smoke drift down over the locomotive like a funereal drape.

"Pay the man," said Ruth, collecting her packages and preparing to leave the saloon.

In retrospect, it might not have been the happy day that I recalled. Abe once said to me, "A man is given only a handful of happy days, if he's lucky. Only fools and drunkards believe otherwise."

We rode through the evening and on into night. I was glad when Ruth fell asleep, though she gave me hell when she awoke for letting her new hat get crushed against my shoulder. When we arrived in Springfield, my mouth tasting like cinders, we were worn out and longing for bed. We walked home to our house on Eighth Street in the ordinary silence that comes of weariness. The town was abed, all except for its drunk, a fellow named Dugan, and a mongrel dog licking a piece of greasy butcher's paper at the curb.

In May of '65, I would stand in that same station when Abe and his son Willie, in their coffins, were brought home from Washington. I was there as a friend of the Lincoln family; otherwise, I doubt I would have gotten near the funeral train or the borrowed hearse that carried Abe to the statehouse for his own eulogy and, on the next day, to Oak Ridge Cemetery to be "folded away in time's violet-scented handkerchief"—not with 100,000 mourners filling the town.

Abe seemed to have had an intimation of his fate. He said to me, while we were making our customary survey of the traffic passing the corner of Sixth and Adams streets, "I will never be an old man."

I recall a solitary bugler standing on the rear platform of the "Lincoln Special," as the funeral train was called. He made so mournful a music that the mob wept in its thousands and tens of thousands. Moran was his name. He had lost an eye at the Battle of Five Forks. General Grant himself gave him the Medal of Honor. According to a newspaper account I read, the boy had named his trumpet "Joshua."

−8−

DURING THE 1850S, SOLDIERS ROUNDED up rogue bands of hostiles that refused the hospitality of the reservations and herded them into Indian Territory. Massacres were common on both sides of the moral argument, whose resolution few could foresee. Fewer still could guess that the union would, in less than ten years' time, be ripped apart. Like others, I believed that we had more to fear from the savages than from the secessionists.

"Fear makes us martial," you once said. "Thus do brutes beget brutes on good men."

Between skirmishes, buffalo hunts were a favorite pastime of the men and good exercise for their mounts. I rode out with them once and discovered in the chase and kill an ecstasy that verged on the religious. The Indians revere the bison because of that rapture, which opens their hearts to the earth and to their gods. They also admire the animal's enormous vitality. Despite its speed and power, a troop of cavalry could slaughter a hundred in an hour and strip them of their coats, with which to warm their winter bivouacs in the high plains. Hides were also prized as gifts to send east to loved ones, who'd have them made into muffs, polar hats, and lap rugs. Ruth no longer needed them, having grown indifferent to the cold. I did send a buffalo skin to Charlotte and another to Tess. I thought you might disapprove of robing yourself in an animal carcass, or Carlo would have objected to the smell.

By this time, I had sold the Springfield house and, after taking Charlotte east to live with Tess, moved into the fort. My needs were few. I never felt the itch to acquire or possess. I had been a divinity student and was then an army chaplain, two occupations that discouraged luxurious living. I'd been fortunate to have had a wife who was neither vain nor a spendthrift—a robust farm girl used to hardship and privation.

Otherwise, the years leading up to the Mormon Rebellion passed uneventfully for me. Sunday mornings, I would preach to the troops, then ride into town to repeat the sermon to my Lutheran congregation, which may have been startled by a gristly figure of speech apposite for the cavalry. After Ruth's death, my manner coarsened, and I grew my beard to the limit of army tolerance. I looked as the "prophet of loneliness" might have, if he had exchanged his sackcloth for a blue serge suit and gold buttons.

Was I lonely?

Yes, but no lonelier than the other men at the fort—or,

for that matter, the people of my civilian flock. No lonelier than Ruth must have been before our marriage (and, perhaps, during it) or, as I suspect, than you are now in a Homestead without your ally Carlo. It would be banal to say that we are all lonely, but it is the truth notwithstanding and one that poets, for all their fine words, cannot make any more endurable. Most can put aside their loneliness and carry on with the life given them to use and then to forfeit. Soldiers seem gifted at forgetting.

My ministry to the men was becoming more and more about ceremony. I'd repeat the words of the service for the dead without feeling their significance. In the tomb, the "rock of ages" where we'll spend all that's left of time in waiting, words die without so much as an echo to recall them. Far from home, men die; no words can help them; no tears are shed over their corpses. Blood and salt—these are the human residue.

During my first year in Springfield, I rode with the cavalry south into "Little Egypt." Renegades had jumped a reservation and captured the saltworks on the Saline River, near the town of Equality. The tribe had ceded the Great Salt Springs in 1803. Still rankling from the treaty's terms, the renegades were demanding its return. They hadn't a hope in hell of getting the land back. They were just one more band of discontented redskins. In those days, there were many such, even among those whose lives had been given over to whiskey and idleness.

I did not care for Indians. I judged them to be less civilized and more inscrutable than the Mexicans we'd hunted.

In that the savages had gods of their own, I considered them outside my remit. I told myself that the deities to whom they prayed should look after the red men and their souls, if they had any. At the Saline River, my care was for the soldiers and the whites living in Equality.

The soldiers finished off the Indians in two hours. We lost five men; one, a private from Ohio, took twenty minutes to pass from this world into the next. I had time to hear him talk—between groans—about his wife and child, his grocery store in Greenville, and his sins, which were trivial. I said the words of my trade and, pressing his hand in mine, assured him of the glory to come—once he had been "raised above the sorrows and temptations of the present world."

Do you see how impossible it would have been to have Charlotte with me? The country was becoming dangerous.

That night, we camped by "Nigger Spring." Since few white men were willing to mine salt, the work was largely done by slaves. In the morning, the sentries shot deer that had come down to the river to lick salt from the rocks.

I overhead a soldier say, "It was good sport," and didn't know if he had meant the deer or the Indians.

After breakfast, I rode some distance to the Garden of the Gods Wilderness. The place was wondrous strange, and what gods might have once roamed there must have been fearsome. Gigantic slabs of sandstone thrust upward, amid pinnacles and spires, caves and imposing arches of rock. The mysterious formations reminded me of the *moai*, the Easter Island statues described by Captain Cook in his journal. The gods of the island paradise proved helpless against smallpox and consumption, which exterminated the inhabitants in spite of their prayers and sacrifices.

Speaking of Cook's journal, I penned my own account of the Mexican War. After Ruth's death, I felt at a loss and cast about for something to distract me. Having few merits beyond the attractive light it shed on me, the manuscript deserved to be put into the stove, but I couldn't bring myself to destroy it.

You would have been enthralled by the Gods Wilderness, its otherworldly canyons, bluffs, and ridges. I recall your girlish interest in geology and your sketches of volcanoes. That was a long time ago, and time, in its slow passing, erodes and deforms more than rocks. It tells eloquently and appallingly on a human face. I wonder if it has finally told on yours.

You must think me hard. Life is hard, and the heart grows mineral the longer it beats time within it. In your corner room, safe within your father's house—regardless of his severity—you can have no conception of what people alive in the world outside the pages of your books endure— the scrabbling for necessities, the clutching at what they don't need but nonetheless want, the moral dilemmas all but the meanest of them face. I was privy to it; I had learned to see inside the hearts of men and could not, in conscience, turn away, though what I saw there often offended me. That is the *pastor's* dilemma. A prophet can call down ruin on his people, but the pastor must chasten and forgive—or play his part so well that none suspects that he has perjured himself.

"What of mercy?" I can hear you ask in a voice a timid nun might use to interrogate the beast inside a man.

Mercy takes a terrible toll.

Seven years after we rode against the saltworks, I put Ruth into the ground with small hope of resurrection. Although I had pronounced the requisite words with the persuasiveness of a conjuror, I could not then nor can I now picture her dressed in heavenly raiment, singing *Hallelujah* in her flat midwestern voice.

I'm reminded of the Sunday morning that Ruth impudently altered the Easter hymn to express an irreligious joy:

"The dough has risen! *Hallelujah*!
  In the oven the loaf will go!
  Sing yeast's praises! *Hallelujah*!
  Soon our bellies will be full!"

I took comfort in the army, in which a man can satisfy a desire for solitude and mitigate its loneliness among other men. At the fort, I befriended an Indiana man a few years older than I, named Arnold Tauber. Born in Wittenberg, Saxony, he'd emigrated when he was twenty. That he came from Martin Luther's native town pleased me, even if I no longer revered the heretical German. I sometimes wished I could purchase the remission of my sins—not those of the flesh, which scarcely interested me, but the sin of a doubting mind.

For a soldier, Tauber was quiet and scholarly. He considered himself "a student of time" and carried with him

Gibbon's *The History of the Decline and Fall of the Roman Empire*. One or another of its volumes would be in the pocket of his sack coat or, when he was on horseback, in his saddlebag. He relished the idea that, by Gibbon's light and his own saturnine disposition, the United States was already in decline—the golden age of the republic debased past redeeming.

I disagreed. We'd won vast territories from the Mexicans; we had discovered the richest gold fields in history; railroads were beginning their slow progress across the continent. Two thousand miles of an untouched empire lay between Council Bluffs, on the Missouri River, and the Pacific Ocean. Wherever aborigines stood in the way of our unyielding westward advance, they would be removed by historical necessity. Necessity relieved me of moral qualms. My disturbing recollections of the Mexican War had been absorbed by the national memory of glorious battles won.

I said none of this to Tauber. He could be contentious, an aspect of his character I didn't care for. Nodding, I would hear him out and, now and then, interject a catarrhal sound to prove that I was listening. I disliked controversy, and, when it loomed, I'd challenge Tauber to a game of backgammon, played according to Edmond Hoyle's treatise, a book which also belonged to the eccentric cavalryman.

Having few vices and those few being venial, Tauber was a suitable companion for a parson. We drank spirits, but not immoderately. We swore like gentlemen, not like troopers. We wagered pennies and never flew into rages over our losses. We went to the saloon but sat at a table rather than leaned against the bar like the roughnecks and hooligans. By our frowns, we made known our disapproval, which meant no more to them than it would to a boy chastised by his teacher for rude noises. Periodically, but without unreasonable frequency, Tauber would be overcome by "passion" and visit a house in which such pressures as beset even a Christian man could be relieved. Afterward, he returned to the barracks and, by a smiling absence of remorse, I knew that he'd been innocent of lust and had taken a woman "medicinally," so to speak.

"Men are nothing but whiskers and socks in constant need of darning," you once chided me when I was preening over some virtue I imagined I possessed.

Your low opinion of my sex has oftentimes seemed to me correct.

My wife's death aside, I recall those days in Springfield fondly. The world had yet to enter an age of universal jangle and uproar. On Sunday mornings, the choir sang of a "Jesus, meek and gentle," who had not yet "loosed the fateful lightning of His terrible swift sword" or been "trampling out the vintage where the grapes of wrath are stored." We fretted over the hostiles, who were interested in collecting scalps rather than in staking claims to what, in their minds, belonged to them. They could be subdued, without too much trouble, by a company of cavalrymen. We believed that the Indians were of a degenerate race and worthy of the lice infesting them.

So I thought then. Most people did. Most still do. It's easier to belittle and defame. We can resolve moral issues with less soul-searching if the cards are marked, the terms of the debate manipulated, or the points in a chain of doubtful logic deliberately smudged like a decimal in an embezzler's ledger book. While each of us believes he keeps his own accounts, in actuality the books are held by a power greater than congresses, parliaments, presidents, kings, and emperors. We carry on like warrior ants, which believe the universe is contained in an anthill, and the outcome of their great wars decides the fate of all.

What power, you ask, could possibly be greater than that wielded by despots?

Enmity. Hatred as the primal urge and prime mover, capable of toppling all forms of government, even the most tyrannical. I sometimes thought that you had been infected with that same nihilism; your verses, in their disregard of grammar and sense, could be the warrants of anarchy, the symptoms of a disease. But then I remembered your words: "Ecstasy is ungrammatical, and never more so than in our faithless age."

In the spring of '56, Tauber and I decided to use our furlough to see the prehistoric teeth unearthed two years before by Hayden during his exploration of the Upper Missouri, on exhibit at the Chicago History Museum. I'd read an extract from the *Proceedings of the Academy of Natural Sciences of Philadelphia*, in which paleontologist Joseph Leidy identified them as the dental remains of a dinosaur, the first to be discovered in North America. I recalled your pencil sketches of footprints made by primeval beasts that reigned long before the Flood drowned our hens and cows—even, in your words, "before God descended from His heaven to create our world, since saurian monsters are not reported in Genesis." That was also Tauber's notion. He could be as fantastical and blasphemous as you. I speculated that dinosaurs might have been the aboriginal inhabitants of the Gods Wilderness, which everywhere bore evidence of titanic strain.

"These teeth confirm Gibbon's theory of rise and fall on a geologic scale," said Tauber while we stood peering through a glass case, in awe of the monstrous teeth.

What emotion would I feel were I suddenly confronted by the creature itself? Something other than awe—terror, more likely. A terror greater than I have ever felt for Him.

"They belonged to a dragon," I said, half in earnest, half in jest. I finished the thought in my unspoken voice, which will often speak the truth: a dragon on which the Whore of Babylon might have sat. I blushed at my imaginings.

Later, as we were idling among the exhibits concerning great civilizations of the past, Tauber said, "It was not only Rome that had its rise and fall."

I grunted, having grown tired of Mr. Gibbon and his theory.

We walked slowly through the ancient world, past the Sumerians, Egyptians, Minoans, Hittites, Babylonians, Greeks, Etruscans. Each of those vanished empires had been condensed and neatly fitted into a diorama. One day, vestiges of our own aboriginal civilizations will be gathering dust inside display cases, forgotten by an America mad for progress and the new.

Life is continuous action, I thought. Memory and history are tableaux.

Leaving the museum at closing time, we went to an eating house and ordered beefsteaks, which, the waiter assured us, "only yesterday were on the hoof at the slaughterhouse." We sat nonchalantly among the "gentry," miners and gamblers, mostly, who'd been lucky, disdaining them for their fancy clothes. Ours were travel-stained, and our beards were not in the least á la mode. The room was gilt, marble, and leather, but the steak tasted suspiciously like buffalo, and the four-bit cigars stank.

Afterward, we went to a minstrel show at McVicker's Theater on Madison. We laughed at the antics of Jim Crow and Zip Coon, their blacked-up faces greasy in the glare of the calcium footlights. Less amusing acts followed, whose indecencies incited the gentlemen to throw coins onto the stage and the ladies to blush into the depths of their décolletage. The sly innuendo made me squirm, and I was relieved when John Wilkes Booth performed Hamlet's famous soliloquy. If I'd known that, on an April night to come, he would shoot Abe Lincoln inside Ford's Theatre, I'd have killed him then and there—God's commandment to the contrary be damned!

If I had killed him, what then? Someone else would have risen to take his place like a figure in a piece of clockwork. At Harvard, I once saw a mechanical model of the universe. Small brass balls revolved in lunar and planetary orbits around a brazen sun. I cannot picture the Creator's hand on the crank.

"It sounds like one of Mr. Poe's tales," you said after I had described the mechanism.

"How so?" I asked curiously, being fond of his fiction.

"The plotting is inexorable and pitiless, like a railroad timetable or the guillotine."

"You're being whimsical again."

"*Whimsical* is a word that people use to belittle their less conventional neighbors," you replied, as wide-eyed as the Sphinx in a blast of desert sunlight.

–9–

THE TIMES WERE BLOODY. Whether or not death will be ample in the future, none can tell, unless Carlo were to break its seal and send you word in "Dog" or Morse. Dogs are said to be alert to the vibrations of the spirit world, and no dog could be more so than Carlo now that he's no longer with us. I would not write about those years if I did not think that, in your reclusion, they might have escaped notice. They were momentous even for me, who had no part to play in the Kansas–Missouri Border War, which was both a rehearsal and an accelerant for the war whose outcome would be the destruction or the preservation of the union.

What made them momentous?

My predestined encounter with John Brown. He was the needle and the scarlet thread that stitched a gory seam that led from Kansas to Harper's Ferry and to our most reck-less, costly civil strife. His was the thread that strengthened me in a calling that did not answer to God, but to man, although, in my weakness and my fear, I have wavered.

What do you know about the Border War? If reports of it were heard in your scriptorium and the pantry where you sometimes hid among the jars of peaches, plums, and piccalilli to escape your "pontiff's" dogmas, you may skip my brief history of those troublesome times. Besides, that was one war that took place without me, for which mercy I am grateful.

In May 1856, seven hundred proslavery partisans sacked Lawrence, Kansas, destroying two abolitionist newspapers (deemed "seditious"), the Free State Hotel (a "fortress" and an "arsenal"), and the home of Charles Robinson, commander in chief of the Free State militia (a "nigger-lover"). As if Lawrence were Jerusalem, John Brown, together with his sons, rose up like a vengeful prophet and hacked to death three slave catchers and two militants with swords at Pottawatomie Creek.

Men love the taste of other men's blood. Hasn't it always been so, Emily?

That August, John Reid's Border Ruffians, armed with guns, cutlasses, and a cannon stolen from the United States arsenal at Liberty, Missouri, seized Osawatomie, on the Osage River, where "Captain" Brown and his sons had been staying with the Reverend Samuel Adair. In retaliation, Brown attacked Reid's four hundred men. Outnumbered ten to one and evidently forsaken by the Lord of Hosts, Brown's "army" retreated. In reprisal, the Ruffians brought "fire and sword" to the Kansas town before advancing on the antislavery stronghold at Topeka, hoping to raze it, as well. Brown's son Frederick was killed in the skirmish. Other of his sons would follow him, until the old man himself died "on the rugged cross."

When he returned to Osawatomie and found it reduced to char and chimney stones, Brown told his adherents, "God sees it. I have only a short time to live—only one death to die, and I will die fighting for His cause. There will be no more peace in this land until slavery is done for. I will give them something else to do than extend slave territory. I will carry this war into Africa."

I detested slavery as much as did Thoreau, Emerson, or Garrison, but I was sworn to uphold the Constitution and took my orders from the colonel at the fort, who, according to the chain of command, took his from President Pierce. God whispered no contravening order into my ear. I gave thanks to Him for His silence. Neither side of the Border War, or the issue of popular sovereignty versus federalism, was guiltless. The proslavery gang wanted to get rich, using slaves to cultivate the territory, while much of the antislavery faction—called "Free-Soilers"—objected on economic grounds: Human bondage, a source of free labor, was unfair competition. The preservation of the union ought to have been—as it would be during the War of Succession—the aim of government and the chief duty of the army. But in the case of Bleeding Kansas, Franklin Pierce and his administration wished to see slavery thrive. I saw Pierce once, in a sick tent, during the capture of

Mexico City; he'd been struck down by the flux. It was the nation's misfortune that he survived.

On Independence Day in 1856, Pierce ordered troops stationed at Fort Leavenworth and Fort Riley, Kansas, to Topeka—there to disband the Free State convention, convened after a congressional investigation had found that the proslavery government at Lecompton had been illegally elected. Thousands of Missourians had crossed into Kansas to vote against a Free State. Armed men bent on stuffing ballot boxes had undermined democracy in the territory.

I have a yellowing scrap of vociferous prose by Benjamin Franklin Stringfellow, ripped from the *Squatter Sovereign*. (I could not help remembering the young type-setter at Hannibal.) The article asservated (there's a bloody word!) his faction's commitment "to repel this Northern invasion and make Kansas a Slave State; though our rivers should be covered with the blood of their victims and the carcasses of the Abolitionists should be so numerous in the territory as to breed disease and sickness, we will not be deterred from our purpose."

I copied it in a letter to you, and you wrote back, "Thus do the words of Butchers enter the Gazette, while those of the Bakers of Bread and Makers of Candlesticks go unnoticed and unheard." You understand the language men use to incite, to wound, to crush, and to damn. Your poems sometimes bleed.

"I write from the heart," you once said. "All else is penmanship." Yours is like the tracks of some small, nervous bird in the snow.

One letter from that time seemed to have been written by staggering fingers.

March 26

He, to whom I might have yielded without the Warrant, is dead. The Bolt arrived—I heard the thundering recessional—and left my heart undressed against the stunning CHILL.

Your Widowed Emily

I guessed that it was your father's clerk, Benjamin Newton, who had died, and I was glad because you had cared for him.

Those were violent, lawless years, when the territory was splintered by the passions and prejudices of men, most of whom were too poor to own slaves. They seemed to have nothing to do with us as we hunted Indians on the other side of the Mississippi. But a rag of char cloth and a phosphorus match can burn down a forest, and a cannon shot can start a war, whose real origins go unnoticed. History is a bluff: Time's true story is told in the bones of a million buffalo and a million humans, in a single bullet fated centuries before to find its mark, in a man raised up in goodness and laid low by hatred, or in someone else who lived in anonymity and died in obscurity but contributed, nonetheless, to a chain of events ending in catastrophe. I'm not a historian, and this account of the Border War is the merest sketch and no more a facsimile of events than a tintype is of a human being.

The last act of the tragedy of Bleeding Kansas was the massacre beside the Marais des Cygnes River. A fragile peace would follow, until all strife was subsumed under the Civil War, which made the bloody grappling that preceded it seem innocent.

On May 19, 1858, Charles Hamilton, a proslaver, crossed into Kansas Territory with thirty Ruffians on some mischief. On their way back to Missouri, they captured eleven Free Staters, none of whom was armed. Hamilton marched them into a ravine and, before ordering his men to shoot, fired the first bullet to prove his mettle or, perhaps, to satisfy desire, whose consummation is sometimes murder. Only five Kansas men were killed that day, but their deaths outraged the North. (Lieutenant Pearson would have scoffed to hear the "incident" called a massacre.)

Perhaps you read the poem by John Greenleaf Whittier—these lines in particular:

> With a vain plea for mercy
> No stout knee was crooked;
> In the mouths of the rifles
> Right manly they looked.
> How paled the May sunshine,
> O Marais du Cygne!
> On death for the strong life,
> On red grass for green!

I've seen that "red grass." I wonder if Whittier, a Quaker, has, though I admire his boldness as an abolitionist. I read "Le Marais du Cygne" in *The Atlantic Monthly*. Have you sent them any of your things? To my ear, he is a great poet. Frankly, your verses vex me. A rubble of broken sentences, pretty fragments. A tiny universe of words wrenched from common parlance and imprinted with your own private legend. Is *swan* in your Lexicon, along with *mermaid*, *hummingbird*, *fly*, and the irritable *gnat*?

What if each night a word or two departed from your Lexicon? Would the world grow less—the universal dictionary having been abridged? Would the universe diminish as it would if an astronomer, having trained his telescope on the night sky, discovered that Mars had vanished? What if I should shut my eyes tonight and say the Lord's Prayer, only to find that I had no word for Heavenly Father? In time, the astronomer would forget there'd been a fourth planet from the sun named Mars, and I that there had ever been words commending my soul to His mercy. We would live, henceforth, without Mars and mercy; we would make do.

These are the thoughts that come to a man who cannot always fall asleep during the terrible hours between Vigils and Matins. I'll tell you one last story of my time in Springfield before it passes into memory—or history; they are, I sometimes think, one and the same.

−10−

IN THE SUMMER OF 1856, I came down with "yellow jack." It was another of the beads—I can scarcely call them "pearls"—strung on the thread of my autobiography, a thread as fine as what the spider spins and as adamantine as the cable with which John Roebling knits his suspension aqueducts and bridges. That sickness nearly unto death was the most disturbing episode during my residency at the fort, which was, except for occasional melees with the savages, peaceable. (Outside our jurisdiction, Bleeding Kansas would be left to other men to staunch.) Gripped by the illness, I prayed incoherently, unless it was the natural language of angels or of Eden that I spoke—a fiery Pentecostal tongue prompted by fever. Yellowed by jaundice and parched with thirst, I cast out of myself not devils, but what the Spanish call *vómito negro*.

The sickness was thought to travel in the holds of steamboats, like weevils in cotton bales. A scourge on us, it came upriver from New Orleans and Mississippi and into the slave pens and warehouses at St. Louis. Some maintain that the soldiers returning from the Mexican occupation brought the fever with them into towns and forts far north of its natural range. (If this was the case, then the "greasers" were taking their revenge.)

During the three days of my "harrowing"—call it that—I had a dream, a single dream, as it seems to me now. I was on my way home from Mexico. I carried a sugar skull, which I never put down until I arrived at your house. It was night, the house silent. In the parlor, Edward was lying in a coffin lighted by tall candles. You sat at a dining table like Miss Havisham's in Dickens's *Great Expectations*, shrouded in spiders' webs, felted with dust, and garlanded with ancient orange blossoms, which, though dead for half a century, miraculously had not dropped their petals. I laid the skull before you like an offering to Mictecacihuatl. You stared at it and then, having picked it up at last, began to eat it.

"*Me encanta el sabor de la muerte*," you said. "I love the taste of death."

On the third day of my illness, the fever let go its hold. I was too worn and wearied to leave the infirmary. The doctor, a captain and a self-styled atheist, interrogated me playfully.

"Having escaped the jaws of death and being a spiritual man, did you see, perchance, an angel or the Grim Reaper with his hourglass and scythe? Or might you have noticed a shining light without apparent source, as some have claimed during their reconnaissance in the world to come? I've not had an opportunity to scout the borderlands, except as ether affords, and I'm curious to know what I shall discover in the great beyond."

"I saw nothing," I said brusquely, unwilling to tell him my dream, which was a private matter.

"Pity," said the doctor. "Have you read Edgar Poe's tale 'The Facts in the Case of M. Valdemar'?"

"I have not."

"It's a perfect horror! I'll tell it to you, if you like. It should be of special relevance."

Do you know the story, Emily? It *is* a perfect horror.

In Poe's tale, Ernest Valdemar, in the final stage of consumption, allows himself to be mesmerized while on his deathbed by a friend hoping that the dying man will be capable of reporting his sensations at the point of death. That point, however, becomes an unexpectedly protracted one. Valdemar endures seven months of hypnagogia, a state of suspended animation, in which one is neither asleep nor awake, dead nor alive. At the end of Poe's tale, the mesmerist questions the still-dying man—or so he is believed to be—hoping to hear what it is that waits for us all.

"'M. Valdemar, can you explain to us what are your feelings or wishes now?'

"'For God's sake!—quick!—quick!—put me to sleep—or, quick!—waken me!—quick!—I say to you that I am dead!'"

Abruptly awakened from his mesmeric trance, Valdemar disintegrates without betraying the secret of the afterlife.

"Had you the opportunity, would you communicate conclusive proof that God exists to all the unbelievers and skeptics, as well as those others torn between faith and doubt?" asked the inquisitorial doctor after having finished his synopsis of Poe's story. "Or proof that He is not? What a service to humankind you would perform, Robert, though the clergy would find itself unemployed!"

"The Bible is proof and assurance enough," I said, lying.

"A mealymouthed prig of a parson would say that!" he replied contemptuously.

I closed my eyes and pretended to fall asleep.

"Be careful you don't follow M. Valdemar into his special hell," admonished the doctor with glee. Quoting from another of Poe's infernal works, he gibbered theatrically, "'. . . it was dark—all dark—the intense and utter rayless-ness of the Night that endureth for evermore.'"

I struggled to keep my eyes closed, so as not to let him see my terror. Never mind that I was a Christian and a minister, I hated the man!

Earlier, I wrote that your verses seem like rubble. Maybe this is as it should be. At some point in its history, one cannot tell if a house is being built or torn down. Rubble, possibly, is all of which we can be certain. I've never been to Rome, but a priest I met during the late war told me that the walls of the Coliseum bear the teeth marks of time. Time rends; we rend one another; all is ruin and catastrophe. When setting out to write the book I mentioned earlier—the one I could not bring myself to burn—I had thought that there was no fact or feeling that could not be caught with words. I was wrong. Your poems are sieves that catch at least something of the wreckage.

Do you fear death in whatever likeness it will choose to show itself? I'd rather meet the Grim Reaper with his scythe than the hideous and unseen cause of yellow fever, cholera, or lockjaw. Give me a death, an angel, a demon I can see! My faith has not the strength to overcome death's uncertainty, never mind its sting.

In Utah, I became an angel of death when I reaped a blasted soul.

–11–

WHEN THE MORMON PIONEERS IMMIGRATED to the Great Basin after their expulsion from Illinois, they settled in what was then Mexico's northern wilderness, which once had belonged to the Indians. After our annexation of Mexican territory, the Mormons again found themselves living in the United States. For them, as for the Indians, there could be no escaping the juggernaut. History is a backward glance to the first murder, the first theft, the first instance of lawlessness, the first usurper and belligerent, whose name was Cain.

I arrived in the territory in the fall of 1857. Had I been clothed in the white samite of righteousness, I could have howled anathemas against the Mormons, as most good Christians did. My brothers of the cloth were horrified by plural marriage and the so-called gold plates shown in a vision to Joseph Smith by the angel Moroni. Religious persons of that time, or this, would never acknowledge that God might have left His holy writ far from Palestine, on a hill in Manchester, New York. Were he alive, I do believe most Americans would have wished Joseph Smith nailed to a cross for the mischief he'd caused. If they could have laid their hands on his bones, they'd have ground them into dust—or, being a practical people—into fertilizer, the ignoble end for bison bones.

Having little faith left in the church, in the goodwill of the United States, or in myself, I did not much care which side in the rebellion prevailed. I was, however, made uncomfortable by the bloodlust common to them both. Had my hearing been uncanny like the dog's, I might have heard the ancient chain that holds fast earth to heaven groan— to strike a pretty figure—its iron links having rusted during merciless ages past. I might've been living among the Aztecs, waiting at the foot of the Pyramid of the Moon for a gutted corpse to be flung down and its severed head placed devoutly on the wall of skulls.

Let me set down a gloss of the Utah War's politics and conduct before I confess my sin. I know that you don't care much for history, Emily, but most of us are forced to live within its coils, in a wider, more turbulent world than the Homestead and the Evergreens or the verses of Elizabeth Browning. (Or do I wrong you?) Whatever you may think of it, history is essential to the understanding of my story, which is threaded through the nation's own. Had I gone to preach in some New England town, time's needle would still have snagged me, as it does everyone. Each of us is a separate thread wound on the same spool.

Popular sovereignty, a dogma upheld by the Democratic Party in some measure to protect the South's "peculiar institution," led—by one of history's unforeseen roundabouts— to the Utah War, or "Mormon Rebellion," as we called it. Stephen Douglas, Lincoln's old adversary from Illinois, had not defended the "Saints" because he was tolerant of their views; his espousal of popular sovereignty and the maintenance of slavery demanded it. He'd have contradicted his party's chief tenet had he advocated the rights of the proslavery faction but denied Mormons the prerogatives of ecclesiastical government and plural marriage. They called it "celestial," to put a pleasing face on infamy.

When the Democrat James Buchanan took office in March 1857, he intended to unwind Mormonism, abhorrent to Americans because of polygamy, from the tightening noose of popular sovereignty, which would, in just a few years, choke the union almost past reviving. Stephen Douglas, like many other Democrats, was now insisting that the Mormon "ulcer" be cut out.

In June, Buchanan declared the Territory of Utah to be in rebellion for refusing to submit to authority—not that in heaven, but the greater one in Washington. In July, 2,500 soldiers left Fort Leavenworth to depose Brigham Young as Utah's territorial governor and to install a "Gentile" in his place. The Utah Expedition would be the scalpel to rid the territory of its distemper.

By late summer, Young had declared martial law, fortified the passes leading to Salt Lake Valley, recalled the missionaries, and raised the Nauvoo Legion, the Mormon militia, to defend Zion against the federal invaders. Lot Smith and a detachment of militia engaged our army at the border of the "Kingdom of God." That fall, Smith's men burned fifty-two provisions wagons destined for the expeditionary force. That winter, we were forced to bivouac at the foot of the Wahsatch Mountains, in the ruins of Fort Bridger, burned by the Legion in anticipation of our attack. Without adequate shelter and supplies, we were cold, hungry, and miserable.

I'm a New Englander and used to the cold, but nothing

had prepared me for the hardships of a Utah winter under canvas, with scarcely a wall of the old fort left standing to protect us from the icy winds. Again and again, the snow would fall, and we'd try to keep pace with our shovels. At first, men of lower rank did the work, but soon we all lent a hand. It was the only way to keep warm. I'd shiver, shovel, sweat, stop, freeze, and shovel—all the while thinking of you, snug in your "mansion," with fires burning in the grates. In the end, I put my books in the stove to enjoy a temporary respite from that chill and futile cycle. I burned *Hamlet*, *Timon of Athens*, and *The Winter's Tale* first, Washington Irving's comic history of Manhattan next, and finally Milton's *Paradise Lost*—for its lake of fire. I kept the Bible partly because of a superstitious fear of its desecration, partly because, as a chaplain, I required it. I preached each Sunday, though it was the hymns the men enjoyed because they could bellow their lungs and stamp their feet and ignite a tiny fire in their bones. I doubt they listened to me prate about the rightness of our cause, the depravity of the Mormons, and the paradise awaiting us if we would only do our duty here on earth. What bosh! By February, I'm sure there was not a man among my flock who would not have preferred hellfire to heaven's tepid joys.

I became acquainted with a young captain who, like me, had been stationed at a fort in Illinois. He was too dogmatic to be likable, but, to pass the time in our winter fastness, we'd talk. Concerning "Buchanan's War," his opinions were orthodox, unless, like me, he was afraid to reveal his disapproval. Men are never so cautious as they are in war, because, in war, they are never so ready to accuse one another of disloyalty. Liberal ideas are the product of an armchair, a glass of something warming, and the smell of roasted meat arriving from the kitchen. Privation and hunger breed discontent, as surely as lice do other lice on broken men.

The captain's name was Ethan Gant, originally of New Jersey. He had graduated from Princeton and had studied physical geography with Arnold Guyot, whose *Earth and Man, Lectures on Comparative Physical Geography, in Its Relation to the History of Mankind* he had read and disliked.

"Guyot's geography is not an inventory of earth's disparate features but a concatenation of related ones," he said. "This I agree with. But he sees in a landscape the revelation of God's design. While I'm not an unbeliever, I strongly doubt that God would have expressed His secret purposes in a mountain range or on the ocean bottom. Guyot is like a Hebrew Cabalist hunting for angels among letters of an ancient alphabet. You're a minister of God, Robert, what is your opinion?"

"My opinion . . .?" In a stupor because of the cold, I'd been only half-listening.

"Does He reveal His features in a landscape?"

I smiled at the memory of your school notebook, in which you'd drawn the footsteps of prehistoric beasts.

"You find me amusing?" he asked petulantly.

"Not at all, Ethan. I was remembering a friend." I was silent a moment, and then I said, "I scarcely know anymore if I believe in God, much less in expressions of divine intent on earth or in the heavens."

He glared at me, and I was surprised by his disapproval. We'd often spoken about God and, like schoolboys, had debated His existence—more in boredom than with genuine interest. He'd assumed that I was devout, an assumption that left him free to play the devil's advocate. I guessed that it was not my religious uncertainty that had shocked him. Had I been anyone else, it would not have mattered. Because I was his chaplain, he couldn't tolerate my lack of conviction regardless of his own doubts. I expect I seemed to him no better than a counterfeiter. I'd abused his trust. My ministry, far from home, in the valley of the shadow of death—or, to be factual, in the valley of the Wahsatch and Oquirrh Mountains—was a fraud.

We made small talk briefly before he walked away "to reckon the valley down below." Gant was a good officer and well respected by his men and his superiors. His knowledge of geography also made him invaluable, and he could often be seen with a telescope trained on a distant plain or mountain pass. Whether he was earnestly searching for the enemy or a trace of Him in the folds of the snow-covered hills, I could not say. During that Utah winter, he might have yearned to prove Guyot right.

Ten months later, I would search the crags of John Brown's face for a sign of God's approval and see there only what a man would show for whom martyrdom was a victory.

I recall one other serious conversation we had that winter, whose subject engendered in us an equal and genuine outrage: the Mountain Meadows Massacre. On September 7, the Baker-Fancher wagon train had been attacked in southern Utah by the militia, which claimed that six of the party were army spies. The emigrants withstood the siege until, on the eleventh, the Mormons raised the white flag. They offered the gentiles safe passage through the valley if they would lay down their arms and promise never to return. Later on, disguised as Paiutes, the Mormons attacked the unarmed party. Save for the infants, all 120 emigrants were murdered.

"*Butchered* would be more apt!" growled Gant, who had been sewing on a button. "They found hanks of hair— *women's hair*—hanging from sagebrush, as well as shreds of their clothes, and children's, too, and, for a mile along the Old Spanish Trail, mutilated corpses."

Feeling obliged by my office, I muttered the invocation from the Order of the Burial of the Dead: "O Lord Jesus Christ, Who wilt come again to judge the quick and the dead, and call forth all who sleep in the graves, either to the resurrection of life or the resurrection of condemnation."

We'd heard rumors of the massacre, but few among us could credit them. Men had yet to witness farmers' fields harrowed by mortar shells and sown with gore and shattered limbs, creeks turned red, as though Aaron had stirred them with his miraculous staff, raw ditches heaped with corpses, muskets clutched in their blackened hands, and row upon row of sickbeds, white and crimson, like gravestones brightened by poppies.

That's too pretty a description for anything as ugly as

war—isn't it, Emily? There is no way to tell of it in words
. . . no way to set down its horrors with ink on paper. I'd
have to write it in blood, gall, excrement, mud, soot, with
the rheumy discharge of the dying, with the tears of the
wounded—with more blood. I'd have to take bone, teeth,
and ashes and, with a mortar and pestle, turn what was
human into powder. Then, like a witch at her cauldron, I'd
mix those foul ingredients together, and, with that reeking
ink, I'd write *war* on human parchment.

"I met an infantry sergeant this morning who'd seen the
aftermath of the carnage with his own eyes," said Gant,
"else I could not have believed it. You know how soldiers
love stories."

"We all do," I said irrelevantly. Though they are, in their
embroidery, useless, I thought. Poetry even more so. Pho-
tographs like those by Brady and O'Sullivan are what's
needed to say—however mutely—what war is.

"I would not have believed that men—even Mormon
men—were capable of such an atrocity," said Gant. Anger
had misshapen his face. "It cannot be allowed to go unpun-
ished! We must hunt them down and hang them!" he cried
with the fervor of Jeremiah.

One-hundred-and-twenty men, women, and children—
this was a class of slaughter all its own, with no word to
signify its enormity. We were on our way to wars of annihilation, which we had been rehearsing with the Indians and
the Mexicans. Soon white men would kill other white men
by the thousands and the tens of thousands. We would need
a new arithmetic of slaughter, and the ledgers would grow

fat with bloodred entries declaring the nation's bankruptcy and a hunger only flesh and more flesh could appease.

"We must do as John Brown advocates," snarled Gant, biting off the thread and tugging at the button on his tunic. "Take 'an eye for an eye, a tooth for a tooth.'"

His ferocity surprised me. I saw hatred in his eyes and a nearly overmastering rage in the tremor of his hand as he jabbed the needle into the spool of thread.

There was blood on John Brown's hands, I said to myself, though it might not have been innocent.

"Well, what do *you* have to say, Robert?" asked Gant with a stern look.

I suppose, because of my silence, he'd begun to think me indifferent to the carnage. You know how people can be suspicious of those who do not hate as they do. It is a perversion of John 13:34, when Jesus said to His disciples, ". . . love one another; as I have loved you, that ye also love one another."

"I hardly know what to say," I replied truthfully.

He gazed at me in that mistrustful way of his, and I knew that I'd better say something.

"I can hardly take it in." No, that wouldn't do. "I've never heard of such infamy." Not enough fire. "I'd like to see them shot down like the dogs they are!"

Instantly, I thought of Carlo and was sorry for the comparison, one which, loving dogs, I did not mean. The simile and the vehemence in which I'd uttered it appeared to satisfy Gant. He eased his body's spring, which had tensed instinctively against me.

"Yes, yes, Robert. Hanging is too good for them. Shooting—or burning them, like the heretics they are—that's what they deserve. Would you strike the match?" he asked slyly.

I could not meet his gaze. The odd thing, Emily, was that, in my heart, I did revile the perpetrators and did think they ought to be cut to pieces like the slave catchers at Pottawatomie Creek. There is a contrariety in our kind, however, that will sometimes insist on entertaining an opposing thought and, out of spite, on defying the majority. Most have the good sense to conceal their opinion, although there will always be some who behave like the small man who provokes a much larger one so that he can have the satisfaction of a bloody nose. The situation was grotesque. I wanted to tell Gant that the Mormons had been driven to desperate, even heinous measures by our aggression, but I kept my mouth shut. I tasted ashes; Gant was poking at the fire with a stick, whether to inflame it or his own passion, I couldn't tell.

As a man of the cloth, if not a Catholic during the Inquisition or a Puritan at the Salem witch trials, I was expected to denounce Mormon depravity.

"You're a parson—don't you think every last one of Brigham Young's gang of idolaters should be exterminated?"

I wanted to ask him whether we should also murder women and children. A braver man would have asked. A true Christian would have also. But at the time, I was hardly either. I did, however, say, "Our mission is to remove Young from office and replace him with Buchanan's man.

We're here to restore the authority of the United States and the Constitution and nothing else. The commission of atrocities should be left to the other side."

Although my voice had broken like that of a boy in need of his first shave, I felt the warmth of satisfaction suffuse me.

Gant frowned. "Reverend Watkins has something different to say about our mission among the infidels."

"Watkins is a fire-breathing Baptist," I replied, "and would just as soon see us burn in hell than picnic in paradise."

Gant and I never spoke much after that. He was not the only soldier in the territory with a low opinion of the Mormons or of mankind in general. Morale had gone down along with the provisions and the temperature. The country was inhospitable; the Mormons were welcome to it! If we could have had a battle or two—even if we'd lost—we would have felt better for it. The Nauvoo Legion was as elusive as the Mexican irregulars had been, choosing not to engage us but, rather, to harass our flanks, cut off our supplies, stampede our horses, and deprive us of forage by setting fire to their fields. After Young ordered the evacuation of Salt Lake City, the townspeople prepared to burn their shops and houses to the ground. The farmers chose to set fire to their barns rather than to sell us so much as an egg! We were hungry, but not so that we would have killed them for their eggs. We brooded and waited. If only there'd been a battle to rouse us from our apathy! We'd have shaken off our indifference as a dog does rain.

I think we knew well before its end that the war against Utah's Mormons was a farce. It marked a milestone on my road to perdition, or—forgive the arrogance—another Station on the way to my Calvary. I ought to blush for shame to have drawn so overweening a comparison, but I was, by then, devoid of it. It had been drained from me like blood drawn by a phlebotomist, leaving my soul ashen.

–12–

ARNOLD TAUBER WAS AMONG THE FIRST reinforcements to arrive from Kansas, where he'd been posted. Still a corporal, he had no interest in promotion; his military service was a lengthy sabbatical in which he could read and write his own history of the world, as he would grandly describe the notebook in which he constantly scratched, although he never offered to let me read it. Although but recently arrived in the territory, he had already lost his mount to a Mormon-set brush fire.

"Not even Mexicans would deliberately kill a horse!" he said indignantly. "It must be true what they say about the Mormons: They eat their dogs and beat their wives."

Sick to death of the Mormons and their enormities, I did not reply. Unlike Gant, Arnold was content to let the matter drop.

He had been given picket duty on the western perimeter, above the ruins of the fort. I would sometimes keep him company. I remember an afternoon when an immense sky could have convinced an atheist to believe in a Supreme

Being, not excepting Joseph Smith's or the Muslims' or the Aztecs'. Who can claim to know His mind? The Wahsatch Mountains, their granite shoulders bluish white, presided over a solemn reaffirmation of belief, but the moment was short-lived, and my heart would once again fill up with snow.

"I'm damned sick of it!" grumbled Arnold.

I didn't know whether he meant the winter, the war, or his own weariness. The Navuoo Legion favored night raids, which kept us sleepless in our tents.

"Have you burned 'Rome'?" I asked wryly, alluding to his beloved Gibbon.

"No, though I've been tempted: It's a fat book and would keep me warm awhile."

"Private Endicott can play Nero with his fiddle if you do," I said, hoping to cheer him.

He stopped his pacing, put the butt of his rifle on the ground, and rested, as though it were a staff and he a shepherd overlooking a drove of rocks. For a picket to halt without reason was a violation of the regulations.

"Johnston can shoot me if he wants," he said. I watched the smoke of his breath leak out between his fingers as he blew into his cupped hands. "Not even Moroni could get through those snowed-in passes."

My eyes must have glazed over in reverie, because he asked, "What're you thinking about, Robert?"

"My daughter," I replied, shaking off the memory of her mewling and puking on my lap.

"Where is she now?"

"Still in Amherst, living with my aunt."

"I have a son," he said. "Edward Gibbon Tauber. He's in Indiana with his mother."

There was nothing more to be said by either of us. Arnold shouldered his musket and began to pace the ridge again.

Toward the end of the rebellion, I happened on a Mormon militiaman shortly after he had died. I'd heard him scream; he was horribly burned. The Mormons liked to set fire to dry grass upwind of our wagons in the hope of engulfing them. But the wind had abruptly changed, and he'd been caught by the blaze intended for us.

I jumped from the wagon in which I'd been riding with Chaplain Watkins. He'd been boring me with a preview of his Sunday-morning sermon, when he would once again bully the men with the threat of annihilation. I knelt beside the dead man, conquering an urge to vomit, and began to cry. It was too much—it was all too much to bear! Watkins caught up to me and, having pulled me from the corpse, railed against my "unmanly display."

I pushed him away as a child would a parent who has said something mean.

"He was the enemy!" said Watkins coldly, and, for an instant, I saw not the scrawny Baptist preacher from Kentucky, but Agamemnon at Troy, before he was murdered in his tub. "You should be giving thanks to the Almighty for having rid the earth of another infidel!" he thundered, as though he were in his Sunday pulpit, chastising the Danville Baptists.

Always, always murder has ruled us—in ancient days

and in the days at hand. We are born to be cut down. It is a fairy tale to say that we will be reborn as grass or as anything else. We are a burnt stick, I thought, as I smelled the Mormon's roasted flesh.

"He's dead," I said.

Much later, I understood that those two words were, in their bald finality, as pathetic as Christ's last uttered on the cross, "It is finished," and I felt His Passion for the very first time.

"Even in death, a Mormon infidel is our sworn enemy and God's!" Watkins hissed. "His pollution would sicken the river Jordan, and his unholy angel sow the Jezreel Valley with salt!"

He was raving, and I was sick with disgust. I shook him off and put my hand into the charred rag of the dead man's coat and drew out the Book of Mormon, bound in black leather and marvelously unharmed. Beside himself, Watkins leaped at me, and we grappled fiercely on the ground.

"Burn it!" he shrieked like a Pharisee in a Passion play. "Burn that blasphemous book, or you will burn in everlasting fire!" I held fast to the book and managed to knock Watkins down. "Traitor! Apostate!" he shouted.

I don't know why I fought him. I don't know why I held on to the Mormon's book. It meant nothing to me. The dead man meant nothing to me. I was sick of fighting. I wanted to go home. I wanted to see my daughter. I wanted to forget all about the Mexican War, the Border War, and the Utah War.

Watkins picked himself up from the scorched earth and

came at me, this time with a heavy stick. He cudgeled me twice across the shoulders, hard enough to make me yelp. Enraged, I took the stick from him and brought it crashing down on his head. He dropped, heavy as a sack of grain. I felt his pulse, lifted his eyelid, put my ear to his chest, and I realized I had killed him. As though I'd crushed the serpent's head beneath my heel, I rejoiced, took up the Mormon's Bible, and turned to the final passage, which should, I reasoned, concern redemption or last things. I read the words—convinced of their futility—that I had been given in order to understand His absence.

> "And now I bid unto all, farewell. I soon go to rest in the paradise of God, until my spirit and body shall again reunite, and I am brought forth triumphant through the air, to meet you before the pleasing bar of the great Jehovah, the Eternal Judge of both quick and dead. Amen."

I had Watkins's blood on my hands. I wiped them on the grass the fire had spared. I ran to the wagon for a shovel, and then I dragged Watkins by the ankles beyond a low rise of reddish dirt. I was someone else, and, as someone else, I began to dig a hole—a grave in which to dump the body. The wind rose from nowhere and said, "This is not the way."

It was God's voice I'd heard in the wind—ours or the Mormon's. Unless the voice had been my own. I was distressed—too feeble a word! Distraught, then. I felt as a man very likely does when the rope is put around his neck or what the rope feels in anticipation of bearing—to the limit of its strength—the weight of a man. Mad thoughts! But no matter whose voice I had heard, I took heed. I dragged Watkins to the wagon and laid him among bales of hay meant for the famished horses.

I drove the wagon to Colonel Johnston's, and, waiting outside his tent, I wondered what I would tell him: "I killed Captain Watkins," or "Captain Watkins was killed by Paiutes," loyal to the Mormons. I knew what I *ought* to say. I knew what God wanted to hear, and I knew what you would think of me if, out of cowardice, I did not say it. I also knew the consequences of having killed a brother officer, regardless of mitigating circumstances. What mitigation could there be for one who had given comfort to an enemy, whether quick or dead? Soon enough, I'd be in Watkins's promised hell, tasting brimstone, which, he had assured us, is more unpalatable than castor oil and just as efficacious—unless the Mormons were right and I would be pardoned at "the pleasing bar of the great Jehovah" for having shown mercy to one of His elect by praying for him in the words of his own prophet.

I was afraid, and when I was called inside to report, I did what anyone in his right mind would have done: I lied. And with the lie, I gave up all claims to God's blessing and was, at last, emptied of faith in Him and in myself. I was Adam fallen once again, nevermore to get up.

I left the tent, ostensibly a free man, but I knew I had consigned myself to the prison of self-loathing. How very fortunate Emily is, I thought, to suffer no greater duress than what her gossamer chains impose. Forgive me for belittling your pain. Next to cowardice, self-pity is my most unattractive quality, and possibly my most enduring. At that moment on the wind-scoured hillside, my eyes watering with Mormon dust, I wanted *not to be*. A funny phrase, but true for so many of our kind. I thought of Shakespeare's Dane, whipped by doubt. I thought of Judas at the end of his rope. He'd betrayed his Lord. I'd betrayed myself, as well as the trust the church and the army had placed in me. I prayed to God Almighty to make me other than I was, to weld me to a purpose that would please Him.

"Give me back the faith I had as a child," I muttered, as if it had been He who had taken it. "Make me worthy of your creation. Forgive me for having lied and murdered. Forgive me my vanity."

If only my fervent wish to be washed clean had not, in time, cooled. If only my heart had not already been excised by the obsidian knife.

Harper's Ferry

Remorse—is Memory—awake—
—Emily Dickinson

–1–

"Y OU LOOK LIKE A MAN WHO WAS DELIVERED from the belly of a whale, only to find himself washed up among cannibals."

With those words, you greeted me in the doorway of the Dickinson family "mansion." We hadn't seen each other since 1855, but you could not bring yourself to show me tenderness—if not that, then kindness. Always your hand and mouth must do your spiteful muse's bidding. Carlo wriggled past you and licked my hands, as Odysseus's dog, Argus, had once welcomed him home from the windy plains of Troy.

"I've been in hell!" I said with a jauntiness I did not feel. Men must play their part, regardless of their true feelings, which are often unknown even to themselves.

After the rebellion had been put down, I returned to Springfield and resumed my duties at the fort. In mid-December, I used my leave to visit Charlotte, Tess, and you in Amherst. Your family had moved from North

Pleasant Street to a stately house on Main—the Homestead, where you have taken refuge, as if in a storm cellar in the eye of a hurricane.

"You've been in 'Zion,'" you replied. "What news of the Kingdom of God?"

Brigham Young had finally renounced his dream of a Mormon Zion, and the Saints had accepted Buchanan's pardon for their sedition. Humbled, they had laid down their muskets, sabers, and bayonets fashioned from scythes. In time—where even gods grow old—Zion will forfeit its splendid isolation to western expansion. America's new frontier will be ruled neither by theocrats nor statesmen, but by another sort of visionary: the plutocrat. Of the three, which will prove the more grasping and corrupt only time will tell.

"*No pasó nada*," I said. "It came to nothing."

"And so shall we all."

I could think of nothing to say.

"In the meantime, have you brought me some little gift?" you asked in a way that could have been mistaken for flirtatious. "A Paiute blanket, perhaps."

I reached into my coat pocket and took out a smooth stone, which I'd picked up nearby the body of the dead Mormon, where it might well have lain—obedient to the law of inertia—for millennia.

"A stone," you said, weighing it in the palm of your hand. "Very pretty."

"Its name is Urim," I said in a voice rich with mystical solemnity. "Together with its companion stone,

Thummim, it embellished the sacred breastplate worn by the high priest of Israel. Both were lost when Nebuchadnezzar sacked Jerusalem." I was enjoying myself at your expense. "Then, in 1823, instructed by the angel Moroni, Joseph Smith unearthed them on a hill called 'Cumorah,' some twenty miles from Rochester. Fitted into silver spectacles, they served Smith as lenses, by which he was able to translate the gold plates of Mormon. The stones are said to possess the power of divination. Perhaps you can use Urim to unveil the truth."

"The truth is too bashful for common eyes, but thank you, Robert."

I shrugged. "I'm only sorry that the original diamond has long since turned into common quartz."

"Even Divinity must degrade in such a caustic age as ours," you replied, gazing at the object in your hand as though it *were* a precious gem.

The dog barked.

"Carlo, like Mr. Emerson, does not care for dogmas of any kind."

Having gone into the parlor, I imagined I saw Edward's stark shadow in the room and felt its chill. As if guessing my thoughts, you said gaily, "The Homestead is too stifling for ghosts, which are fond of damp and drafty houses."

"How is he?" I asked, sitting deliberately in his chair. There could be no question of whom I meant. There was room in that house for only one "he." I fancied that I could smell his Macassar oil and cigars beneath the pervasive odors of dog and sanctity.

"Father is always Father."

And you, Emily, were always the gnome.

"And your mother?"

"Melancholy."

"And Vinnie?"

"Plump and toothsome."

"And Austin?"

"Austin sleeps in the tomb next door."

"And your muse?"

"She raps my knuckles because my rhymes are slant and scourges me for croaking in common meter. I wish I were Barrett Browning. She is an invalid, too, you know."

"You are not an invalid, Emily!"

"Underneath my stays, I am all rickets."

My eyes roved the walls of the room and settled on a landscape in oil depicting the expulsion of Adam and Eve from an Eden resembling an ancient Theban ruin.

"It's called *The Wreckage of Eden*," you said. "I bought it from an itinerant painter who had been to Bedlam.

"'. . . Look on my works, ye Mighty, and despair!'
   Nothing beside remains. Round the decay
   Of that colossal wreck, boundless and bare
   The lone and level sands stretch far away.

"Would you like to tell me about Buchanan's war, which the world calls 'Blunder'? Now that I am older, my hearing has improved, even though my poor eyes are sometimes plagued by fancies."

"No," I replied. "I'd rather forget."

"As you wish." We were silent for a time while the dust of time laid down a shroud that not even Margaret, your industrious maid, could stop. "What do you make of little Charlotte?" you asked, breaking the silence as one would sweep away a cobweb with a broom.

"She didn't know me."

"She does not remember you. Be patient with her; she's only a child."

"I didn't think I would miss her until I did, and now her mind's made up against me."

"Nonsense! She's a little girl whose mind has not yet been fitted with a head screw."

You were thinking not of Charlotte, but of yourself. What is your pain or mine to that of someone made to wear the Spanish boot, someone who is drawn and quartered and burned at the stake, or, like Henry Thoreau's brother, John, dies of lockjaw? What is it to that of the walking dead I'd later see at Andersonville? Or even to the travail of women giving birth to something far more vital than a verse. We are both poseurs, and our lives tableaux.

"I'm in your debt for having looked after her," I said in lieu of anything self-righteous.

"I hardly did that. I am, you know, too preoccupied by words—those nails, which will not, howsoever I hammer them, seal the coffin shut."

Then you did the most unexpected thing. Do you recall? You laughed like a bawd, deeply and immodestly. I'd never heard the like from you. And then, just as abruptly, you became the wren—shy and dun.

"When you returned to us from Mexico, there was also snow. We walked through the pine woods as far as Puffer's Pond. You shook down snow onto me that had been nesting in a bough."

"Let's go there now, Emily."

"Only Eskimos walk abroad today."

The room was uncomfortably warm; you'd poked at the fire to make the apple wood spark and crackle. I felt like shutting my eyes. Apparently, I did, for when I opened them, the parlor was empty, except for Carlo, asleep in his wicker bed. I supposed that you had gone upstairs to scribble. The afternoon had passed into evening, and eventide shadows had rolled into the room. Then I heard noise in the kitchen, and, going to investigate, I found you among the pots and pans.

"Father will be wanting his dinner," you said. "You were sleeping so soundly, I hated to wake you. Mother is upstairs with a headache. Will you stay? We're having fish. Whenever I eat it, I fancy myself P. T. Barnum's Feejee Mermaid."

I did not feel up to an encounter with your father.

"We wish he would return to Congress and regulate the nation. Father would free the bounden slaves, all except those on Main Street, whom he keeps enchained behind the hemlock hedges." You fell silent for a moment and then said absently, "And yet he is necessary, should lightning strike; he was a fireman, after all."

I could not bear to stay a moment's longer in that house. I could not bear *you*, Emily.

"I promised Tess I'd have dinner with her and Charlotte."

You nodded. Did you divine the lie? Maybe so, if Urim were in your apron pocket.

–2–

THE FOLLOWING MORNING, AUSTIN AND I went hunting in the woods by Mill River, where, eleven years earlier, you and I had watched ice floes caught in the current slip over the lip of the weir. We took Carlo with us, not to harry squirrels, but to mitigate uncomfortable silences. A dog is an excellent envoy when conversation stalls. When I had last seen your brother, he had been an awkward eighteen-year-old. I didn't know him now except as a composite sketched by your letters. That morning, traipsing through the snow while Carlo snapped at wind-sown flakes, I was pleased to find Austin grown into a likely and likable young man of twenty-nine. He was competent, a fair shot, and, if not talkative, neither was he dour. There was an element of the grim in him, however; it was not always evident, but a melancholy strain would emerge— a darkness of mood, which seemed a Dickinson family trait. I wondered how he and Sue got on and hoped their marriage was happy. He had been good to Charlotte, who called him "Uncle," and for this, I was in his debt.

Austin had borrowed the surety of the law; it propped

him up just as I had once been by God's law. By this time, only the starch in my cassock kept me erect. I envied him: The law of men seemed more certain than God's. Farmer Gilles wants to buy a piece of land. He has it surveyed, assures himself that it is clear of encumbrances, bargains, pays the purchase price, files the deed, and the land is his to keep, sell, or leave to his heirs. There is clarity in the transaction, whereas there is only faith for those who enter into a divine covenant. I believe in little enough, although my cynicism is not ever-present nor my gloom unrelieved. In my ambivalence, I'm like most people, except the saints, who are always in the light, and lunatics, whose day is always night.

Austin showed no interest in the Utah War or in the intervening years since we had last met. His lack of curiosity pleased me: I had no wish to relive them. I'd thought they had been put away for good, until this recollection prompted me to open memory's drawer and bring the faded images into the light again. Unlike the scent of violet, mixed with the not unpleasant odor of ancient dust that escapes Tess's opened dresser drawer, memory's smell can sometimes take one's breath away.

"Do you enjoy practicing law with your father?"

"It has, at times, its satisfactions," he replied unsatisfactorily. Well, I had my anthill to moil in, and Austin had his.

We were leaning against the leeside of a granite outcropping, kicking snow from our boots while we caught our breath; walking was hard where snow had recently fallen. Carlo lay on his belly, nosing a chip of wood, unmindful of the cold and wet.

No doubt you will want to know the color of the sky, what sounds the forest made, whether there were squirrels, and, if so, whether they were red, gray, or brown, if a fitful wind sent the loose snow whirling up like wraiths, whether the river groaned above the reach where the ice was thick.

The sky was white, unless it happened to be blue. The squirrels, I think, were gray. The woods murmured, twigs snapped, avalanches of wet snow thudded to the ground, and the river did, on occasion, groan.

"Mr. Emerson is coming from Concord to address the lyceum and will be stopping at the Evergreens," said Austin. He'd spoken as if he had announced the imminent arrival of Moses from Mount Sinai. "He stays with us whenever he's in town. Some time ago, Mr. Thoreau was our guest. Father is well connected, as you might expect." I licked my lips, which the wind had chapped. "You're welcome to join us for tea tomorrow."

We roamed the woods for another hour. Austin shot a pheasant. I found that I had no taste for killing birds or small mammals. Carlo chased a red fox, vivid against the snow. Tired, Austin and I spoke fitfully of this and that. I do recall something striking that he said about you.

"Emily would have us all believe she is a captive in her dungeon, when, in fact, she is the warder."

Although I was curious to know what he'd meant by his trenchant observation, I could not bring myself to ask. I was like someone who happens on a scene too horrible to speak of, even to himself. What would you say, Emily, if you were here in more than just my thoughts?

We trudged home, Carlo worrying the dead bird in Austin's bag.

−3−

I ARRIVED AT THE EVERGREENS AT THREE O'CLOCK and shook hands gravely with Mr. Emerson. His handsome appearance and boyish smile belied his reputation as the country's most serious-minded essayist, whose "Nature" I had read in Springfield. Arnold Guyot had also discerned divinity in the natural world, but, unlike Emerson, his opinions were barbed. In the winter of 1859, I could see neither atom nor elephant that bore evidence of God's handiwork. Having grown tired of His creation, He was an absent landlord, whose tenants fended for themselves.

Emerson was in Amherst to speak at an antislavery meeting to be held that night. Sitting in Austin's parlor, he talked about John Brown, who, at that moment, was escorting eleven fugitive slaves to Detroit and thence, by ferry, to Canada. Not even a Transcendentalist could have guessed that Brown was also moving toward his Calvary. Emerson read from the speech he intended to deliver at the lyceum. Since you were indisposed at the time, I'll set it down here.

Who makes the abolitionist? The slave-holder. The sentiment of mercy is the natural recoil which the laws of the universe provide to protect mankind from destruction by savage passions. And our blind statesmen go up and down, with committees of vigilance and safety, hunting for the origin of this new heresy. They will need a very vigilant committee indeed to find its birthplace, and a very strong force to root it out. For the arch-abolitionist, older than Brown, and older than the Shenandoah Mountains, is Love, whose other name is Justice, which was before Alfred, before Lycurgus, before slavery, and will be after it.

"And what of Pottawatomie Creek?" I asked, reminding Emerson of the bloody affair in Kansas, in which Brown and his followers had hacked to death a handful of pro-slavery men.

I had accosted the great man in the conservatory, where he'd gone to enjoy a moment's solitude and the warmth of the sun magnified by the room's glass panes. I regretted my incivility instantly and asked his pardon.

"Not at all," he replied graciously. He steered me by the elbow to the library. "Austin tells me you are an army chaplain who has seen the wars."

"Mr. Robert Winter," I said, introducing myself.

"The *Reverend* Robert Winter," he said, as though to confirm my identity for us both.

I nodded, not wishing to make anything one way or the other of my omission.

"Shall we talk a moment?"

We sat and took each other's measure. I was careful to hold his gaze, though his eyes bored into mine with disconcerting intensity.

"It is difficult, perhaps impossible," he said in a conciliatory tone, "for us to justify John Brown's actions at Pottawatomie, despite the fact that those who died there were not innocents."

I nearly reminded him that, as an ordained minister, he could be expected to frown on murder, but I saw the hypocrisy in the reproach now that I, too, had shed blood, whose virtue or viciousness none but God could assay.

"But I believe that history will approve Brown's act and overlook his method because of the high ideals that prompted him. Brown is an idealist who intercedes on behalf of the voiceless and despised poor—a saint who takes up arms against wicked men. It's little enough for me to endure a troubled conscience in a cause for which he is prepared to give his life."

I would soon have reason to remember those words.

"I understand from Austin that you were in Mexico in '47," he said, signaling a change of subject.

"And at the beginning of '48, yes, I was."

He asked for my impressions of that country, which I gave him. My experience of the Día de los Muertos he found of special interest. He knew about the Aztec rites, of course, but he was unfamiliar with the Mexicans' macabre holiday celebrated on the first day of November, which, as I have written, impressed me. He was fascinated by my account of Mictlantecuhtli, la Calavera Catrina, the *ofrendas*, and the sugar skulls, whose taste he was eager for me to describe.

"The Spanish temper can be dark and cruel," he said. "Spaniards seem closer to death and suffering than most other civilized races. The Inquisition and their abuse of native peoples are proof enough—and who but a Spaniard could have painted *Saturn Devouring His Son*?"

I said nothing about the burning and looting of Hua-mantla or our nation's persecution of the Indians. He would have caught the stink of my hypocrisy soon enough. The discussion of morality belongs to the schoolroom, where it is less likely to offend or embarrass.

My eyes had glazed over, and I blinked to wake them in time to hear Emerson descanting on the Spanish tempera-ment. "When Washington Irving was the American min-ister to Spain, he sent me a little book on the Inquisition and its instruments of torture. Until then, I had thought my knowledge of men would have prepared me for most anything. I was wrong. I was appalled—stricken—made ill by what I saw in that book. I do not read in Spanish, but the illustrations were sufficient to my comprehension."

The mere names of the tortures—too inhuman to be called "ingenious"—are likewise sufficient: the Judas chair, the head screw, the Spanish boot, the breast ripper, the tongue ripper, the iron maiden, the brazen bull, the pear of anguish, the *strappado*, the Spanish donkey, the knee split-ter, the heretic's fork, death by sawing a man or woman down the middle—let this last brutality stand for the rest in its supreme terror and ineffable cruelty. It makes the Romans seem kind for having only crucified Christ.

If Emerson had meant his gazette of horrors as a parable, it fell on thorns. I was in no mood for conundrums or cautionary tales. I had reached the point at which a man can go no further without tumbling into an abyss. The Sage of Concord invited me to hear him speak that night, but I excused myself. I would rather have gone to a barn dance or gotten drunk like an ordinary man unconcerned by the evil that men do.

A thin, well-dressed negro came into the room. He had just arrived by train from Boston. Emerson introduced us, and, when I shook the stranger's hand, I noticed that the left one was missing.

"Reverend Winter, I would like you to be acquainted with my friend and colleague Mr. Samuel Long. Mr. Long, the Reverend Winter, recently returned from Zion, in the Territory of Utah."

We shook hands solemnly, and I hoped there would be no ensuing discussion of the Mormons or their unsuccessful rebellion.

"Mr. Long will also be addressing the society tonight. He has his own story to tell——"

"As does each of us, Waldo."

I marveled at the negro's familiarity, but Emerson appeared to take no notice.

"You are right to remind me, Samuel. Each writes his

own autobiography, if not with ink, then with some other medium equally impermanent."

"With blood?" asked the negro.

"If the occasion calls for it, but even blood and the memory of blood fade."

The other man seemed as though he would disagree, but the moment passed.

"Your thoughts, Reverend Winter?" asked Emerson, turning his penetrating gaze on me.

"I'm sure Mr. Winter would have much to say on the subject of blood, but I am famished for something more substantial than words," said Long. "Even yours, Waldo."

I felt obliged to Long for the diversion. The disadvantage of experience is that one is constantly asked to describe it to the curious. The man who stays at home is seldom pestered by his neighbors, and rarely by biographers.

I excused myself to both gentlemen and, having bid my host and his other guests good-bye, left the Evergreens. Before going home to dine with Tess and Charlotte, I stopped next door at the Homestead.

"Why weren't you at your brother's?" I asked, standing with my back to the hearth fire. A book lay open on your lap like a charmed bird.

"I feared there would not be oxygen enough for two luminaries of the age to burn brightly," you replied mischievously.

"You were missed."

"I'm sure they mistook a shadow in the corner of the room for me and smiled in its direction, as though it were the wallflower of Amherst, wilting at the sight of Canova's

Cupid and Psyche being naughty on the green marble mantelpiece. My brother is a connoisseur of objets d'art, some of which can make a lady blush."

I sat on the ottoman and glowered.

"Is Mr. Emerson fascinating?" you asked.

"He's a good man, I think, and persuasive."

"I have the better part of him on the bookshelf upstairs next to Euripides, whose work was also subversive for its time."

"You would have enjoyed the afternoon," I said impatiently.

"He is too magnetic a personality, I am told; I would have fainted to hear him speak, and his eyes, had they fallen on me, would have made me evaporate into a cloud. I might then have distilled a little rain to water Austin's plants—he and Sue are neglectful of their green charges."

Annoyed, I wanted to pick up the bowl of nasturtiums and send it flying. Instead, I asked you what you were reading.

"George Sand's *Mauprat*," you replied, taking the book from your lap and, having laid the silk ribbon between the pages, closing it.

"Ah, the lady novelist who wears men's trousers!" I said to spite you.

"I should like to wear men's trousers, too."

I didn't know whether to laugh or rebuke you. "Whatever for?"

"To shock Father."

"Do you hate him so very much, then?"

You set George Sand beside you, smoothed your dress, and said, in the offhand manner of a woman remarking on the milliner's newest fabrics, "There was a surgeon in Philadelphia, Dr. Mütter, who had learned to reconstruct the human face in Paris."

"All things novel and obscene begin in Paris," I replied peevishly.

"I didn't realize you are such a Calvinist, Robert! You should retire your sack coat for a Geneva gown."

I uttered a few syllables indicative of disapproval.

"If I were brave enough, I'd have the telltale warrants of my sex amputated."

Your fantastic notions often embarrassed, but never before had they appalled me.

"I think living shut up in this house has driven you mad."

"If I were a man," you said in a kind of reverie, "I'd kill my father, as Oedipus did his."

"I think you are in earnest!" I cried, feeling afraid.

"I *am* in earnest, Robert. How else am I to escape? And poor Vinnie—and Austin, too, whom Father installed in the Evergreens to keep him close. A fitting name for a cemetery! And yet . . . and yet, I love him, for I must. It says so in the covenants."

"What covenants?"

"Those that bind by a gravity more imperative than Isaac Newton's, which concerns the attraction of apples and of planets, but not that of one human heart to another."

"Love . . ." Because Ruth and mine had been brief, I sensed that I'd missed its fullness and peace.

"That, or its opposite," you replied with a shrug of your narrow shoulders.

Always the ironist!

I studied your diminutive frame, your weak chin, your wan face and was sorry to have sneered at you. I'm sorry now, Emily, though, despite your smallness and reclusiveness, you are no more vulnerable or timid than an asp.

"Fathers have their place in the universe," you said. "And we, their children, are pilgrim planets in orbit around them. That, sir, is the way of things—reprove them as I might."

You stood abruptly and went into the kitchen. I heard an iron door creak open and close.

"I have a roast in the oven," you said upon your return. "The kitchen is a domain where male tyranny dare not show itself."

"There was a negro man at your brother's . . . Samuel Long. He lacked his left hand."

"The manumitted and mutilated slave, yes, I know of him. His story is dreadful, and Mr. Emerson and Mr. Thoreau were the saving of him, or so Austin insists."

"He seemed disinclined to tell his story."

"It is written on his back. I'm not being fanciful, Robert. If you want the translation, he's in town to give his testimony before God and the abolitionists. They say he speaks most movingly of his bondage and escape."

"I'm going home tonight to see if I have a father's instinct. I've neglected my child."

"She may blossom in your absence," you said thoughtfully as you picked a nasturtium to pieces with nervous fingers.

I recalled Emerson's allusion to Goya's ghastly painting of infanticide and shuddered.

"Still . . ." My voice trailed off toward an admission of helplessness.

"Of course you must try," you said perfunctorily.

Silence settled on the room like a shroud.

"Do you like Poe's things?" I asked, because my mind had been tending toward the grim atmosphere of his tales.

"One does not care to be reminded."

"Of what?"

"One can have the bird or else the shadow it leaves upon the lawn."

"Poe, also, believed in affinities," I said.

"His are knit of iron cables, mine of gossamer. You may judge for yourself which is the stronger."

I wished that you were still with me, Ruth. I longed for your plain speech and common sense.

That night, when Aunt Tess laid a serving platter on the dining table, laden with white potatoes encircling a shank of lamb, Charlotte recited a stanza from Wordsworth.

"Rest, little young One, rest; thou hast forgot the day
    When my father found thee first in places far away;
    Many flocks were on the hills, but thou wert owned
        by none,
    And thy mother from thy side for evermore was
        gone.'"

Tess gathered Charlotte into her arms and called her "dear child."

"Did you teach her to say that?"

"Heaven's no! It was Miss Emily, of course."

"Aunt Emily did," repeated Charlotte, nodding her pretty head.

"She's always teaching the little one something or other."

I should have been grateful, but your repellent fantasy of metamorphosing into a man under the surgeon's knife oppressed me. You had meant to provoke because of my disdain for George Sand, but that you could conceive of anything so monstrous dismayed me. I would have forbidden you to see the girl, but what reason could I give Tess or Charlotte, who adored you? I hadn't the words to tell the cause of my uneasiness.

You once told me, "In a storm, we can shed words, as a tree does leaves, until we stand naked and mute before our God." Naked and mute in spirit, I had none before me, save that of the Aztecs or of the Spaniards—gods with teeth that gnashed and rent.

After supper, Charlotte and I drew pictures on her slate, played hide-and-seek, told each other what shapes we saw in the fire, and sang "Pretty Maids All in a Row." Having grown tired at last, she went upstairs with Tess to prepare for bed. When I went to kiss her good night, she asked for a story, but I couldn't think of any except as might illustrate a homily or an admonishment. She wouldn't let go of my hand until I'd told her one, so I made up a tale about a girl who returns home from far away every first of November and eats barley sugar candy.

Later, sitting beside Tess on the sofa, I wondered aloud what judgment would be passed on me, what punishment meted out for my neglect. There was no answer either from her or from the silent ones who judge and punish—only the steady *click*, *click*, *click* of knitting needles.

–4–

THE FOLLOWING WEEK, AUSTIN INVITED ME to accompany him to Boston. We traveled on the Amherst and Belchertown line to Palmer, where we made our connection. I hadn't been on an excursion since Ruth and I had gone to Hannibal, and the unspooling view of fields, meadows, hamlets, and towns outside the window held me rapt.

"The Minotaur escaped the Golden Age into one of rust and soot," you once remarked. "Like Father, the poor creature has become saturnine and out of sorts."

Maybe so, but I thrilled to ride the degenerate minotaur of iron and smoke, even though a speck of grit blew into my eye and made it weep for nothing but itself.

Your brother had an appointment with William Ticknor, of Ticknor and Fields, at their office on Washington Street. At Emerson's recommendation, Hawthorne had made Austin his plenipotentiary in matters regarding his published works. Hawthorne and his family were then living in England. Arriving early, we waited in the anteroom. Austin perused a contract, and, in the silence of the thickly carpeted room, I could hear snatches of a conversation issuing from Ticknor's private office. At two o'clock, the door opened, and a negro gentleman emerged, his hand clasping that of Ticknor, who stood behind him in the doorway. The negro's other cuff was empty.

"Mr. Long!" I said, very much surprised. "I hadn't expected to meet you here."

"Mr. Ticknor and I have known each other for some time. Mr. William Ticknor, please be acquainted with the Reverend Winter."

"Good day to you, sir," said the publisher cordially.

"And to you, sir," I replied.

"Austin," said the negro, giving his hand to your brother, who took it warmly in his own. "I hope you and Mrs. Dickinson are well."

"Tolerably so, thank you, Samuel."

"I am glad to hear it. Please give Sue my regards. And now, gentlemen, if you'll excuse me, Mr. Garrison will be champing at the bit for his article," said Long, winding a scarf around his neck and turning to leave. At the time, he was a correspondent for *The Liberator*, William Lloyd Garrison's abolitionist paper, also located in Boston.

"I have not given up hope!" called Ticknor as the other man went out the front door.

"I've been trying to persuade him to let us publish his reminiscences of Thoreau when they were neighbors in Walden Woods," he said to us in explanation. "He's a stubborn and self-effacing man."

"Excuse me," I said. "I'd like a word with Mr. Long."

I went outside and caught up with him on the sidewalk. "Mr. Long . . ."

"Yes? Do you wish to speak to me?"

"I must apologize for having missed your testimony on the day we met in Amherst. I was not myself."

"We cannot always be ourselves," he replied graciously. "It is the times we live in."

He shrank from the curb when a cab swerved toward him to avoid a newsboy in its path.

"I read an excerpt from your remarks in the Amherst paper. I thought what you said was very fine indeed."

"I would do better were I fiery, but I have not John Brown's gift for oratory."

"I overheard you and Mr. Ticknor talking about John Brown just now."

"He is a man often talked about these days."

"What do you think of him, besides his oratory?"

"I don't think they can be considered apart."

"Yes, but what do you think of *him*?" I repeated, perhaps too insistently.

"Are you asking me because I am a negro?"

"Yes."

My frankness must have appealed to him, because he answered my question with equal candor.

"I think he is insane." I opened my mouth to speak, but he went on. "But insanity for such a man is not that of the Bedlamite or the poor deluded souls locked up at Bellevue. It is nearer to that of ecstatic visionaries, such as Saint John of Patmos, Christopher Smart, Christ—if you'll forgive me, Reverend, for my blasphemy—and my friend Thoreau, although he's more likely to go into fits of ecstasy over a Jesus bug than the Lamb of God."

"I've been troubled by Brown ever since Pottawatomie," I said doggedly.

"Tell me, Robert, are you also troubled by the sacking of Lawrence and the burning of Osawatomie? Are you—I take it we are speaking of your conscience?" I nodded yes. "Was it troubled by Nat Turner's rebellion but not by the four million souls who suffer bondage as if it were their just desert?"

Until that moment, the contradiction had been felt like a rash, general and unfocused. Till then, I'd never heard the matter put so simply; a child could have taken Samuel Long's point.

"I will miss my deadline if I don't hurry," he said.

"Did you ever meet him?" I asked, grasping his elbow to detain him a moment longer.

"In the fall of 1857, when he spoke at the Concord town hall."

"Did he move you?" My vehemence surprised us both.

"As if he'd been the Baptist come again. Now, I really must go, Mr. Winter!"

I let go of his elbow. He tipped his hat and walked toward the *Liberator* offices.

"Godspeed!" I called after him.

I went back inside and waited for Austin to conclude his business. I took a manuscript from my case; I'd brought what I hoped would be the making of a book of my own about my experiences during the Mexican War, augmented by reminiscences of the Mormon Rebellion. Yes, Emily, the same narcissistic foolishness I mentioned earlier.

Their business at an end, the door to Ticknor's office opened, and the two men came into the anteroom.

"I have a manuscript!" I blurted, holding the papers in my hands as though they were the stone tablets of Moses or the gold plates of Joseph Smith.

Frowning, Austin snuffled in disapproval; I had kept the pages a secret from him during the train ride. "Coals to Newcastle," he muttered under his breath.

"Does it have a title?" asked Ticknor with a smile.

"*A Chaplain's Journey.*"

"You were a chaplain?"

"I've been one since the Mexican War."

"If you'll leave it with me, I'll read it when I can."

"Thank you."

"I make no promises. We receive a number of manuscripts, since it is our business to publish them, if they should happen to interest us."

I nodded like a simpleton. Vanity of vanities—the itch to inflict one's every gripe and flutter of the heart on a reader, as if writing were a sickness and, at the same time, its cure!

If you were here with me now, Emily, I would say, "You have offered up your days and nights to the vainest of vanities"—as have I, though mine is of a different sort.

Ticknor bid us good afternoon and returned to his office, carrying my sheaf of papers.

Your brother was good enough to make no further mention of my presumptuousness, which had clearly embarrassed him. We dined and made desultory conversation, as two people will who have talked enough for one day. We walked to our hotel near the Common and, before going inside to bed, lingered on the sidewalk, looking at the blooms of gaslight shining coldly through the bare trees.

"They are a splendid sight!" I said, letting a ghost of warm breath escape into the night.

"When Thoreau first saw them lit in Amherst, he complained that they dimmed the stars, 'which are more glorious than they.'" Austin paused a moment to smile. "Henry is that way."

I thought he must be a crank. Later, when I said as much to you, you replied, "Henry's boots are too big for the parlor."

After Austin and I returned to Amherst, I went to visit you at the Homestead. It had snowed again. Did it always snow when we were together?

Do you recall that evening, Emily? The sun was low down in the west, its fires belittled by gaslight caught in the nets of winter branches, while candles illuminating the windows of the houses along the street throbbed with a coppery gleam more wonderful than gold. The light fell in pale oblongs onto the snow, and the mansion seemed a world apart, which it was. A sleigh was waiting on the snowy path—the coachman nearly hidden under a blanket. The horse snorted plumes of smoke and fitfully pawed the icebound earth, causing the harness bells to ring out its misery with each shake of its heavy head. Weighted down by snow, the spruce trees leaned.

When I arrived, your new friend Kate was just leaving. I caught a glimpse of her as she turned to kiss your cheek in the entrance hall. She was darkly attractive, perhaps even beautiful; her hair dark beneath a black hat, her eyes dark behind a black veil, her elegant figure unabashed by dark furs. I gave her my arm—glad of the night, which hid the flush of warmth I could feel spreading across my cheeks—and helped her—gallantly, I hoped—into the sleigh. Her hands lay inside a fur muff; I covered her lap with a rug, embarrassed by the intimacy. She thanked me, I nodded to the driver, who touched the horse's sodden flank with the whip, and the sleigh drove off into the snow-illumined night. Turning, I thought I saw Sue scowling at a window behind the hedge.

I watched you nervously fixing your hair—a strand of which had come undone—like an actress about to walk onstage. You'd taken to dressing it "after the fashion of Elizabeth Barrett, whose husband also writes poems." For a moment, we regarded each other in mutual confusion and puzzlement. Then you led me into the parlor.

"Forgive me for not introducing my friend," you said, wrapping your shawl around your thin shoulders. "The snow and the hour did not wish it."

"I could not help noticing her black veil."

"She is recently widowed," you replied, and then with something like a blush, you let me know that you did not wish to speak of her.

Although I was intrigued—*entranced* is the better word—I let the matter drop. Without any real interest and with little coherence, I related my trip to Boston, Austin's meeting with Ticknor, and my own happenstance encounter with

Samuel Long. I did not refer to our brief exchange concerning John Brown, to whom I found myself giving increasing thought. I knew you did not share my fascination for the abolitionist, and, suddenly feeling tired and absurd, I wished you good night.

Lying in bed, I grew peevish at the thought of how frivolous the tribe of scribblers can be. You are the poet of the divided self. Poe recorded, in prose, the depravity of lives diverted from the commonplace. Abraham Lincoln, however, was the prophet of a disintegrating nation—an eventuality far more terrible in its consequences than "The Fall of the House of Usher" or the minor tragedies played out inside the Homestead.

In Utah, I'd read about Abe's nomination at the convention in Springfield as the Republican candidate for the United States Senate. I could picture his oddly fashioned but kindly face—clean-shaven then—as he stood—all the length and lank of him—to accept his party's blessing. I saw, in my mind's eye, resoluteness, sadness, and misgiving on that face. He would lose the seat to Stephen Douglas, author of the Kansas–Nebraska Act of 1854, which had created a proslavery empire from Indian Territory, the Territory of New Mexico, and Texas. Douglas campaigned against Lincoln on a platform of popular sovereignty, or rule by the people, even if they cast their votes for slavery and murder. I fear this issue will be with us always—a stone the union cannot pass. Lincoln was not then an abolitionist, but he detested slavery because of what it threatened: the destruction of the United States, an end made inevitable by *Dred Scott v. Sanford*. The infamous Supreme Court decision declared that a negro—freedman or slave—could not, by law, be a citizen and that the federal government had no authority to forbid slavery in the territories.

Did you read Abe's speech, Emily? It thrilled me, and it scared me when I read it in *The Deseret News*, whose motto is "Truth and Liberty," published by the Mormons in Salt Lake City.

> "A house divided against itself cannot stand." I believe this government cannot endure, permanently half *slave* and half *free*. I do not expect the Union to be *dissolved*—I do not expect the house to *fall*—but I *do* expect it will cease to be divided. It will become *all* one thing, or *all* the other. Either the *opponents* of slavery, will arrest the further spread of it, and place it where the public mind shall rest in the belief that it is in course of ultimate extinction; or its *advocates* will push it forward, till it shall become alike lawful in *all* the States, *old* as well as *new*—*North* as well as *South*.

With the shrewdness of a Yankee lawyer, Abe likely foresaw the division of the house, the legatees at loggerheads—its fall a judgment on them both for having failed to arbitrate their differences. War was inevitable, for neither side would concede. Did he look across the years and see himself as the man who would save the house from ruin?

Did he hear an overture of disaster played to the wistful tune of "Dixie"? Did he smell—the instant before he closed his eyes forever—the stink of martyrdom in the gunpowder wafting from a theater balcony? When John Wilkes Booth had shaken a warning finger at him two years earlier, during a performance, in Washington, of *The Marble Heart*, did the president's own heart turn momentarily cold?

<h2 style="text-align:center">–5–</h2>

THE FOLLOWING DAY, I RETURNED to the Homestead to ask you about the mysterious widow. No sooner had I broached the subject, however, than you flared and insisted that I mind my own business, which was my daughter, Charlotte, and not "Mrs. Kate," as you called her.

"I won't mention her again," I said peevishly.

"How was your trip to Boston?" You'd meant to be conciliatory, but my back was up.

"I told you last night!"

"Did you? I don't recall. I was not myself last night."

I served you Samuel Long's words with vinegar. "'We cannot always be ourselves.'"

"That is very true and very wise, Robert," you agreed with a warmth that checked the falling barometer of my spirits.

I followed you into the conservatory.

"My favorite room of all," you said happily. "I call it mine even if I have no deed to it except as use and enjoyment grant. My demons don't pursue me here, and Father does only occasionally, to see the yellow ox-eyed daisies."

"He is master of the house, nonetheless."

"He is not my *Master*," you replied with a glance that could've been mistaken either for coyness or a dampened ferocity. As a rule, you concealed your anger like a snarled thread inside the bosom of your dress.

Startled by the peculiar emphasis that had fallen on the word *master*, I asked, "Who, then, is he?"

"'He maketh me to lie down . . .'" you replied distractedly.

"Is Christ your Master?" I asked doubtfully.

"Not He, though he wore a beard and bore his wounds in silence."

My patience was at an end. "Who, then?"

You would not say, and I was left to wonder if it might not be Sam Bowles, the bearded "Arabian" editor of the *Springfield Republican,* whom you favored with letters and poems; the pale, but beardless, Reverend Wadsworth of Philadelphia; your muse; or—no, the idea was appalling! Emily, forgive me for having entertained it. Like Poe and Hawthorne, I'm too ready to believe that the monstrous and impossible must be the case when the truth is hidden. Is there something dark and unnatural—an unspeakable strain—in American literature?

"See how the sky comes in at the windows? We might be standing in a glass house such as angels live in."

The conservatory was cheerful and did indeed seem to enclose an otherworldly air and light. You sat on a cane chair, and I on another, staring out at the vast azure wastes.

"The Sun is not a gentleman," you said. "His temper's hot, his clothing garish, and he is indifferent to the thirsty cattle lowing in the withered grass. I much prefer the Moon, who creeps in at night and, motherly, comforts me with a silver touch upon my cheek. But no sooner has she left the room than demons come to vex me and nightmares nicker in the corners."

You rose from the chair and paced the room in agitation.

"What is the matter now, Emily?"

"Why, nothing. Nothing is the matter."

You took your seat again.

"Or say, instead, that 'nothing is the natter,' for I have been nattering about nothing at all. Dangling from the edge of a precipice can make one giddy with talk."

I let it go, too tired to keep up with you. I remarked on the cactus plants, looking out of place in dour, wintry Amherst.

"They are what I know of Mexico, and all I need of it."

"I hope Carlo still enjoys the serape," I said unkindly. "Or did it long ago fall to pieces?"

The serape was apparently too trivial a subject for discussion.

"I love the cactus; It's been, as Sir Walter Raleigh said of his tobacco pouch, *'Comes meus fuit in illo miserrimo tempore.'* He was my companion at that most miserable time."

I studied the freckles on your face and once again decided that I liked them.

"Do you want to hear a story, Robert?"

"If you tell it plainly."

"There once was a porcupine. It grew tired at last of its wanderings. It stopped where it happened to be and stood there—stock-still—for what, to a porcupine, was an eternity. At long last, it took root and became a cactus. Ever since, it has given generously of its sharpened quills and has also kept the curious at a distance. I could ask for no better friend."

Abe Lincoln might have enjoyed your fable. I did not.

"It was not plain enough."

You made a face. I shifted restlessly in my chair.

"Would you like tea or coffee? Some toast and marmalade? I've been impolite not to have asked before this."

"No, thank you."

You fell silent and then abruptly asked, "Robert, can we pretend there is a wall between us like Bottom's loamy, roughcast wall pierced by an imaginary cranny through which Pyramus and Thisbe whispered?" You peered quizzically at me through an aperture made by your thumbs and fingers.

"I don't understand."

"I would like you to hear my confession," you said in all seriousness.

"I'm not a priest!"

"And I am not contrite!"

"Emily, what is it you want from me?"

"To air my mind. I do as much for the quilts and blankets, but for all that I am a gnome, I'm still too large for the airing cupboard."

"I won't hear your confession," I said. I had done as much for the murderer Manzanero, then why not you?

"Mr. Emerson says that 'all friendship is confession.'"

"Then I will listen to what you have to say as a friend."

You seemed ready to speak your mind, then apparently changed it.

"No, Robert, it is not as a friend that I would speak to you now."

"If you are neither penitent nor friend now, what are you?"

"A woman ravished by an alien god."

I shivered at the thought of Mictlantecuhtli, his body clamped to yours.

Sensing my horror, you recanted savagery for ordinary Christian despair. "A woman in the wilderness to whom He has turned a deaf ear, if you like."

I did not like it at all. Though I had lost my sense of a vocation, I could still shudder at impiety.

"Is the casting out of demons beyond your strength?" You seemed pitiable, but only for a moment, for your next question irked me. "Are you a man of little faith, or is it merely that you are a little man?"

I shook my head with the solemnity of a self-righteous man withholding mercy. I could have heard your confession and offered absolution, if reluctantly; the Lutheran church favors public penance and forgiveness above a private grant, which appears too like the Roman sacrament to be encouraged. But something gnawed at me—a thing I did not wish to know. A secret. The thought of its revelation frightened me. It whispered like a draft in an unused room while, outside, snow was freshly mortaring the Homestead's mustard-colored bricks.

Carlo came into the conservatory. He walked like the old man he was in dog years. He licked my hands kindly, and I was grateful to him for his unfeigned and uncalculating affection.

"I'll tell Carlo, then," you said as he went over to your side and rested his chin on your knee. "He has been my constant confessor and can be counted on not to break the seal."

Did you glare at me, Emily? I think you did. In spite of it, I foolishly asked, "Won't you let me marry you, at least?" (Strange to have said "at least.") I was as astonished as you were by my absurd proposal, after what had passed between us. Had I set myself on fire, I could not have given you more reason to be shocked. I waited to be scolded and sent away, but you laughed so hard, the dog cowered.

"Robert, I will not be 'bridaled.'"

I stood and nearly leaped at you. I held you by the wrist. It was all I could do not to take you by the throat. At that moment, I hated you. You must have known; you must have seen it in my eyes and heard it in the rasp of my quickened breath.

You did not make a sound. Suddenly, your mouth relaxed its grimace, and your face was lighted by a beatific smile. Abject, I let go of your wrist and resumed my seat opposite yours.

"Forgive me," I said contritely. "I will never again presume to ask."

"I am indentured here," you said gravely. "Fate has made me the scribe of our pettiness and misfortunes."

"I'll be leaving Amherst soon," I said, having made up my mind at that instant.

"Will you return to the army?" Your voice bespoke a genuine interest now that you were safe from my advances. "Will you go back to Springfield?"

"Not to Springfield. A chaplain's post is vacant at Washington City."

"By the map, you will be nearer Charlotte and Tess."

"Yes," I replied. To you, as well, I thought, although I knew my suit was hopeless.

"Will there be war, Robert?"

"I'm certain of it." Despite the shameful compromises and bloodshed of the previous decade, I knew that war would come. "The fuse may have already been lit, or is about to be. It takes only a little powder to blow up a dam."

"Or to pull down a house," you said softly, almost absently.

Were you thinking of the "house" in Lincoln's aphorism or the Homestead, presided over by your autocratic father? In your heart, did you wish him dead and buried beneath the rubble of your verses?

"Rat is on the stairs," you said.

"I don't understand you," I replied wearily.

"I'm ungraspable, like a ball of quicksilver that children love to mash under their thumbs; it disperses for an instant, only to reconvene without a particle of loss."

I sighed.

"I must start dinner; I would not wish to be chastised for dereliction of kitchen duties."

"I'll be going, then."

I followed you into the vestibule, where my coat, hat, and scarf were hanging.

"Will you visit me tomorrow?" you asked as I stepped outside into the cold March air.

"No, I have business to attend to before leaving for Washington. And I want to spend the remaining time with Charlotte."

"Of course," you said, visibly relieved.

"Good-bye, Emily."

I tipped my hat as I had done a dozen years before when I first met you outside North College and had nearly fled.

"We'll go our own way now, with our own words," you said in parting.

I never saw you again, though, upon my return to Amherst after Harper's Ferry, we spoke briefly like a confessor and his penitent.

−6−

ON MY LAST NIGHT IN AMHERST, Charlotte and I were guests at the Evergreens. You did not come, sending Carlo as your envoy. Austin and Sue were genuinely hospitable. They cosseted Charlotte, who roughhoused with Carlo and fed him little cakes from the table until he was sick. None seemed to mind. I thought that you stayed at home because you were afraid I would force my attentions on you again.

I was angry. You're well out of it, I told myself. She is not half the woman Ruth was; I'm only sorry I didn't realize it while she was alive—*and Ruth had been alive in every atom.* God forgive me those times when I was anything less than kind. Well, even Adam and Eve fell out over an apple. You and your Master are welcome to each other! I said to myself.

"What are your plans?" asked Austin.

We had gone into his workroom to smoke cigars, which the ladies abominated. They did not begrudge us whiskey in moderation, which we took with a little water for propriety's sake. I was looking forward to life among rough-and-ready men, far from Amherst. I had begun to tire of it and of you. I was glad that you'd rebuffed me. I was glad to have no ties.

Yes, there was Charlotte! But I knew by then that I could not care for her as a father should. I send her money and little gifts. Next year, I'll see her enrolled at Amherst Academy and, afterward, at Mount Holyoke. She will follow in your wake—no, I would not wish your widow's way on her. You are cut off from the ordinary concerns of our kind. They whirl around you, as if on a madly turning wheel.

"You seem vexed," said Austin, letting out a cloud of bluish smoke, which obscured a daub leaning on an easel. The painting—an empty meadow under snow—seemed tinged with gloom, as if by your father's shadow, although Edward, disapproving of your brother's pastime, refused to set foot inside the studio.

"I thought that Emily would be here this evening."

"She would have been . . ."

I looked at him closely, waiting for him to finish the sentence. "Well?"

"If she had not had another of her spells," he said hesitantly.

"What kind of spell?" I asked skeptically, for I knew you to be as flighty as a shuttlecock.

"Nervous fits." He stubbed out his cigar in a broken piece of pottery. "It's a family secret, Robert, which I trust you will keep."

His tone was one of admonishment, accompanied by a stern gaze that pierced mine to the quick, or whatever in the eyes resembles that most tender of flesh. With his moody, handsome face, he might have been a fiery-haired Heathcliff come from the Yorkshire Moors, or from the pages of Emily Brontë's novel. When words engulf and sting, they are as fearsome as fens and nettles.

"I had no idea."

"I thought it right that you should know."

"I am sorry for her."

"In a previous century, she would have been burned at the stake for consorting with the devil. In our enlightened age, she'd only be shut up in an asylum. We have made progress," he said with an irony whose intention, I supposed, was to make me an accomplice in the family's shame.

I had grown tolerant during my descent from the child-like innocence of the seminarian. Experience broadens the mind, as they never tire of saying. It also makes the moral high ground shrink beneath one's feet. By now, I had little left to stand on, while, all around me, the choirs of the righteous and the anathemas of the lily-white vied in raucousness with the stokers of hellfire and the howling of the damned.

"Emily became very much agitated last night and has kept to her bed all day."

Was I to blame? If so, I'm sorry.

"She sent her good wishes by Carlo."

Carlo had, indeed, carried a small scroll fastened to his collar, which Austin took from his pocket and gave me to read.

> Forgive—as Friends must always do each other— my absence. My Volcano was uncorked last night, & I have yet to emerge fully from its lava, whose heat has left me flushed. We exchanged Farewells enough yesterday, & when my hand is again tractable, I will write you—if you'll only let me know the place.
>
> Yours with a good will,
> Emily
>
> P.S. By now you must be sick of oysters & whist— necessities at Brother's table.

"Despite her illness, she's not so weak as most suppose," said Austin, having finished his whiskey.

"She's a catamount," I said, "that meows to dissemble its ferocity."

"Sometimes I think the Homestead is a cockpit where she and Father are fighting for their lives."

"They hate——"

"Not hate."

"Then what?"

"I don't know. But whatever it is, they require it—it is their atmosphere. They must feel a tightening in the chest to assure themselves that they're alive."

He might have been describing my own grappling with the Father of us all.

We fell silent, and I heard Charlotte's young voice piping in the other room.

"Are you happy being a lawyer in your father's firm?"

I couldn't have said what had motivated my question: spite, sympathetic curiosity, or a mixture of the two—more than likely that.

"I wanted to paint landscapes," admitted Austin. "I fancied myself another Church or George Bingham. I dreamed of a studio in New York City or Chicago. But Father got his way, and I have only moved next door."

Of the two, I thought the law the better trade.

"I should not have told you about Emily," said Austin abruptly. "But you're a clergyman and can be entrusted with a secret."

"Will you tell her that I know?"

He acknowledged our complicity with a nod of his head, while I remembered Manzanero.

Your brother's parting words to me that night were, "You

are wrong if you believe Father to be entirely at fault where Emily is concerned: He protects her."

While we walked home to Aunt Tess's, I held Charlotte's small hand in mine and tried to say something by which I would be remembered, as Hector had spoken to Andromache and his son before leaving for Troy, where a spear whose sole purpose was to kill him awaited. Destiny, if not a Divinity, does shape our ends, rough-hew them how we will. My end, when it comes, will be unheroic and unworthy of a classic age. Ours is the age of lead, and I will fall in some sordid place far from grace and any affectionate heart.

"The snow looks pretty in the moonlight."

"Yes, it does, Father," replied Charlotte, picking up and setting down one foot after another in its drifts, like a Red Indian stalking his prey.

"When you were a baby," I said, "I carried you to the Lincolns' house, in Springfield. The snow lay deep around me, and I was scared that I might drop you into it and you'd be lost until the spring."

She fell silent, contemplating my morbid fancy, I suppose, and then she said in the serious manner of a child, "I am much taller now, Father, so you needn't worry."

In the morning, I took the train to Boston and, from there, a coastal schooner south on the Atlantic to Chesapeake Bay, and thence up the Potomac to Washington City, where I arrived at my new posting on March 21, 1859.

I wrote you with my new address, and you wrote in return.

Robert——

Now that you know ALL, I hope you will soon forget your Witch, who must bear her Demons as she may. They feed me savories—even as they gnaw heart & vitals. It is—I suppose—a fair exchange. They are like the worm, which eats common dirt and—in gratitude for its supper—casts a rich loam that gardeners prize for their anemones. Or they are like the grit that rubs the Oyster's silken lining into Pearl. Pythia must be housebound to serve the god that puts words in her mouth.

Carlo sends his love.

Emily

P.S. Father will never allow me to stray far from the Homestead, lest I suffer the Ducking Stool, Pillory, or Stake. We will see each other again, Robert, if fairy tales are true. Until then—or in lieu of Perpetuity—please make do with my Image, which Alchemy has caused to appear on base metal. I have sat only twice before for a portrait—the wren is too shy to sit for long.

With the letter, you had included a daguerreotype taken by Mr. J. C. Spooner, of Springfield, Massachusetts. Your eyes betrayed a nervousness, as if the wren were, indeed, about to take flight.

I carried your portrait during the drama at Harper's Ferry

and, later, through the endless night of civil war, when all the house lights went out. It wasn't love that would not let me part with it. When I was a small boy, I became afraid to leave the house after having seen a runaway horse trample a woman in the street. Although Aunt Tess wasn't a Catholic, she gave me a Saint Christopher medal to wear around my neck. "It will keep you safe," she said. I wore it like an amulet against evil, which has been loose in the world since the first couple's final notice and eviction, when Adam got his stoop, and Eve her stain. I don't believe anymore in a saintly intercessor, but I do believe in the existence of EVIL. (You would capitalize it thus, and you'd be right to acknowledge its supremacy even within the world in miniature of the printed page.) I carried the daguerreotype for the same absurd reason that I wore the holy medal. We're a superstitious race, afraid, like children, of being in a world where we are often alone.

At the seminary, I was fascinated by an icon that had once hung in an Eastern Orthodox church. The artist had given the image of Saint Christopher the head of a dog. Carlo, whom you have called your "demon dog," may be a watchful saint, protecting you from the martyrdom you seem bent on achieving.

> Ripped from Radiance into common day,
> Then, by a midwife's slap, made to rid
> My lungs of atoms drawn in the dustless
> Atmosphere of Heaven—where the lead

For the Bullet that will one day bless
Me poured—ardent—into the mold—
My iron christening cup—

What bullet did you fear, Emily? Do you fear it still, or have you found a way to live without terror, in spite of your conviction that you're standing in its path? The resolve to go on regardless of misgivings was one of Lincoln's strengths. It carried him into Ford's Theatre on the night of April 14, 1865. Would I have had the courage, belief, and love to have stood in the bullet's path the instant John Wilkes Booth fired his derringer? Would I be as brave as Giles Corey and reply to my inquisitor, "More weight"?

–7–

QUARTERED AT THE WASHINGTON NAVY YARD, on the Potomac's eastern branch, I performed the duties of chaplain for sixty men assigned to army ordinance and a detachment of marines stationed at the I Street barracks. My arrival coincided with the thaw of winter's frozen mud augmented by March rain. The dreary city's inhabitants were either dispirited or else half mad with visions of patronage as they traipsed the unpaved streets in search of government contracts, appointments, and military commissions. There were more swine rooting in the sloughs and gutters than statesmen sitting in the halls of Congress. At the ragged end of winter 1859, Washington may have been the dirtiest capital on earth, excepting that of the Hottentots.

I would often visit the "Castle," as the Smithsonian Institution's red sandstone edifice was called, mostly to see the canvases of John Mix Stanley. I admired his paintings of the western frontier and California, through which he'd traveled with General Kearny's expedition at the time of the Mexican War. I felt an affinity for Stanley, as well as envy of his artistry. I wished I had been called to be a painter of what the eye can see instead of a spy on the souls of men. His landscapes contain an atmospheric light—the luminosity evident in the Hudson River School of artists; in Stanley's work, however, the land is untamed. His paintings are to theirs as a headland is to a hummock, a mountain gorge to a sylvan grotto, or a torrent to a brook.

At the navy yard, I became acquainted with an army surgeon by the name of Edward Fenzil. In many ways, he was charming, even fascinating. He'd been a friend of Edgar Poe, in the winter of '44, when the writer was living in Philadelphia. There was, in Fenzil, a grotesque strain that precluded intimacy. He was given to brooding, interrupted by a manic intensity that alarmed me. He was strange, as a man might well have become in the presence of a macabre nature such as Poe's. Fenzil's imaginative faculty was highly developed, and he enjoyed telling outrageous stories of his winter as a protégé of the gothic master. Fenzil also drank and took ether. In spite of my aversion for the man, he was an unusually skillful surgeon.

Fenzil had an appreciation for painting, which served us as common ground. I could not help being infuriated, however, by his criticism of John Stanley's pictures.

During a visit to the Castle one May afternoon, he called Stanley's landscapes banal and affectless. The light that I considered splendid in them he thought "too optimistic." He preferred the dark horrors of Goya, Jacques-Fabian Gautier d'Agoty, and Hieronymus Bosch. In Fenzil's opinion, those artists had caught the germ of human nature, which no school of polite dabblers could ever hope to do. Returning to our quarters, he begged me to take ether with him, so that I might enjoy a respite from "the monsters." Ether, he claimed, produced a dreamless sleep, undisturbed by night terrors detained behind a *cordon sanitaire*, the name given by the French to the quarantine of those sickened by the Black Death. He likened the anodyne to the holy water of an exorcist.

"I will do no such thing!" I shouted, frightened by his words. Strong drink was one thing, ether or opiates quite another.

"Then you must resign yourself to an ordinary life," he said with a sigh.

After that, I kept my distance from him insofar as it was possible. The surgeon and the chaplain are comrades in sickness and in death; in war, the sickbed too often is succeeded by the deathbed and the grave.

Could he read your mind, Emily, even Fenzil would be shocked by the grotesque fancies that writhe there like Medusa's snakes. Pardon an extravagant turn of phrase; his dark imagination—fretted by his master Edgar Poe's—must have rubbed off on me. I am susceptible to stronger wills and larger minds—such as yours, Emily. Austin was right when he said you are not the harmless spinster you pretend to be.

In Washington, I became fond of a likable private of marines named Luke Quinn, an Irish immigrant who had enlisted in '55. He'd worked as a drencher and pickler at a Brooklyn tannery near "the Swamp," and, keen on baseball, would go to Red Hook on Sunday afternoons to watch the Excelsior Club play. When the men garrisoned at the marine barracks played a game of ball, they would insist on my being umpire, though they swallowed my Sunday-morning sermons like ipecac, because, in Luke's words, "If you can't trust a padre, who can you trust?"

Who, indeed?

"Thanks, Reverend," Luke would say politely after the game was finished or the ball hopelessly lost in the marsh bordering the west side of the yard, as impenetrable as the morass that mired the pilgrim Christian for his sins in Bunyan's allegory.

"*De nada,*" I would reply, as Manzanero had done after I had shriven him.

Nada means "nothing," Emily, and if you listen closely when the word is pronounced—solemnly, as it begs to be heard—you can hear a deep bell toll, as if for the end of days.

Na-da! Na-da! According to John Donne, it rings for us all.

Luke and I used to walk the back streets and alleys and relish the iniquitous sights. Even now, I have no idea why I took pleasure in the slatterns, whores, sharps, pickpockets, cutthroats, and confidence men, which abound in every city, save the celestial. I suppose I preened myself on being a righteous man, though there was more hypocrisy in me than probity. As for Luke, I think he was afraid of what would likely come to pass and, by resisting temptation, hoped to get on the good side of the Lord. Chaste and a teetotaler, unnatural virtues in a marine, he couldn't have accrued many sins in his young life. In the taprooms, we drank root beer and talked a good deal of horseshit. On Sunday afternoons, after I'd admonished my flock against the pleasing aspects of vice, he and I would listen to a military band perform patriotic hymns of the thrilling martial sort. We behaved like two altar boys, shoes shined, hair combed, and ears clean, to hear the trump of doom resound and cheer the Lord when He rode down the sky in His fiery chariot.

Our friendship came abruptly to an end during the siege of the engine house at Harper's Ferry, when John Brown shot Luke through the abdomen. He did so with a "Beecher's Bible," the name bestowed on the rifles shipped to "Captain" Brown in crates marked BIBLES by the abolitionist Henry Ward Beecher, of New England—a ruse whose aim was slaughter, however well intentioned.

−8−

YOUR LETTERS TO ME WHILE I WAS IN WASHINGTON were as dazzling as the butterflies transfixed by pins in your father's study. But I had to wait for Austin's visit to hear of your attachment to Kate Scott, the dark, mysterious woman whom I'd helped into a sleigh three months before.

"They are often together," he said after ordering a roast chicken to divide between us.

I had taken your brother to dine at the Old Ebbitt Grill, a block from the White House. Buchanan was sitting at a corner table, together with his secretary of state and a man whom the landlord identified for us as a Louisiana cotton magnate. "A lord of the lash!" he called him with such acrimony that I feared he would spit on the floor, as is the custom in saloons frequented by rude men. Heads together, they were talking in low voices, like a knot of conspirators.

Austin took a draft of his ale and said, "I'm troubled by Emily's fascination for that woman. There is something unwholesome about it." He repented of his remark and hurried to recant it. "I don't mean that their friendship is in any way improper! But the woman has set tongues wagging—well, you know what Amherst is like. And she has made conquests—Sam Bowles, in particular." As if in an aside, Austin muttered with a distracted air, "Even my own wife seems smitten by her! I wish to God she would return to Cooperstown forthwith!"

I felt a cold draft on my neck, although the sweat had come out on my forehead.

"You've gone pale, Robert. Are you all right?"

"It's nothing. I'm bothered sometimes by a fever I caught in Mexico."

Austin looked at me doubtfully and then said, "Father detests her."

A fact that makes her doubly attractive to your sister, I told myself.

"He calls her 'Sappho.'"

Now it was Austin's turn to shiver.

Were you conscious of the uneasiness your friendship with "that woman" caused? Or could the scandal have been spice for your daily gruel?

I hurriedly changed the subject. "Have you seen Charlotte recently?"

"I have, and she is well." I thought he glanced disapprovingly at me, but maybe not. "Tess continues to dote on her. I'm fond of the imp myself."

"I'm glad to hear it and very much obliged to you, Austin."

"Not at all. When will you be home again?"

Amherst was no longer home. The Washington Navy Yard was what passed for one that spring, summer, and early fall, but I couldn't admit my disloyalty to Austin, who was so kind to Charlotte.

"I don't know," I told him, and then I uttered a short sentence without embellishment, in a voice devoid of emotion, as if I were predicting rain—four words that would bear on the very idea of home for nearly three million men. "There will be war."

"Do you think so, Robert?" he asked nervously. He was

not yet the glum, determined squire whom time would anoint with thinning hair and side-whiskers.

"I am convinced of it."

"Soon?"

"Next year or the year after."

I looked up sharply at the others in the room, thinking I would find them leaning forward expectantly in their chairs to hear what I'd say next, but they appeared oblivious to the closet drama being played out beneath an engraved reproduction of George Munger's watercolor *The President's House*—a sobering reminder of the burning of Washington City during the British occupation in 1812. I hoped the picture was not prophetic.

"Father also thinks there will be war, which is the reason I'm here in Washington," said Austin soberly. "I met with Sumner this morning."

Senator Charles Sumner, of Massachusetts, was as efficacious as John Brown in inciting antislavery opinion in the North against the slave power. In 1856, after the sack of Lawrence, South Carolina congressman Preston Brooks nearly beat the Massachusetts man to death with a heavy walking stick for having vilified his cousin, a Democratic congressman and slaveholder, for having taken "the harlot, slavery" as his "mistress."

"What business did you have with him?" I asked, happy to have left Kate Scott in the wake of our conversation.

"Sumner is chairman of the Senate Committee on Foreign Relations, and, if war is imminent, our clients can benefit from his European connections. The adverse effect of hostilities on commercial interests will be catastrophic unless they can be sheltered abroad. Sumner is a powerful man in Congress, and I admire him in spite of his lavender trousers."

I nodded my head knowingly, although I did not care whether their interests or their heads went to hell in a handbasket.

My well-being must have been on your brother's mind, because he returned to the theme of my rootless existence. I was, in equal parts, touched by his solicitude and irritated by his officiousness.

"Robert, is this enough?"

His hand indicated the dining room, but it was meant to take in the capital, the army, and perhaps even my chaplaincy, which may have seemed frayed as an old cassock to his discerning eyes.

I sat up straight in my chair and postured self-importantly like most everyone else in Washington, which, like capital cities the world over, was as much a theater stage as a seat of government.

"A modicum of contentment is all that a man can hope for who believes himself to be in the service of honorable ends," I replied. "I leave happiness to fools and brides."

What tripe! Even now I blush to recall those words and the mincing manner in which I spoke them.

Austin did not appear to mind my pomposity; perhaps the business of law and his visits to Washington had inured him to shameful displays of self-love.

"I wish you well, Robert, in your vocation. We'll pray for you if war does come."

I thanked him, and we parted that night as friends.

FEARFUL & EXCITING INTELLIGENCE!

SLAVE UPRISING AT HARPER'S FERRY!

Conspiracy of Negroes in Virginia & Maryland.

U.S. Arsenal Raided, Blood Shed & Lives Lost!

Slaves Armed with Rifles & Pikes.

Terror on the Train——Hostages Taken——

Telegraph Wires Cut——Massacre of Civilians——

Thousands of Army Rifles Seized by Negroes.

Slave Insurrection Spreads to the Interior.

EXTRA-ORDINARY MASSACRE FEARED!

&c.   &c.   &c.

Fenzil and I were thrown together unexpectedly on October 17, the day following John Brown's raid on the federal arsenal at Harper's Ferry, Virginia. With him, were sixteen white men, including three of his sons, three free negroes, one freed slave, and one fugitive slave. They were equipped with Sharp's carbines and had brought with them 950 iron pikes, with which to arm the slaves expected to revolt in the vicinity of the town, which stood beneath high bluffs, at the confluence of the Shenandoah and Potomac Rivers.

The night before, a Sunday, the "Provisional Army," as Brown grandiosely referred to his meager force, had taken hostages, cut telegraph wires, seized a train, overcome the guard, and quickly gained control of the arsenal, where 100,000 army muskets and rifles were stored. By his action, Brown intended nothing less than the overthrow of slavery, believing that, as news of the insurrection spread, blacks would rise up against their masters, kill them if they must, and join him in his holy war against the South.

On the afternoon of Monday, October 17, President Buchanan ordered the marines at the Washington barracks to put down the rebellion, under the command of Lieutenant Colonel Robert E. Lee, who would, two and a half years later, lead a great and vengeful host against us as general of the Army of Northern Virginia. And in reply to "Dixie," the boys in blue would sing "John Brown's body lies a-mouldering in the grave. His soul's marching on!" History is the superb ironist and cuckolder. We came to arrest John Brown and ended in martyring him.

It *is* strange, Emily, how the circumstances surrounding our lives appear haphazardly assembled, like a crowd come to watch a building burn. If we could only ascend high enough—in a balloon, say—to some supreme vantage point, the purpose of our lives might show clear through the muddle and perplexity, like gold nuggets in a pan.

At three o'clock that afternoon, we boarded a Baltimore and Ohio train for Harper's Ferry. We took two twelve-pound howitzers and enough ammunition to subdue a thousand fanatics. At the time, we didn't know the strength of our adversary, nor were we aware that the Virginia militia, as well as local farmers and shopkeepers, had skirmished with Brown's tiny force and taken the bridge across the Potomac, by which it might have escaped into the mountains. The telegraph had been rendered useless, and, if not for the eastbound train, which Brown had stopped, then foolishly let pass, we would not have known of the raid at all. The "fearful intelligence" was reported by the train's conductor on reaching Baltimore.

The slave revolt, on which Brown had been relying to swell his ranks, did not occur. None mutinied, and no abolitionist joined the Provisional Army. The raid's first fatality was a colored man named Hayward Shepherd, a porter on the express train that had been fired on and stopped by Brown's men. Even with a wagonload of guns, twenty-two untrained marauders had no hope of withstanding an assault by a force ten times their number.

On the train from Washington, I was too distracted to notice the scenery. It could have been polar snows or the Arabian Desert for all I knew of it. I was always so when I went into battle. For all their indecent songs and bravado, the marines who shared the train with me were also apprehensive. How could it have been otherwise? No one knows better than a man who has been to war how fearful a thing war is.

"People say niggers remember their savage ways, soon as they get shut of white folk," one marine told another, sitting together on the seat behind me. "Don't matter if they got Jesus in them or not, they turn animal when the chains come off. They'll cut a man open and unravel his tripes before the poor bastard's finished squirting his tobacco."

"I'm not scared of no man on earth, but I'm scared of niggers. I know a man in Georgia who once saw a black take the whip out of the hand of a driver, who'd just given him twenty stripes, and stuff the handle down his throat. 'There is no more fearful sight than a negro who's lost his mind,' my friend said."

"I've heard tales of them eating white people raw."

I recalled the white cannibals among the Donner Party.

"John Reid's Ruffians were right to kill the abolitionists."

"If I get 'Old Brown' in my sights, I'll send him straight to hell!"

When the Civil War began, I remembered those two men and wondered whether they had joined the boys in oatmeal gray or kept their blue sack coats. The Confederate army was born at the siege at Harper's Ferry; it grew from the Virginia militia, but John Brown was the spur for all that followed. History is an unending roundabout, on which we fool ourselves into believing that we are in the vanguard of events, when, in actuality, we are merely chasing one another's tails.

The marines' nervous energy soon flagged and most of

them slept, or pretended to sleep, or smoked pensively. Only Luke Quinn appeared calm as he read a Testament given him by the Pennsylvania Bible Society when his train had stopped at North Philadelphia Station on the way to Washington.

You should have been a chaplain instead of me, I thought as I watched his head bowed over the Good Book's thin pages.

I had killed a man in the Valley of the Great Salt Lake— a man, like me, of God. My conscience gnawed at me not for having cut short his life—he was a mean son of a bitch—but for having broken the principal commandment of a God whose silence I could scarcely justify, one who seemed unconcerned by our growing inclination to tear one another to pieces. And yet, as the train hurtled toward a destination as inevitable as it was dangerous, I felt myself better suited to a life of violence than one of peace.

"What do you think we'll find at Harper's Ferry?" asked Fenzil, who sat beside me.

He was chewing his nails, not because he was afraid, but because it was his habit—a repellent one for a surgeon, I thought.

"I don't know," I replied, trying to dissemble my fear.

We had both read the report published hastily in a special edition of *The National Era,* a Washington abolitionist paper. Our blood had cooled to read that the slaves were armed with rifles and—more terrifying still—pikes and that the rebellion was spreading into the South. It took little imagination to picture fierce black men in rags, impaling white men, women, and children in their beds and dooryards.

EXTRA-ORDINARY MASSACRE FEARED!

I shut my eyes and saw in my mind's night the blood of the wicked and of the innocent soaking the dusty streets, homes and businesses afire, fields sown with salt, barns pulled down, cattle slaughtered, and the corpses of proslavery men hanging from lampposts, assuming the village had lampposts. If not, any tree would do; violent death is not particular. I opened my eyes and saw, outside the window, that the light, which had been keeping pace with us in the ribbon of dirty ditch water beside the tracks, had dimmed.

"I expect we'll both be run off our feet by this time tomorrow," said Fenzil.

I grunted in reply.

"We'll make a delightful party of four," he said. I looked at him quizzically. "The surgeon, the chaplain, the beneficiary of our quite different skills, and, if things go wrong for him, the grave digger."

My eyes had begun to water because of the tobacco smoke that filled the carriage with a bluish ghost.

"There's nothing to cry about, Winter," said Fenzil with the easy cruelty of our kind.

When our train arrived at Harper's Ferry, the militia had already attacked the arsenal and forced Brown and his men to take refuge inside the engine room next door. Two dozen hostages had been rescued from the armory guardroom, and two of Brown's sons, Watson and Oliver, had been shot dead.

You will want to know my impressions of the town and countryside thereabouts.

An idyllic landscape of dramatic heights, woodland, rivers, and meadows, which would have moved Edmund Spenser to write a pastoral. Thus are we betrayed by first impressions and by *words*. Rancor, envy, and fear doubtless ran through Harper's Ferry like a vein of rust, as they do everywhere on earth. Spenser's sheep were sick, his shepherds and their lasses poxed.

Outwardly, the leaves were those of autumn; the wind rustled them, turning them this way and that. The rivers were broad and sandy-bottomed. The fish were abundant, and, if the rivers sounded discordant, it was only the noise of guns and cannon, the alarms and shouts of men that made them seem so. Mankind is a boil on Nature's back.

Fenzil and I were billeted in the post office. From that time until the end of the uprising, we would have to lay aside our hostilities and work together, bound by the mortal complication, which our two professions sought, each in its own way, to unknot.

"If you were to read any of these letters, Robert, you'd be disappointed. For all the to-and-fro of words, we still don't seem able to find the right ones."

"What would be the *right* words?" I asked, curious, for once, to hear what Fenzil had to say.

"Those that disarm before a blow is struck . . . endear before anger hardens the heart . . . console before a heart is broken past mending. Words that—what is it you padres say?—'turn swords into plowshares.'"

His reply had verged on prayer, uttered with an uncharacteristic earnestness, which surprised me. To have shown his feelings no doubt embarrassed him, as a lady would be whose petticoats had peeked out from the bottom of her skirts. He quickly hid them from me.

"Do you think John Brown could be right?" I asked impulsively.

I watched in amazement as his face, which had a moment earlier been frank and open, recomposed itself into a mask.

"The army relieves us of moral misgiving," he replied, neither with a smile nor a smirk. In his voice, however, I sensed his relief. "I have my doctoring and you your ministering. We'll leave right and wrong to God and the generals."

And that, dear Emily, concluded my first night in Harper's Ferry—peaceful enough for a siege, although shots were exchanged long after the moon had set, according to the sentries and to the evidence of my dreams, which were troubled and noisy with rifle and musket fire.

On Tuesday morning, October 18, Lieutenant Colonel Lee sent his aide-de-camp, J. E. B. Stuart, under a white flag of truce, to negotiate Brown's surrender. Brown refused with more dignity than indignation (surprising in that his son Watson had been shot dead while carrying a white flag). Having received his answer, Stuart ordered Lieutenant Greene and his squad against the engine house. Sledgehammers proving useless on the iron-bossed doors, Greene and ten marines battered them down with a heavy ladder. Once inside, the lieutenant knocked Brown senseless with a saber blow to the back of the neck. Before he dropped, he had fired wildly, hitting Luke Quinn in the gut. He gasped his last breath without benefit of clergy or so much as a kind word to send him on his way. The way led to a fearsome darkness. Thus is it ever, though we light candles, pray, and say "Amen."

Afterward, as I knelt over his body, I recalled a fragment from a story told in some Greek or Latin text read long before at Gettysburg: Charon's *obol*, a coin placed in the mouth of a corpse, with which to pay the ferryman for crossing the river Styx. By now, I thought that one notion of the afterlife was as true or false as another. Had I not absolved Manzanero of his sins? Hadn't I read the words of the angel Moroni over a dead Mormon? Then why not put a penny in Luke's mouth? I'd have daubed him with mud and plastered him with turkey feathers if, in so doing, I could have ensured him of a kind and merciful welcome by whatever Divinity was prepared to receive him.

Brown's dead were also left to me, including the freed black Dangerfield Newby, whose ears had been cut off as souvenirs. I mumbled over the corpses—I might have recited the names of the baseball players on the Brooklyn Excelsiors team or the capital cities of the United States for all the significance I gave to them. To be truthful, I wished Brown and his men damned to hell. If Luke had not taken a fatal bullet, I might have felt otherwise. Thus do our opinions seesaw on the fulcrum of circumstance.

Fenzil had his work cut out for him, sewing up the wounded. Private Ruppert had been shot in the face during the storming of the engine house, and his wound was the most grievous of any I had seen. Fenzil whipstitched the torn flesh and then, like a tailor having finished with his needle and thread, leaned against a wall and quietly smoked a cigar—his once-spotless apron decorated ingloriously with the gore of friend and foe alike.

"What do you smell, Robert?" he asked, offering me a cigar. Thinking that he'd meant the cigar smoke, I replied, "Good Virginia tobacco."

"I mean after a fracas—what stink is in your nostrils, what taste in your mouth?"

"A gritty taste, an acrid smell," I replied, blowing smoke into the reeking atmosphere of the engine room, which now served us as a field hospital. The dead were stacked up outside like cordwood waiting for winter. A winter that seemed to have no end would take us unawares at Fredericksburg, in '62.

"I smell rancid butter," he said. "I taste pennies on the tongue."

The spoiled body of Christ in a weevily Communion cracker and Charon's *obol*.

By the end of the day—one, it has since been said, which made the Civil War impossible to evade—Fenzil and I wanted only to sleep in our post office billet. We did so after having first anesthetized ourselves with a draft of ether.

–9–

JOHN BROWN AND SIX OF THE SURVIVING SOLDIERS of liberation—nine had escaped us—were taken to Charles Town, seven miles from the arsenal, to be tried and hanged for treason, conspiracy, and murder. I accompanied them reluctantly, having charge over their souls, however much their recent actions may have cast doubt on their salvation. I would remain there until, on December 2, time ceased for Brown and eternity or extinction commenced. I wouldn't stay to watch the remnant of his misguided or—who knows?—inspired followers march to the gallows.

You might have thought we were on a picnic. The marines loafed like careless boys. They played baseball with a peg leg, which, they boasted, had once belonged to Santa Anna. They fished for brown trout and smallmouth bass. They sang all manner of songs—comical, minstrel, and bawdy. They were no more inclined to hymn singing than boys are. They courted and danced with the village girls after a barn raising like red-faced country clods lit by corn whiskey. Ordinarily serious and often severe, Lee tolerated their high jinks. He, too, may have had an inkling of what would soon be visited on them and on the nation—a war as terrible as any of old Egypt's plagues.

With iron gray hair seemingly galvanized by a lightning bolt, grizzled beard, hectic eyes, and a gift for apocalyptic pronouncements, Brown seemed a veritable Moses. Fenzil saw to the prophet's wounds while he sat in his jail cell with a Bible for solace. He did not repent of the mischief he had caused. If he grieved for his sons, none ever knew. In the meantime, the men waited with a patience out of all character for the machinery of the law—Virginia law—to grind on toward a foregone conclusion: John Brown would be hanged—and good riddance to him!

"Say what you like about 'Old Brown,' he's an impressive fellow," said Fenzil, taking the rocking chair next to mine on the front porch of the courthouse, where the abolitionist's trial would be conducted. "He suffers his wound in disdainful silence, knowing all the time that he has an appointment with the hangman. I tell you, Winter, the man scares me—his eyes do when they clamp on mine! I can see fire glittering in them—whether the devil's or Divinity's, I could not say."

I pictured the fire that burned atop the Pyramid of the Moon, where the Aztec priests offered the vitals of the sacrificed to the dread god Mictlantecuhtli. Time is woven with the bright and dismal threads of our kind's darkest raptures into a serape worn in the Dance of the Dead.

"I would not look into his eyes," I said pensively—an admonition intended as much for me as for the surgeon—the to-and-fro of whose rocking, I noticed irritably, was contrary to my own.

"No, I shan't do so again," replied Fenzil without the edge of ridicule with which he usually spoke to me.

He was skeptical of faith and, at the same time, liked to mock me for my manifest lack of it. I was, for him, a curiosity that would have graced the shelves of Thomas Mütter's "museum" of grotesqueries, which, in Philadelphia, at the start of his career, Fenzil had tended—a collection as repulsive as P. T. Barnum's. There, at Jefferson Medical College, he had met Edgar Poe. And there, he had assisted Dr. Mütter—yes, the same surgeon whose transfiguring knife you wished for. The circumference of a human life is indeed small.

"Do you have any sympathies for Brown?" I asked Fenzil, arresting him in mid-rock with my hand.

"I've been wrung dry of finer feelings," he replied.

He got up from his rocker and walked across the street to the jailhouse—whether to talk to the guards or Brown, I couldn't have guessed.

Whenever I could, I'd go off by myself. My mind was turning with outlandish ideas. Once entertained, ideas can't be recalled, nor can one throw a *cordon sanitaire* around them. They are as contagious as a plague and will jump from one person to another like a flea from a dog. I spent hours loafing amid wild apple trees, their ripe fruit lately spilled onto the ground, causing, by heady decomposition, the air to smell like sour wine. I would lie there, a drunkard under the influence of the mind's intoxicants—more potent than alcohol.

In a poem you sent me, the paper sutured with scarlet thread, as though the words were a wound, you wrote:

> The Aspen leaves
> Turn in the wind
> From Dark to Light—
> Light to Dark again.

None knows to what end
The Breaking Wheel turns—
Whether to convert—rend—
Or to mill us fine.

Was I born and, having been so, bound to discover in John Brown the reason for my life? Is God less powerful than the affinity by which we are held fast one to another? Are there designs that supersede His own? Does a human phenomenon like love exist beyond the Almighty's power to repeal or to annul? If He exists, can we ever be free of Him? Will we ever come into our own as men and women—complete, self-sufficient, and, possessing all and wanting naught, content? Could I have said, as Walt Whitman wrote, "I am satisfied—I see, dance, laugh, sing"?

Toward the end of the six weeks I was in Charles Town, I received a letter from Waldo Emerson, who had heard from your brother of my involvement in the affair.

Bush
Concord, Massachusetts
November 24, 1859

Dear Reverend Winter,

I have had news of you and your whereabouts from our mutual friend Austin Dickinson, who asks to be remembered to you. [Not a word of greeting from you, Emily!] We, the faction advocating the higher purpose for which, we believe, mankind was cast out from a placid, bovine existence before the Fall, are hoping—forlornly, as I can only suppose—that the great man John Brown will be pardoned. His life has been too bound up in what is best for our troubled race, to be sacrificed on the rude altar of vengeance.

He is that new saint, than whom none purer or more brave was ever led by love of men into conflict and death,—the new saint awaiting his martyrdom, and who, if he shall suffer, will make the gallows glorious like the cross.

I beg you to deliver my best wishes and sincerest regards to Mr. Brown. Tell him his friends in Amherst are praying for his liberty and exoneration. We were lifted up, as though by the hand of the Almighty, when he was last among us, at the Concord town hall, on May 8th last.

I am sending this letter to you, Robert, because I do not know if John is allowed mail.

> I remain——
> Your respectful correspondent,
> R. Waldo Emerson

Thoreau had added a postscript for Brown in his skittish hand:

I think that for once the Sharpe's rifles and the revolvers were employed for a righteous cause. Take heart, great soul!

Henry D. Thoreau

Also enclosed in the envelope was a poem by Daniel Ricketson that had recently appeared in the *Springfield Daily Republican*.

Still the warm current flows along his veins,—
His noble heart still beats to freedom true,
And finds a deep response where virtue reigns,—
His soul sublime, and calm as heaven's
own blue.

O thou who hold'st his life-blood in thy hands,
List to the voice of God that speaks within;
His life or death depends on thy commands,—
O, nobly spare him, and escape the sin . . .

However much the "Black Republicans" and Transcendentalists may have petitioned, begged, and clamored for Brown's release, Democrats—north and south—raised their voices in a truculent chorus, foreseeing the dissolution of the union if he were pardoned. In actuality, his pardon had become beside the point: Most of the proslavery congregation declared that the raid on Harper's Ferry had made war inevitable.

"The day of compromise is past. . . . There is no peace for the South in the Union!" decried the *Charleston Mercury*.

"The Harper's Ferry invasion has advanced the cause of Disunion, more than any other event that has happened since the formation of the Government," railed Virginia's *Richmond Enquirer*.

"If Brown and his confederates were fools and madmen at Harper's Ferry, may they not have been such in Kansas also? And if so, who shall say how much of the wrong in that unfortunate territory is justly to be charged against those who were the instigators of these fools and madmen, and who placed in their hands the weapons for violence and bloodshed!" thundered the *New Hampshire Patriot*.

"Brown's acts are but the corollary of black republican 'shrieks for freedom!'" shrieked Springfield's *Illinois State Register*.

"There can no longer be any doubt but what this was a regularly concocted, and premeditated attempt of Abolition Fanatics to overthrow the Government, and emancipate the slaves!" censured the Milledgeville, Georgia, *Federal Union*.

"It was not a negro insurrection at all . . . there were no slaves at all, except one or two, who were seized and held under terror; not one negro or mulatto, except some intruding free negroes, loafing vagabonds from other States . . . it should be more properly described as an invasion of Virginia by a gang of abolitionists, dupes or emissaries of a treasonable fanaticism, going into a peaceful country to scatter 'firebrands, arrows and death!'" fulminated the New Orleans *Times-Picayune*.

Most northerners would have agreed with the New York City *Independent* regarding Brown: "Harper's Ferry was insane, the controlling motive of his demonstration was sublime." But Nathaniel Hawthorne's cranky judgment disturbed me. "Nobody was ever more justly hanged," he wrote, as if possessed by the ghost of his great-great-grandfather John Hathorne, who had helped to send the Salem witches to their deaths.

Still more unsettling was a telegraphed message I received from Abe Lincoln: "An enthusiast broods over the oppression of a people till he fancies himself commissioned by Heaven to liberate them."

By such contentious opinions was the union divided over Brown's deed or misdeed. Was it a step toward emancipation or a misstep into war? I was as divided as the nation itself. While I waited for him to be tried and most likely hanged, I did not know what to believe or in whom to place my trust. Bewildered by contrary voices, I felt my faith, which had been weakened as a man's strength is by blood-letting, dissolve like a wafer on the tongue. How often in the past had I tasted that bitterness? How often had a child-like belief in goodness returned and drenched my tongue in its honey only to turn again to gall?

On Wednesday, November 2, Brown received his death sentence. You have sometimes complained that words "slip and slide on meaning's treacherous ice." But words denoting the body's extinction are unequivocal. In a month's time, John Brown would ascend the gallows stairs, and, having played his final role and taking no curtain call, would break his neck at the end of a rope.

Was Brown insane?

I heard him exchange words with a spectator in the courtroom who had come to hear the abolitionist's doom pronounced:

"To set the slaves free would sacrifice the life of every man in this community."

"I do not think so," replied Brown coolly.

"I know it," insisted the spectator, who, like Herod before him, wanted the head of the Baptist on a plate. "I think you are fanatical."

"And I think you are fanatical," retorted Brown. "'Whom the gods would destroy they first made mad,' and you are mad."

I think, Emily, that we are all mad.

–10–

ON THE MORNING BEFORE HIS EXECUTION, Lieutenant Colonel Lee summoned me to his temporary headquarters. When I entered the room, he was staring out the window at the oaks. Caught by a gust of wind, their gold and scarlet leaves were scattered on the courthouse lawn, where an ornamental cannon from the War of 1812 and a pyramid of iron balls stood, as if in waiting for the next raid of militant abolitionists to appear from out of the North. Hearing me enter, he broke the thread of his stare and the train of his thought and turned to regard me.

"Captain Winter," he said, those sad eyes of his fixed on mine.

"Yes, sir!" I saluted—rather smartly, I thought.

"At ease, Captain."

I relaxed, although not entirely, because Lee's ramrod backbone, whether he was sitting his horse or on a chair, shamed me, who was so often slumped. You know how poor my posture is, Emily—hardly befitting an army captain or a minster of God, who might be expected to carry himself with dignity, having borrowed a particle of His uprightness.

"You were in Mexico during the war."

"Yes, sir, Colonel Lee." And there I had pondered the savagery of ancient gods.

"And in Utah, during the rebellion."

"Yes, sir." And there I'd blasphemed and murdered.

"Then you've witnessed acts of bloody violence few of your kind have."

I supposed that by "your kind" he meant God's ministers, and I nodded in the affirmative.

"Would you say that your sense of duty is as strong as it was before joining the army?"

I thought it best to lie. "Yes, sir."

"Good," he said without the ring of conviction with which he ordinarily spoke. "I'm told the men like you."

"I'm glad to hear it, sir." Whether they respected me as their pastor was another matter.

My gaze escaped his and studied a crack in the ceiling, which formed the letter z.

Zealot, I said to myself. Brown . . . Garrison . . . Stephen Douglas . . . Brooks . . . Brigham Young . . . Buchanan . . . One day the world will be incinerated by zealotry.

"I've also been told that you have not been careful of John Brown's soul."

"Sir?" I was taken aback by Lee's remark.

"In all these weeks he has been incarcerated, you've not been to see him."

I felt my shoulders round and my spine turn into a swag of chain.

"No, I have not, sir."

"Why is that?"

"He killed a young friend of mine!" I blurted.

"Private Quinn."

"Yes, sir."

I know now that my avoidance of the condemned man had more to do with my uneasy admiration for him than with the death of my young friend by his hand. I had seen too much of death to be altogether affected by any one instance of it, and I was not convinced of the justice of the sentence passed on Brown. Emerson and Thoreau considered him a great man. Who was I to believe otherwise? I was embarrassed by Brown's imminent death—yes, *embarrassed*—as if I myself were to be his executioner. I doubt that Lee would have indulged my delicate feelings.

"You will visit him tonight in his cell," he ordered. "Even a villain like 'Old Brown' is entitled to his last meal and his Last Rites on his last night on earth before the Last Judgment."

"Yes, sir." Extreme Unction was not mine to give, but I held my tongue.

He stood and said, with the utmost severity, "Captain Winter, you will give Mr. Brown the comforts of your Savior!"

"Sir!" I replied with a tremor in my voice, wondering whether Lee had a different Savior or even none at all. Perhaps he had no need of one.

I saluted and went outside, feeling like a boy returned once more to the playground after a caning from his teacher. I stood and watched two negroes raking leaves from the courthouse lawn. They neither shuffled nor sang, nor were they sullen. I didn't know if they were slaves or freemen. I only knew that they were men, and the thought staggered me, as if I had never before entertained it in the presence of negroes.

All that afternoon, I worried about my visit, wondering what I should say to Brown. I wondered—and feared— what he would say to me. There are certain words that, having been said, will stay with us, as if we were shut up for eternity with a pesky fly, which had also been granted everlasting life: *buzz*, *buzz*, *buzz*—an unrelenting noise provided by the Grand Inquisitor.

> Our God shall come, and shall not keep silence: a
> fire shall devour before Him. And it shall be very
> tempestuous round about Him.

At eight o'clock, on the night of December 1, which would be Brown's last among the living, his guard admitted me to the cell. Sounds were amplified unnaturally: The warder's keys jangled as if the music of the spheres had turned sour; the iron door groaned as though God were pulling a monstrous tooth from earth's granite jaw; a cricket in a dusky corner chirped as would a catapult being ratcheted into place; an insomniac bird outside the barred window raised a hue and cry as it will at the approach of doomsday. My eyes magnified each effect of light and dark: The glow of the lamp trembled in the darkness, while the blackness under the cot could have been an entrance to ancient Night. John Brown, wearing a frock coat and collarless shirt, appeared to exceed the dimensions of his jail.

He must have sensed my fear, because he invited me kindly to sit in the cell's only chair and to drink a glass of the cider he had requested. I did as he asked. The cider, which was not hard, nonetheless scorched my insides like the most ardent spirits.

"Your plain cider has a powerful effect," I said, setting the glass on the desk where he had been writing. "It's like the miraculous jug at Cana, in which Christ turned water into wine."

"Thus does the word of God, like purest water on the tongue, burn the soul of any man who heeds it," replied Brown, his eyes glittering in the light from the smoky oil lamp.

"Do you still maintain that you did right at Harper's Ferry and Pottawatomie?" I asked abruptly.

I hadn't intended to interrogate him. I had been ordained by the church, commissioned by the army, and charged by Lee to urge him to repent and, in exchange for his contrition, offer him deliverance, if not exoneration and freedom. At that instant, I realized that my life had been tending toward this fatal conjunction, in a narrow cell in Charles Town—not two hundred miles from Appomattox Courthouse, where Robert E. Lee would, in less than six years' time, surrender his sword to Ulysses S. Grant, commanding general of a victorious Union army.

"Mr. Winter." In his eyes, I supposed I was unworthy of my clerical title or military rank. "Are you asking as a pastor or as an army captain?"

"I'm asking as a man who has lost himself!" I replied with more heat than was necessary and a good deal more candor. I'd surprised myself by disclosing an intimate matter to a man whose motives I could hardly fathom. He didn't appear surprised, however; he was the sort of man who inspired unreasoning devotion.

"We are all lost," he said, sparing pity neither for us nor himself.

His face was seamed, as a man's can sometimes be, which has looked too long on the iniquity of others (never mind his own).

"But you have only to follow Colonel Lee's orders to ease your conscience."

"Mr. Brown, I am not Lee's spy!" I cried indignantly. "I am a man of God."

"And I tell *you*, Mr. Winter, that we are all God's spies, waiting to reveal the secrets we keep even from ourselves.

I will do so tomorrow afternoon before Him who sits in judgment of us all."

"You can be of no help to me!" I said bitterly, like a child whose father has failed to comfort him.

"I am not the shepherd here," he reminded me, and I was ashamed.

"'We lie down in our shame, and our confusion covereth us,'" he said, as if he had looked into my mind and seen its turmoil. "But we must behave as if we were not confused. We must believe that He has whispered in our ears the plan of His intricate design and our purpose within it. *That* is the meaning of faith, is it not?"

"I no longer have faith," I moaned like Goodman Brown after having seen his wife, Faith, dance naked with the witches in the forest of Salem.

"Don't look to God to restore it!" In Brown's voice, I heard His wrath. "It is for you to find what you yourself have lost."

Suddenly, I wanted to fall to my knees and beg God's mercy from Brown. I wanted him to deliver me from the maze into which I had wandered. I wanted my heart to be made pure and my conscience washed clean. I wanted to confess to this man, who I had hoped would confess to me. I wanted to call him "Father."

"I killed a man," I said softly.

He put his hand on my arm and peered into my eyes. The fierceness had gone from his, and he looked at me with sympathy, even affection.

"Did you do right in killing him?"

I shook my head ruefully. "I broke God's commandment."

"If you had not killed this man, would you feel lighter in spirit, untroubled and clean?"

"I would!" I cried in self-pity.

"Then you would be just another person who failed to act in order to escape a burden, whether it be fear of censure, punishment, or a heavy heart. To do God's work, we must oftentimes suffer an unclean spirit and a tormented conscience. That is the sacrifice we make to Him. That is the gift we can give to Him. To endure shame and, if required of us, to die an ignominious death—even if we must endure the intolerable pain of His absence throughout all eternity. This is the measure by which we judge whether we are honest and upright or not. It is, in my opinion, the greatest service a man can render unto God, even if he be damned for it."

"And if we are wrong? Suppose we have misheard God or misunderstood His wishes?"

"Was the Almighty wrong when He created man, although man turned out to be a bitter disappointment? He could easily have undone His handiwork and destroyed the race, but He did not. He learned to live with us, His greatest mistake, and we must learn to live with ours. And if, in spite of my intentions, Pottawatomie and Harper's Ferry were wrong, I will die with them on my conscience, knowing that I acted for the right reasons. I offer Him my errors, as well as my banishment from His sight. And God said, 'So then because thou art lukewarm, and neither cold nor hot, I will spew thee out of my mouth.' I was hot to do His bidding, and if He chooses to spew me out into the void, it is for reasons of His own, which must be inscrutable to us."

He paused and allowed the silence, which rounds out our brief lives, to be restored in the room, in which we waited for morning and the appointed hour when eternity would yawn in the field where the noose awaited, certain of its purpose, faithful to its master, obedient to the forces that had gathered at Charles Town—some to forestall civil war and others to hasten it.

"No man sent me here; it was my own prompting and that of my Maker. I acknowledge no master in human form," said Brown when the silence had grown intolerable.

"If only His promptings were clear and unequivocal!" I groaned.

"You have only to look around you to be certain of His will," he replied sadly. "Pity the poor in bondage that have none to help them; that is why I am here; not to gratify any personal animosity, revenge, or vindictive spirit."

I would not have been surprised if the night outside the window had suddenly turned to radiant day, so very moved was I by Brown's faith and surety. Had he been dressed in white instead of a black frock coat, rusty with age, I could have taken him for an angel.

"Even if you can no longer believe in the efficacy of Grace, in Divine Providence, in salvation and last judgment, in the words of your calling, in goodness and mercy, you must *act as if you do believe in them.*"

"Would you like to pray, John Brown?" I asked him in a voice very near to breaking.

"Pray for yourself!" he said sharply. "Pray for the negroes and pray for the abolitionists—that they will keep faith with their black brothers."

"Will you pray *for me,* John Brown?" I asked, meek as a child frightened by the dark.

"I will remember you in the next world," he replied, "and you will do well to remember that we are 'strangers and pilgrims on the earth.'" And then he wished me good night.

The next morning—I could not tell you if it rained or snowed or dazzled us with sunshine—"Captain" Brown walked to the scaffold in the purposeful way he had always walked, with his head bowed not in fear or sorrow, but in meditation. Fifteen hundred soldiers were there to see him hang, including, although I didn't know it then, John Wilkes Booth, a private in the Richmond Greys. I detested them and the curiosity with which they regarded the morbid scene, as though an interesting tableau had been arranged for their entertainment. (The newspapers would call it "picturesque.") I must admit, however, that I, too, was curious to know how the great man—yes, by now I thought him so—would conduct himself.

He climbed the wooden stairs that led to eternity, which is quite a different thing from immortality, without an awkward step, a cowed look at us, or so much as a tremor in his hand. I saw Colonel Lee standing erect near the gallows, as if waiting for Brown to fall to pieces. But Brown neither fell nor faltered. He took the gallows like a stage, although he had nothing more dramatic to utter than "Do not keep me needlessly waiting" to the executioner before his stoical countenance disappeared beneath a white hood.

They kept him waiting a full ten minutes while the military cadets formed up around the scaffold, and then he was dropped like a sack of meal. Instantly, he became a shell, a hull, a void around which the once-living flesh suffers its natural corruption. What Brown did become, in fact, was the match that lit the powder keg that nearly blew the nation to kingdom come. He was, according to Melville, the "meteor of the war."

During his trial, the grizzled prophet of the coming night had testified to the nation's guilt:

> I John Brown am now quite *certain* that the crimes of this *guilty, land: will* never be purged *away;* but with Blood. I had *as I now think: vainly* flattered myself that without *very much* bloodshed; it might be done. You may dispose of me very easily. I am nearly disposed of now; but this question is still to be settled,—this negro question, I mean; the end of that is not yet.

–11–

I took my Christmas leave in Amherst, returning once again to snow. I stayed five days at Tess's house and enjoyed Charlotte's impish company. I had purchased gifts for them in Boston while I waited for the train to depart: a shawl for Tess and a fur muff for the girl, too large for her small hands. At a stationer's shop on Court Street, I bought you a fountain pen, but, at the last minute, I gave it to Austin. On a table, a pile of books published by Stearns & Company promised to reveal the full extent of what was titled *The Papal Conspiracy Exposed*, in "a Work for Every American Household." Where is Savonarola now? I asked myself. I'd have lighted the match and incinerated that hateful work and its author, Mr. Edward Beecher, D.D., a theologian and an abolitionist who believed that the Antichrist resided in the Vatican and wore red satin slippers. Madness!

I was in a rage that afternoon. I felt I had been burned clean of moral indecisiveness by the white heat of John Brown's rapture. Surely he had been a god, even if a lesser one. Hadn't I seen him radiantly crossing night's immensity when the day that took his life was spent, like the meteor Melville had called him? Didn't the war come, didn't the Union triumph, and weren't the slaves disenthralled—by John Brown, as well as by Abraham Lincoln and his army? None of it, I'm afraid, was Christ's doing.

On Christmas morning, I walked to the Homestead. I knocked at the door after using the boot scraper, to give your father one less reason to be harsh. Vinnie showed me to a chair set outside the north parlor's pocket door. The door was shut. I sat in confusion, wondering if the family had resolved to shun me. Then I heard a rap on the other side of the door, succeeded by two others.

Rap . . . rap, rap!

I held my breath in expectation of I knew not what. Some Christmas mummery, perhaps.

Then your voice arrived from the other side. "Robert." I felt myself tremble with anger. "Robert, is that you?"

Exasperated, I nearly shouted. "Are we to converse in Morse or play at spirit rapping?"

"I seldom see anyone. Upheavals have told on my face, unless the glass lies. Remember me as I was in halcyon days."

And then you scratched at the door with your nails!

"What new mania is this, Emily?"

"I am the tenant in the wall, nibbling at its heart's desire."

I hammered on the door.

"Hush, Robert, you'll disturb eternity, which, excepting thunder, is silent!" I stopped, and you said, "If you like, you can court me as in old-fashioned days, when ladies would blush to see a gentleman stare."

"I want to see you!"

"You have my ear, and I have yours. Faces would only confuse—the way an expression tends one way while utterance goes quite another. Words are what is vital between us."

I sat in my chair like a schoolboy banished to the corner, sullen and defiant.

"I'm sick to death of words!" I might have been admitting to a disgust for suet pudding for all the interest you took in my complaint.

"Austin has told me that you were in Harper's Ferry and at John Brown's execution."

"That's right, I was!" I replied petulantly.

"Was it very terrible?" Your voice, no matter how I

strained to hear your intention, revealed neither sincerity nor dissimulation.

"Not half so terrible as this mockery of yours!"

My reproach went unanswered or unheard.

"Mr. Emerson says that John Brown was a great and good man. Do you think so also?"

I wanted no more of this desultory conversation leading nowhere. I stood and tried to force the door, but you had apparently bolted it from inside.

"You must not carry on so, Robert! Think of me as a ghost. Are you afraid of ghosts? I promise I shan't gibber."

So this is to be my homecoming, I thought. I had arrived in "Ithaca," only to find la Calavera Catrina instead of Penelope. I'd expected piccalilli and was to be served sugar skulls by a madwoman in a white dress! No, I was not to be shown even that much courtesy.

"John Brown would've detested your smug reclusiveness!" Had it a voice, an asp might have spoken thus. "Look to his example, Emily!"

"I would not want such another father," you said coldly. "He would bid us all drink from a poisoned chalice."

"'Thou lovest all devouring words, O thou deceitful tongue.'" I rebuked you, as if I had been standing in a pulpit.

"Too often I've bitten my tongue."

Were you referring to a habitual reticence or to epilepsy, the "sacred disease" that once afflicted and inspired the Oracle at Delphi?

"For Christ's sake, Emily, speak plainly for once!"

"The Hindus arrange things differently. You must be reborn as a woman, Robert, and be my sister."

Again, I banged on the door with my fist—once, twice, thrice—portentously.

"The death knock, Emily—the sound you've waited all your life to hear. Your 'Master' has come with his scythe to harvest you." It was I who gibbered, by now past caring if your father drove me from the house with his ax.

"I've become an abbess of the Abyss," you said as blandly as if you were giving me news of the weather or the asparagus. "Soon I will be as alone as God is."

"Walk with me into town!" I pleaded, knowing that the moment was near when we would be separated forevermore.

"Why would I shamble up and down insipid village streets when eternity's golden minarets shiver at my window?"

I couldn't decide if you were shamming, insane, or rehearsing a wretched part you would, by words and will, one day make your own.

"I heard a bird yesterday whose voice was like Jenny Lind's. Father disapproves of her."

"Why do you allow him to oppress you?"

"He allows me the morning hours to write my verses, believing no harm can come of it, although he would rather I needlepointed Christian mottoes on fine linen to decorate the prison walls. And for this favor, I make his bread, which he prefers to bakers' loaves."

I entertained the idea of breaking down the parlor door with the chair, as the marines had done to the engine house's with a heavy ladder. But the splintering noise and chorus of shocked voices from the parlor would have been too much for *my* nerves. I went to the coat tree, put on my winter things, and strode dramatically out the door and into the snow like Young Werther.

"Old Brown" would have mocked me for my egotism. I was thirty-six years old; you were twenty-nine; we might have been a pair of sulking children. I was determined to be done with you, and I have neither seen your face nor heard your voice since that December morning. Why you continue to write to me, I'll never know, unless your purpose is to reduce human intercourse—all society and friendships— to words. Goddamn them!

–12–

IN SPITE OF MY RESOLUTION AND A RANCOR that would not quit me, I carried your letters and poems, as well as the daguerreotype, all through the bitter years of war. Rarely were you absent from my thoughts, although they were often unkind. I might have called Amherst home and escaped the bloodshed had you shown me kindness. I did not require love; I would not have embarrassed you again by my former importunity. I wanted—wished for—the mystic chords of affection, to alter Abe Lincoln's phrase for my own narrow purpose. I wished for a connection—a bond— to another person. Charlotte was too young and too close in blood to satisfy my need for intimacy, and Tess, by then, too dotty. Ruth was dead, and memory is a thin broth of little nourishment.

During that endless war, whose tokens are, for me, a muddy ditch flooded with rain, a jumble of dead men beside a fence, pigs rooting in shallow graves, green leaves spotted with crimson, gray earth, gray skies, gray bread, gray smoke, gray snow, a hacking cough, musket fire, a fearsome noise like a twig's snapping, which might have been caused by a bushwhacker or a femur shattered by a minié ball—all through that endlessly harrowing war, I did as John Brown had adjured me. That I did so perfunctorily and believed in almost nothing was beside the point. The emptiness I felt was my sacrifice and confirmation of my place on earth—never mind in a future heaven or hell. I was like a man who is kept upright by his suspenders and his bootstraps, by the starch in his shirt and the crease in his pants. My black frock coat with its nine brass buttons was adequate to the performance of my duty.

In this way, I endured.

POSTSCRIPT

Dear Emily,

I have wronged you in this effusion as often as I have shamed myself. To my mind, the one cancels out the other, and, by this arithmetic of compensation, we are acquitted—you by me, and I by you. This, at least, is how I choose to think of the matter and—in lawyers' talk—close the case of Winter v. Dickinson. *I have born you a grudge far longer than is good for me and is deserved by you.*

John Brown has been in my thoughts as often as you or Abe. To him, I owe the greatest debt, though I swear I have yet to resolve the moral questions posed by his life and death. He is as mysterious as any other of the workings of God or—for those days in which I do not believe in Him—the universe, drained of meaning and spelled with a lowercase u. *I've come to agree with Brown that it is better to act wrongly than to do nothing. This conclusion is not sound theology and most likely unpleasing to God's ear and yours, but it is—at times such as these in which we live—what is required of every man and woman who hopes to do some accidental good in the world.*

I was in Andersonville, in May, for the liberation of the remaining Union prisoners held there. I might have gone to sleep in our time, only to have awakened at the foot of the Pyramid of the Moon, so ghastly were the sights and smells of that most notorious of prisons. I had arrived shortly after the arrest of Henry Wirz, the commandant, who will be hanged in November for war crimes, the only man on either side to merit such an ignominious punishment.

I could never have imagined the misery that carried off so many. The word hell *no longer evokes the childish Sunday school picture of fires tended by devils; instead, I think of Andersonville Prison, its fetid swamp, filthy stream, field of noisome excrement, pestilential mosquitoes and biting flies, shallow graves, and human beings so emaciated that not even a louse would seek its nourishment there. I would not have been surprised to see a skull rack, a bloody terrace, and Mictlantecuhtli, his appetite momentarily appeased, grinning in satisfaction.*

Pray send me some saxifrage for the stone in my heart.

I have said all that I know to say, Emily. This reminiscence has turned out to be what a man might write in his jail cell while waiting for the warder to usher him onto the little stage where he will perform his final scene. And if, in ages hence, this text should find itself—by the strange ways of accident or fate—in another's possession, he may not have heard of our bloody affairs. We can only hope—or pray, if faith survives our reckless generation—that the future will be more peaceable than the present and the past have been.

No man can escape dying. Only a few men can escape a premature death while the body is left to shamble through the dust.

You once wrote that a life told in words is like a leaf in winter, when all that remains is a tracery of veins—the skeleton of what had been green, generative, and full of hope. These words of mine have cost me dearly.

Robert W.
Summer 1865

ACKNOWLEDGMENTS

As I have done in the four preceding books in the American Novels Series, I acknowledge my debt to the literature of the American past, the "genetic inheritance" of most every American writer, even those in opposition to its mainstream. Like a faith long ago renounced, the American voices that thrilled and moved me in my youth have returned in my seniority—like the story of Eden itself, which held me in thrall as a child and does so still, even if the Garden is a ruin as sad and irrecoverable as Pompeii.

Time writes its own narrative, which we call history, and history is—in and by time—rewritten according to the excavations and annotations, the memory and forgetfulness of each succeeding generation. History, like fiction, is shaped by necessity. Historical fiction, to which genre this novel most likely belongs, makes its own accommodations with the past. While I have largely cleaved to historical fact, I have enjoyed prerogatives of storytelling, such as anachronism and elision. For example, I have introduced Carlo, Emily's dog, into the Dickinson household a year before he was acquired by the family and taken him a year earlier than his allotted time. I have given Austin the avocation of painter, when he was, in fact, a connoisseur. Emily's reclusion, I should point out, did not begin until 1867.

John Brown's part in the dialogue with Robert Winter is mostly invention, but some of the words I give him to say appear in Thoreau's "A Plea for Captain John Brown," in which the Concord Transcendentalist quotes the trial testimony of "Old Brown." For dramatic unity, I chose to have him speak them in his jail cell rather than in a courtroom.

I have given Emily words of my own to utter and hope to have caught something of her oddities of expression, her mordancy and slant of thought. (My brazen imitations of her verse are best thought of as early drafts of poems she eventually discarded.) With the exception of the epigraphs, I have borrowed neither poem nor phrase from her. I am grateful to Harvard University and Amherst College for their permission to use certain of her verses as epigraphs. I have also taken words from Emerson, Thoreau, and Lincoln and have welded them to utterances attributed to them in the fiction.

I remind readers that the Democratic Party of the day and the then-new Republican Party were—in Lincoln's metaphor—the "house divided" on the issue of popular sovereignty, used as a justification for the legal right to own human beings and as a fulcrum to launch the Civil War. Democratic statesmen like Daniel Webster and Stephen Douglas, as well as Presidents Pierce and Buchanan, aligned themselves with the proslavery faction, while the "Black Republicans," which included Lincoln, championed abolition.

An acknowledgment of my esteem is due again to Bellevue Literary Press—in particular, to my publisher, editor, advocate, and friend, Erika Goldman; to its founding publisher, Jerome Lowenstein, M.D., and to Marjorie DeWitt, Elana Rosenthal, Molly Mikolowski, Joe Gannon, and Carol Edwards, my pricking editorial conscience. My gratitude to my wife is unflagging.

I consulted certain books while writing this fiction: *Emerson Among the Eccentrics: A Group Portrait*, by Carlos Baker; *Lives Like Loaded Guns: Emily Dickinson and Her Family's Feuds*, by Lyndall Gordon; *A Loaded Gun: Emily Dickinson for the 21st Century*, by Jerome Charyn; *The Mormon People: The Making of an American Faith*, by Matthew Bowman; and *The Preacher's Tale: The Civil War Journal of Rev. Francis Springer, Chaplain, U.S. Army of the Frontier*, edited by William Furry. I also relied on the Emily Dickinson Museum website.

I am indebted to the Reverend Dr. Mark Oldenburg, dean of the chapel, Lutheran Theological Seminary at Gettysburg, and the Reverend Dr. Nelson Rivera, associate professor of theology at Moravian Theological Seminary at Bethlehem, Pennsylvania, for their guidance concerning the theology and practice of a nineteenth-century Lutheran minister. I thank Edwin Toro, living in the mountains of Columbia, for the use of his mother tongue.

PERMISSIONS

"She dealt her pretty words like blades" J 479/F 458
    —Line 1
"This world is not conclusion" J 501/F 373
    —Lines 19–20
"Because that you are going" J 1260/F 1314
    —Lines 39–40
"Remorse is memory awake" J 744/F 781
    —Line 1

                                    —Emily Dickinson

ABOUT THE AUTHOR

NORMAN LOCK is the award-winning author of novels, short fiction, and poetry, as well as stage, radio, and screenplays. His most recent books are the short story collection *Love Among the Particles*, a *Shelf Awareness* Best Book of the Year, and four previous books in The American Novels series: *The Boy in His Winter*, a reenvisioning of Mark Twain's classic *The Adventures of Huckleberry Finn*, which Scott Simon of NPR *Weekend Edition* said, "make[s] Huck and Jim so real you expect to get messages from them on your iPhone"; *American Meteor*, an homage to Walt Whitman and William Henry Jackson named a Firecracker Award finalist and *Publishers Weekly* Best Book of the Year; *The Port-Wine Stain*, featuring Edgar Allan Poe and Thomas Dent Mütter, which was also a Firecracker Award finalist; and *A Fugitive in Walden Woods*, a tale that introduced readers to Henry David Thoreau and other famous transcendentalists and abolitionists in a book Barnes & Noble selected as a "Must-Read Indie Novel."

Lock has won The Dactyl Foundation Literary Fiction Award, *The Paris Review* Aga Khan Prize for Fiction, and writing fellowships from the New Jersey State Council on the Arts, the Pennsylvania Council on the Arts, and the National Endowment for the Arts. He lives in Aberdeen, New Jersey, where he is at work on the next books of The American Novels series.

BELLEVUE LITERARY PRESS is devoted to publishing
literary fiction and nonfiction at the intersection of
the arts and sciences because we believe that science and the
humanities are natural companions for understanding the
human experience. With each book we publish, our goal is to
foster a rich, interdisciplinary dialogue that will forge new tools
for thinking and engaging with the world.

To support our press and its mission, and for our full catalogue
of published titles, please visit us at blpress.org.

BELLEVUE LITERARY PRESS

New York